ABERDEEN
CITY LIBRARIES

TOMORROW'S VENGEANCE

Recent Titles by Marcia Talley

The Hannah Ives Mysteries Series

SING IT TO HER BONES
UNBREATHED MEMORIES
OCCASION OF REVENGE
IN DEATH'S SHADOW
THIS ENEMY TOWN
THROUGH THE DARKNESS
DEAD MAN DANCING *
WITHOUT A GRAVE *
ALL THINGS UNDYING *
A QUIET DEATH *
THE LAST REFUGE *
DARK PASSAGE *
TOMORROW'S VENGEANCE *

* available from Severn House

TOMORROW'S VENGEANCE

A Hannah Ives mystery

Marcia Talley

This first world edition published 2014
in Great Britain and the USA by
SEVERN HOUSE PUBLISHERS LTD of
19 Cedar Road, Sutton, Surrey, England, SM2 5DA.

British Library Cataloguing in Publication Data

Talley, Marcia Dutton, 1943-
  Tomorrow's vengeance. – (The Hannah Ives mysteries series)
  1. Ives, Hannah (Fictitious character)–Fiction.
  2. Murder–Investigation–Fiction. 3. Retirement
  communities–Maryland–Fiction. 4. Detective and mystery
  stories.
  I. Title II. Series
  813.5'4-dc23

ISBN-13: 978-0-7278-8364-3 (cased)

All Severn House titles are printed on acid-free paper.

Severn House Publishers support the Forest Stewardship Council™ [FSC™],
the leading international forest certification organisation. All our titles that
are printed on FSC certified paper carry the FSC logo.

Typeset by Palimpsest Book Production Ltd.,
Falkirk, Stirlingshire, Scotland.
Printed and bound in Great Britain by
TJ International, Padstow, Cornwall.

Betty Lee Talley, 1922–2005
Kathryn Lucille Fosher, 1922–2013
and
Mary Lillian Dozier Darden, 1921–2013

'And flights of angels sing thee to thy rest.'

–

William Shakespeare, *Hamlet*, Act 5, Scene 2

ACKNOWLEDGEMENTS

Writing is a solitary business, yet it takes a team to put a novel into the hands of readers. With thanks to my incredible team:

My husband, Barry Talley, who understands what it's like to live with a woman who 'always seems to have a term paper due.'

My editor, Sara Porter, my can-do publicist, Michelle Duff, chairman Edwin Buckhalter, publisher Kate Lyall-Grant and everyone else at Severn House who makes it such an incredibly supportive place for a mystery writer to be.

Tyson Bennett and Elaine Broering, whose generous bids at charity auctions benefitting the Annapolis Opera Company and the United Church of Christ in Lovell, Maine, respectively, earned them the rights to play roles in this novel.

Barbara Jean, for performing her original song, 'Tell Me Your Name,' within the pages of this book. Listen for yourself at www.barbarajeanjazz.com.

Sisters in Crime, for the week-long retreat at the Lodge at Ballantyne in Charlotte, NC, where the final draft of this novel was written.

And once again, thanks to my fellow travelers at various stations on the road to publication – the Annapolis Writers Group: Ray Flynt, Mary Ellen Hughes, Debbi Mack, Sherriel Mattingly, and Bonnie Settle for tough love.

To Kate Charles and Deborah Crombie. When the time comes for me to join a retirement community, I hope you'll be sitting on the porch with me, rocking and knitting and still telling tales.

And, of course, to Vicky Bijur.

'Methought the souls of all that I had murder'd Came to my tent, and every one did threat Tomorrow's vengeance . . .'

William Shakespeare, *Richard III*, Act 5, Scene 3

ONE

'Continuing care retirement communities, or CCRCs . . . offer three types of senior housing in one location, so that older residents can move from one to the other as their need for care increases throughout retirement. These communities allow seniors to stay among friends and near their spouse during the aging process, and for that reason they have grown in popularity over recent decades. The number of older adults living in CCRCs has more than doubled between 1997 and 2007 and now totals 745,000 seniors living in over 1,800 CCRCs. With the boomer generation retiring, we can only expect this number to grow.'

Testimony of Senator Herb Kohl before the Senate
Special Committee on Aging, July 21, 2010.

You can accomplish a lot on the banks of the Chesapeake Bay while stretching your calves in the downward-facing dog pose. What to buy your husband for his birthday. How to use up a bumper crop of early August tomatoes.

After a few minutes of staring at my feet, wondering in a Zen-like way whether I should replace my beat-up Nikes, I shifted to the sphinx position. Once my head cleared, I gazed out over the waters of the bay, tea-brown and placid beneath a cloudless sky baked to a pale blue by the sun.

A sailboat ghosted by as I arranged my limbs in the side plank pose, looking to the casual observer, I supposed, like a woman who'd been knocked to the ground while hailing a cab. I breathed deeply, tensing my abdominal muscles as I'd been instructed.

My stomach rebelled and rumbled, reminding me that it was almost time for the lunch I'd planned to have at Spa Paradiso, the spa that dominated the hill behind me, owned and successfully operated, I'm proud to say, by my daughter, Emily, her husband, Daniel Shemansky, and their relentlessly cheerful and capable staff. Did I want soup or salad, or both?

I folded myself into a lotus position, closed my eyes and tried to focus on my mantra – *kerim, kerim, kerim* – but other thoughts kept intruding, messing with my *wah*, like where the heck had I stored the folding beach chairs?

Sweat slithered down my temples and trickled into my hair. I considered, briefly, diving into the tepid water, but didn't fancy being stung to death by sea nettles, those nasty pearlescent jellyfish that invaded the upper reaches of the bay every mid-summer when the salinity got too high.

Kerim, kerim, kerim. I tried to ignore the splintered spot on my bamboo mat that was digging into my thigh and the dampness of the grass I'd spread the mat upon. *Kerim, kerim, kerim . . .* Damn it! Did I really want to practice yoga three times a week?

Through half-slitted eyes, I considered the serpentine brick wall – about five feet high – that meandered gracefully along the slope of the manicured lawn down to the wide, white sand beach that Spa Paradiso shared with its immediate neighbor, Calvert Colony. Named in honor of Lord Cecil Calvert, the guy who'd founded Maryland back in sixteen-hundred-and-something, the sprawling continuing care retirement community had only recently opened its doors. It was a geritopia so posh – according to my husband, Paul – that if you had to ask how much it cost to buy in there was no way you could afford it.

Kerim, kerim, kerim. The sun warming my cheek. The gentle buzz of bees flitting around a nearby bed of red *valerian* and golden *coreopsis*. The drone of a power mower in the distance and the smell of fresh-cut grass.

A jet ski rooster-tailed by, shattering the quiet. 'Damn,' I muttered again, giving up.

'You *are* alive, then, Hannah,' a familiar voice said.

I turned, squinting, shielding my eyes from the late morning sun. 'Naddie!'

'Am I interrupting?' my old friend asked.

I unfolded my legs and struggled awkwardly to my feet. 'Not really. I was about to call it quits anyway. Honestly,' I said, gesturing toward the jet ski that was departing with all the stealth of a Boeing B-57, 'those things ought to be illegal.'

'He had a kid with him, too,' Naddie added. 'No helmet, no seatbelt.'

As she rattled on about the irresponsible driving habits of jet skiers – getting no objection from me – I rolled up my mat and tucked it under my arm. 'Are you coming or going?' I asked, indicating the entrance to Spa Paradiso.

'I've just had a facial. Can't you tell?' she said, patting her cheeks with the fingertips of both hands.

Naddie – Nadine Smith Gray, retired mystery writer – was in her mid-eighties but had the clear, smooth complexion of someone half her age. From the fresh pinkness of her skin I could tell she'd had a facial, but I also suspected she'd had her hair done, too. Her silver waves had been coaxed into a neat pageboy cut that framed her face and curled gently under her ears, showcasing a pair of art deco earrings acquired, I was sure, at one of the craft shows she liked to frequent. Naddie wore what I always thought of as her summer uniform: an A-line denim skirt that hovered several inches below the knees, a pale pink three-quarter-sleeve scoop-necked T-shirt, and sensible leather sandals. I smiled. 'Join me for lunch?'

She slid her sunglasses up to her forehead, disrupting the orderly march of bangs across her brow. 'No thanks, Hannah. Gotta get home for an appointment with my decorator. Your nose is red,' she added.

I tugged on the brim of my floppy hat. 'And I slathered myself with SPF30, too. Skin cancer doesn't appeal.'

Naddie and I went way back. More than a decade, in fact, to the time I was hired to catalog the novels and personal papers she'd donated to St John's College. For various reasons I hadn't seen Naddie for months, so I was disappointed that she couldn't join me for a meal and some good gal-to-gal gossip. 'Can I walk you to the parking lot, then?'

'I didn't bring my car. I walked.'

'Walked?' My mouth hung open. Naddie lived in Ginger Cove, a retirement community at least eight miles away.

Naddie furrowed her brow. 'You didn't get my change of address card?'

I shook my head, puzzled. 'You've moved? My gosh! Where?'

Naddie stood at the head of a concrete path edged with *liriope* and *pachysandra* that curved gently down the hill from Spa Paradiso and led through a gate to one of the neat brick Georgian-style buildings of Calvert Colony. She pointed vaguely in that direction. 'I bought one of the town homes over there,' she told me.

I sucked in air. 'I thought you were *happy* at Ginger Cove!'

'Oh, I was, Hannah. No complaints. It's just that . . .' She paused. 'Well, I'm one of Calvert Colony's investors, actually.'

'Well, I'll be,' I said, although the news didn't really surprise me. During her successful forty-year career as a novelist, the sales of such mystery classics as *Death Be Not Proud* and *A Talent to Deceive* – now in their umpty-dumpth printing – had earned L.K. Bromley – the name under which Naddie wrote her stories – a place on the list of America's Richest Women. And that was before Tom Cruise optioned her novel, *Triple Jeopardy*, and turned it into a blockbuster movie and popular video game.

Naddie had always been fiscally sensible. Rather than spend her money on a chateau in the south of France, luxury yachts or major league baseball teams, she'd invested in real estate.

'The Baby Boomers are easing into their seventies now,' Naddie explained. 'At least 800,000 older adults are already living in high-end communities like this. The demand can only grow.'

I had learned from my son-in-law that while the plans for Calvert Colony were still on the drawing board, Spa Paradiso had worked out an agreement with the developers to provide spa and health club services to their residents, and I wondered, with some affection now, if my friend Naddie had had anything to do with facilitating that contract. As part of the deal, Dante (the mononym my son-in-law had invented for himself) and his stockholders had ceded some of their land to the Calvert Colony development group.

'Have you toured our campus?' Naddie asked.

'Haven't had time, Naddie. I got an invitation to the grand opening but I was away on a cruise to Bermuda with my sisters, so I missed it. I wandered around a bit while the place was under construction, though. It's pretty impressive.'

Even in its earliest stages, Calvert Colony had sprawled over the old Blackwalnut Creek property, a twenty-acre campus at the end of Bay Ridge Road just east of Annapolis. Before the construction of the Chesapeake Bay Bridge opened up the Atlantic Ocean beaches to vehicular traffic, Washingtonians seeking relief from the stifling summer heat had flocked to Anne Arundel county resorts. Blackwalnut Creek had been one of them. After the popularity of the resorts faded, the Catholic Church had purchased the Blackwalnut property for use as a Jesuit retreat and conference center. Early in our marriage, Paul and I attended a Marriage Enrichment Program at the center, but it had been a little too touchy-feely for us. Trust falls, blindfold walks and bouts of extended eye contact weren't exactly our style. We'd gone home, giggling like children, shared a bottle of wine, chased each other around the bedroom and . . . well, let's just say that was all the 'enrichment' we needed.

After the Jesuits moved on, the Catholic Church sold the prime Chesapeake Bay waterfront property to a development company. According to the Baltimore *Sun*, they needed the money to replenish coffers sorely depleted by cash settlements to victims of pedophile priests.

The centerpiece of the Blackwalnut Resort had been a grand, sprawling, white clapboard New England-style hotel called Blackwalnut Hall. Calvert Colony architects sensibly preserved the hotel – including the charming chapel that the Jesuits had annexed onto its southern side – and it now served as the focus of a development which included an apartment building, six blocks of individualized semi-detached town homes, several dozen two-bedroom single family homes and a scattering of cottages, all connected by narrow winding roads that were just wide enough for two golf carts to pass.

Naddie interrupted my reverie. 'So, what did you think?'

'My first impression?' I paused for effect. 'Wow. Just wow.'

'There's still tons of work to be done, of course, Hannah, but folks have been gradually moving in. The old hotel is nearly full.'

'The newspaper mentioned it was to be a combination of independent and assisted living,' I commented.

'It is,' Naddie said. 'And they've added a secure wing near the chapel to house the memory unit. Blackwalnut Hall serves as our community center, too. Would you like to see?'

I indicated my ragged jogging shorts and stained T-shirt, both soaked with sweat, and spread my arms. 'Now?'

She hesitated a second too long.

'Love to,' I laughed, 'but for everyone's sake I'll need to change.'

'After lunch, then. I'll meet you at the main entrance,' Naddie said. 'Give you the fifty-cent tour.'

I grinned. 'If I don't get the full dollar tour I'll feel cheated.'

'Come to the reception desk in Blackwalnut Hall,' Naddie instructed. She started off down the path. 'Know where that is?'

'In the lobby of the old hotel, right? Hard to miss.' I wiped my face with the hem of my T-shirt.

'See you around two?'

'It's a date.'

Back inside Spa Paradiso, I made my way to the women's locker room, showered and changed back into the black jeans and striped T-shirt I'd arrived in. With my hair still damp, I wandered into the spa's restaurant, studied the specials board and ordered a chicken salad sandwich and a cup of gazpacho which Francois Lesperance, the spa's master chef, served to me personally at a small round table near the swimming pool. While I waited for two o'clock to roll around, feeling content and well-fed, I lay in the atrium on a lounge chair reading a well-thumbed paperback copy of Markus Zusak's *The Book Thief* that somebody had carelessly left behind.

After a while, I closed my eyes. Life was good.

TWO

'The Holy Prophet (peace and blessings of Allah be upon him) has observed: "Let that man be disgraced, and disgraced again and let him be disgraced even more." The people inquired: "O Prophet of God (peace and blessings of Allah be upon you) who is that man?" The Prophet of God (peace and blessings of Allah be upon him) affirmed: "I refer to the man who finds his parents old in age – both of them or one of them – and yet did not earn entitlement to Paradise by rendering good service to them."'

Abu Umamah al Bahili.

'**M**rs Ives. Mrs Ives.' A hand on my shoulder; a gentle shake. My eyes snapped open. Ben, the pool boy, loomed over me. 'Sorry to bother you, but didn't you say you had to be somewhere at two?'

I leapt to my feet so quickly that my head swam. 'What time is it, Ben?' I asked, bracing one arm aganst the wall until the dizziness passed.

'Ten minutes to.'

'Oh, thanks! You're a lifesaver.'

Making a mental note to tip Ben double the next time he brought me a fresh towel, I gathered up my handbag, tucked the orphan paperback into it and headed out.

Blackwalnut Hall was much as I had remembered it from days gone by. A porch, long and deep, ran the length of the front that faced the bay. Eight tall white Doric pillars supported the roof. Rocking chairs were arranged at regular intervals along its length and, since it was mid-afternoon, half of them were already occupied by seniors resting their eyes, reading or simply enjoying the view.

Just as I reached the steps, my cell phone chirped. It was a text message from Naddie. She was running twenty minutes late. I texted back – *OK* – then located an empty rocker between a beautiful Muslim woman and a slumbering, elaborately mustachioed grandpop wearing a red plaid lumberjack shirt, and sat down to wait.

To my left was the dual span of the Chesapeake Bay Bridge, four-and-a-half miles long, the engineering marvel that connected Annapolis to Maryland's eastern shore and to the towns and beaches of the Delmarva Peninsula. Kent Island at its far end was a gray-green swathe on the horizon. I counted five container ships and a car carrier anchored in the mid-distance, awaiting clearance to proceed under the bridge and up into Baltimore Harbor some twenty-five miles to the north, where they would unload and perhaps take on more cargo. Sailing in the opposite direction was *Woodwind*, a seventy-four-foot, three-masted schooner, crammed full of tourists out for an afternoon sail.

'Relaxing, isn't it?' the Muslim woman said. She was dressed in a black skirt and a saffron-yellow, long-sleeved silk blouse. A white headscarf was draped loosely around her neck and completely covered her hair. If she wore the scarf out of modesty, it failed miserably. The hijab framed her face like the Madonna in a Renaissance painting, only serving to draw attention to the woman's extraordinary beauty.

She removed the oversized Jackie Onassis-style sunglasses she wore and turned her violet eyes on me. 'My name is Safa Abaza. Are you new here or just visiting?'

'Just visiting,' I told her. 'I ran into a friend over at the spa and she's promised me a tour. I'm Hannah Ives.'

Safa's pale skin wore the blush of a few too many minutes in the sun, but other than plum-colored lip gloss and something to darken her gracefully arched eyebrows, I detected no trace of makeup.

'Are you visiting, too?' I asked. She looked so fresh, so young that I assumed she couldn't be a resident.

'No, my husband and I live here. In one of the town homes.'

I stared at her for a moment, temporarily speechless. Safa couldn't possibly be as old as fifty-five! Had she discovered a Fountain of Youth somewhere on the property?

As if reading my mind, she said, 'My husband is a good bit older than I, as you probably guessed. I've just turned fifty-one, but Masud is sixty-eight.'

I couldn't believe Safa was as old as fifty-one, either, but decided to take her word for it. 'My husband and I live in down-town Annapolis,' I told her. 'He teaches math at the Naval Academy, so we aren't thinking about retirement just yet. When we do, though, I can think of a lot of worse places than Calvert Colony.'

Safa's eyes sparkled with interest. 'Masud is a professor, too! He's just retired from George Washington University, where he taught for many years at the Institute for Middle East Studies. When my husband first heard about Calvert Colony, we were living in Crofton.' She folded her hands in her lap, was silent for a moment. 'He came for a tour and he liked what he saw, but I never thought we'd actually make the move. It's very unusual for Muslims to go into nursing homes.'

'Well, Calvert Colony isn't exactly a nursing home, is it?' I chuckled. After a couple of moments' thought, I asked, 'Why is that so unusual?'

'The Quran teaches that we must care for our parents as they cared for us as infants. Our children – we have two, a boy and a girl, both grown with families of their own now – are naturally Muslim. When Masud began talking about moving into a retirement community, the children were upset. Our daughter was completely opposed to it. She said *of course* she'd take care of us! But I know my daughter. Her main concern was that if she didn't look after us properly it would reflect badly on her. "Look at Laila!" our friends would say. "There she is shopping at Bloomingdale's, and she's dumped her poor mother and father in a nursing home."'

'Laila's a beautiful name,' I said.

Safa nodded, reached down for her handbag and rummaged about inside. 'This is Laila,' she said, handing me a laminated wallet-sized studio photograph of a woman flanked by two children, the older one standing stiffly at her side, the younger, a toddler, leaning casually into her lap. 'Laila's not wearing a hijab,' I observed as I handed the photograph back to her.

'She wears it for prayers,' Safa explained. 'But otherwise . . .' She shrugged. 'Laila tells her father she's done the research and she believes that wearing the hijab comes from Arab culture and not from Islam. But she gave it up after September eleventh, so I'm certain that anti-Muslim harassment had a lot to do with it. Masud didn't approve, of course,' Safa continued. 'Talking with my husband about the hijab is a lot like talking about abortion with a Tea Party wingnut. A lose-lose situation.' She raised an elegant, beautifully manicured but polish-free finger. 'Laila pointed out – quite correctly, too – that while the Quran requires modesty, it says nothing about keeping your hair covered.' She smiled and was silent for a moment. 'But when she started making trouble about the move to Calvert Colony, Masud turned that argument around on her. The Quran requires that we care for our parents in their old age, he told her, but it doesn't say exactly *how*.' She spread her arms, palms up, taking in the whole expanse of the complex that surrounded us. '*This* is how.'

'My retirement plan involves booking round-the-world cruises on the *Queen Mary Two*,' I joked, although I was half serious. 'Back to back. A beautiful cabin, someone to clean and make it up fresh for you every day, fabulous food, champagne bar, spas and pools, not to mention movies, lectures and Broadway-quality entertainment.' I sighed dramatically. 'Now *that's* assisted living!'

Safa giggled. 'I like how you think, Hannah!'

After a moment, her face grew serious. 'Masud realized that sometimes life sends you challenges that are beyond a child's ability to help, and he didn't want to burden Laila and Roshan.' She leaned forward, inclined her head closer to mine and spoke softly. 'Masud has been diagnosed with Parkinson's disease.'

I started to lay a comforting hand on hers then drew back, not knowing whether the gesture would be misinterpreted. 'I'm so sorry.'

Safa shrugged. '*Insha'Allah*. What can one do? It is early days yet, and Masud has already started medication, so I'm hopeful. One can live a long time with Parkinson's, as you probably know. Look at Michael J. Fox.'

I remembered reading that the youthful *Back to the Future* star had been diagnosed with early-onset Parkinson's disease in 2001. Nevertheless, he had worked fairly steadily as an actor since then, and would be back on television in the fall with a semi-autobiographical sitcom. 'He's certainly done a lot to raise public awareness about the disease,' I said.

'Yes, and it's generous support such as his that gives us hope for a cure.'

'Forgive me if I'm speaking out of turn, Safa, but I think that you and your husband have made the right decision, both for you and for your children.'

Safa nodded in agreement. 'Masud brought me here for a visit, we talked to Mr Bennett, the director, and Masud was happy with what we heard. We are fine for now in our town home, but later? Well, the concept of modesty is accepted here, that was of utmost importance to me.'

'Do you mean the clothing you wear? The hijab?'

Safa blushed. 'That is part of it, but more importantly, should I need one, I must have a woman doctor, and, when the time comes, women who tend to me.'

After I was diagnosed with breast cancer, a male surgeon and a male oncologist had pretty much saved my life, so I was glad the Episcopal Church didn't place such demands on its women.

'What do you do about daily prayers?' I asked. I knew that devout Muslims pray five times throughout the day. We'd once had an airport pickup where the cab driver arrived at the crack of dawn and asked to use our bathroom so he could wash his feet before his sunrise prayer. With some pride, he'd showed us the Qibla app on his iPhone which featured a compass programmed to determine the direction of Mecca from anywhere in the world, even the cab parked in our driveway. What would Mohammed have thought of that? I had marveled at the time. I had a Daily Office app on my iPhone, but had only consulted it twice. The cabbie's devoutness put my half-baked efforts at regular daily prayer to shame.

'Ah, prayers,' Safa repeated. 'This was a real plus, especially for Masud. Calvert Colony built a *musalla*, a place where we can practice *salaat*.' She waved a hand in the direction of the gardens, where a modest building that I had taken for an over-sized, elaborately decorated garden shed was nestled in a grove of young crabapple trees. 'There are only three Muslims in residence now, and I am the only woman, but two more couples will be moving in as soon as the new block of town homes is finished.'

'I hope you don't mind my asking, but you look so, so . . .' I paused, searching for the right word, not wanting to insult her.

'American as apple pie?' she finished for me.

I felt my face flush. 'Yes.'

'So, you noticed!' A laugh bubbled out of her. 'Until I went to college, I lived in McKinney, just north of Dallas, Texas. I met Masud when I was in the Peace Corp teaching English at a lycée in Tunis.'

I'd majored in French at Oberlin College, so I knew she meant a secondary school of some sort, most likely for girls, in Tunisia. '*Donc, vous parlez très bien le français, n'est-ce pas?*'

'*Oui, et je parle aussi l'arabe.* And once the language barrier disappeared,' she continued in English, 'my eyes were opened and I became fascinated with the culture. It was ever so much richer than anything I had experienced before. I was totally sucked in. About halfway through my first year there, I was invited home to dinner by one of my students. Her family pretty much adopted me and treated me like a daughter.'

'Is that when you started wearing the hijab?'

'After a while, it seemed the natural thing to do.'

'Don't you find it confining?'

'Not really. For me, it is a religious act. The hijab tells the world I am a Muslim woman.' She smiled. 'It saves a lot of time, actually. In social situations I usually don't have to explain, "Sorry, I don't drink," or "I don't mean to be rude or anything, but I am a Muslim woman so I don't shake hands with men."'

'I see your point,' I said. 'Like wearing a wedding ring says "hands off" to jerks at professional conferences.'

'Exactly. In Tunisia, Western women are fair game. You wouldn't believe the cat calls I used to get while walking to work. Harmless, mostly, but still.' She turned to me, beaming. 'I can teach you a very useful phrase: *Rude bellick, Allah bish yhizz lsaanik!*'

'Is that the Arabic equivalent of "Your mother wears combat boots?"'

She flashed me a charming, gap-toothed grin. 'It means be careful or God will seize your tongue!'

I laughed out loud. 'I'll have to remember that next time I'm in Tunis.'

'After I began wearing the hijab, Hannah, nobody bothered me. I was safer in the streets of Tunis than I would have been in downtown Dallas, that's for sure. I actually felt liberated.'

Safa's hands suddenly flew to her throat, her fingers rapidly working to adjust the hijab where the fabric folded under her chin. 'You must excuse me,' she said, standing up. 'Masud's waiting. It's time for me to go.' Her eyes flicked sideways.

Where the sidewalk curved around a miniature Japanese maple a man stood, smoking. Masud was not particularly tall but he was dark and handsome, with abundant salt-and-pepper hair combed straight back. He was dressed in black trousers and a short-sleeved white shirt, the collar open. The fabric of the shirt was so sheer that I could read the label on the pack of cigarettes tucked into his breast pocket: Camels. Unfiltered. The only brand with a picture of the factory on the label, my late mother, a lifelong smoker, had always joked.

If Masud had been wearing a bow tie, I thought, as I watched him exhale a stream of smoke into the humid summer air, I might have mistaken him for a handsome waiter.

'Of course,' I told Safa. 'I'm meeting someone, too. But I've enjoyed our conversation and I hope we run into each other again.'

Safa bowed slightly. 'I hope so, too, Hannah.'

After an awkward pause while I considered whether to extend my hand or not, Safa turned and glided down the steps to join her husband. As she reached the bottom step, Masud dropped his cigarette butt on the sidewalk, ground it out with the toe of his sandal, turned abruptly and strode down the path on his own. Safa, like a well-trained puppy, followed several steps behind.

Until he spoke, I'd forgotten about the elderly lumberjack. 'Litterbug!'

'Well,' I said, turning in the old man's direction, 'at least the butt is biodegradable. Have to give the man points for that. No cellulose acetate filters to screw up the Chesapeake Bay ecosystem.'

'Send that goatherder back to the desert.' He folded his arms across his chest and closed his eyes, effectively putting an end to our conversation.

Hoping, for Safa Abaza's sake, that this wasn't the prevailing attitude at Calvert Colony and, as we used to say, a preview of coming attractions, I left the old guy to his snooze and headed inside to track down Naddie.

THREE

'Today's 55-and-over retirement communities are not your grandmother's nursing home. You walk into a stunning lobby with beautiful lighting and carpeting, and there's an art gallery and a restaurant, just like a fine hotel. Some offer everything from entertainment centers with theater seating, videogames and computers, to state-of-the-art gyms with personal trainers where residents can take age-modified Zumba or belly-dancing classes. Some communities have dog parks so that family pets can also feel right at home.'
Annapolis *Gazette,* March 28, 2013, Section B, p. 2.

Directly over a pair of tall walnut doors, whose frosted windows had been replaced with leaded glass, hung a modest sign painted in incised gold capitals on a tasteful blue shield: 'Blackwalnut Hall.' Below, in smaller font, visitors were instructed to kindly check in at reception.

I straight-armed my way through the door, stepped into the lobby and slammed on the brakes. What had once been a dark, claustrophobic gallery where bygone priests had sat, smoked and read such runaway bestsellers as the *Spiritual Exercises of St Ignatius Loyola*, had been transformed into a bright reception area. Light poured into the space from floor-to-ceiling windows, in front of which a double-wide staircase with carved wooden balustrades curved gently up to a mezzanine.

To my right, just beyond the reception desk – which remained where it had always been – an enormous stone fireplace rose like a rockslide, dominating the far end of the lobby, its chimney disappearing into the open rafters. Clustered around the hearth were conversational groupings of comfortable, overstuffed furniture, arranged on oriental carpets the size of your average three-car garage. All around, large, high-quality landscape oils in elaborate gilt frames decorated the wainscotting, which had been painted a warm vanilla.

I whistled softly. The decorators had bought big time into the 'open-concept' idea I kept hearing about on HGTV. Blackwalnut Hall reminded me of a ski lodge I'd once visited in Vail, Colorado.

But what really took my breath away was the fish tank. Nestled in the curve of the staircase, it consisted of a cylinder at least ten feet in diameter and perhaps twice as tall, embellished at the base with elaborate wrought-iron scroll work. Outside of the National Aquarium in Baltimore and some kook in his garage on the Discovery Channel, I had never seen a fish tank so huge. Surrounding the tank were two semi-circular, highly polished walnut benches. A gentleman sat on one of them, his back to me, staring into the crystal-clear water where yellow tangs, electric-blue damsels, orange-and-white clownfish (hello Nemo!), a couple of angelfish and – I squinted – yes, even a lionfish now swam. I stepped forward for a closer look. 'Was that a . . .?' I started to ask the seated gentleman, but I was interrupted.

'May I help you?' someone loudly inquired.

'Sorry,' I said, turning toward the woman behind the reception desk. 'I was mesmerized by the fish tank, I'm afraid.'

'It happens to everyone the first time they see it. Spectacular, isn't it?'

I had to agree. 'It knocked my eyes out. I'm here to meet Nadine Gray,' I told her.

The woman consulted a computer screen on the desk in front of her. 'Right. Mrs Gray called ahead and told us to expect you, Mrs Ives. Would you mind signing in?'

On the highly polished walnut counter an iPad-like device was mounted on a swivel stand. She turned the screen in my direction, and I used the stylus she provided to scrawl a signature in the box after my name. 'Thanks,' I told her. 'I think I'll wait over by the fish.'

I settled down on one of the benches and stared into the tank, half expecting a shark or a killer whale to make an appearance. As if it knew what I was thinking, an eel poked his snake-like head out from behind a sea fan and bared its teeth at me.

'Zen-like, isn't it?' a nearby voice rasped. It belonged to the gentleman I'd noticed earlier. In his mid-seventies, I guessed, dressed in a blue, button-down oxford cloth shirt neatly tucked into a pair of khaki shorts, and secured with a Smathers & Branson needlepoint belt with elephants and martini glasses stitched into it. White socks stuck out of the toes of his sandals.

'It is,' I agreed. 'I could watch sea grass undulate for hours.'

'They cleaned it the other day,' the old man advised me.

I figured he meant the tank. 'Oh, yes?'

He nodded, raising one of the grizzled, fly-away eyebrows that shaded his eyes like awnings. 'Sent two divers down. Masks, fins and all. Extraordinary.' After a moment he added, 'But everything about this place is extraordinary.'

'It's my first visit,' I told him.

His gray eyes fixed on me and moved slowly up and down. 'Checking out one of the town homes, I imagine?'

'Let's just say I'm casing the joint.'

'Well, you'd better hurry, young lady, because from what I hear they're selling like hotcakes.'

Young lady. Nobody'd called me that since George Bush was president. The first one. I was a grandmother three times over. 'I'll give it some thought,' I said with a smile before turning back to my in-depth study of the fish.

'I see you've already met Colonel Greene,' Naddie chirped from behind me a few stress-free minutes later.

I swiveled on the bench, smiled, and patted the empty space next to me. 'The colonel and I have been discussing aquaculture.' It didn't surprise me to find out that the man was a veteran. His 'high and tight' buzzcut was a dead giveaway.

'Get a room!' boomed the colonel, making me jump.

I followed his gaze. A pair of mature gouramis floated by engaged in a lip lock.

Naddie leaned forward, addressing our companion. 'They're not kissing,' she explained gently. 'They're having a discussion over territory.'

He considered her with steel-gray eyes. 'Humph.'

I imagined the colonel wasn't used to being contradicted.

After introducing us formally – Hannah, Nate, Nate, Hannah – Naddie sat down between Nate and me and asked, 'How's Sally, Colonel?'

'Took off in the golf cart after lunch and I haven't seen her since. Damn fool game, if you ask me.'

'Golf?' I was surprised since an article in the local newspaper had mentioned that construction of the Calvert Colony club house and a nine-hole golf course was on hold pending Anne Arundel County approval of the developer's plans for sediment containment in Blackwalnut Creek.

'Bingo,' he barked. 'Every Wednesday at one-thirty. The woman is insane.'

Thinking about the spa's deep pockets, I said, 'I imagine there are some excellent prizes.'

'Oh, sure. Bottles of wine, movie tickets, Macy's gift certificates . . .' Nate paused to draw breath. 'Last week she won a Brazilian wax job. Now what in *hell* is Sally going to do with that, I ask you?'

Next to me Naddie snorted, and I realized she was stifling a laugh. 'Be nice, Nate,' she scolded gently after she had sufficiently recovered. 'The grand prize this week is a Circle Line River Cruise for two. You have to admit that would be pretty cool.'

The colonel shrugged. 'Not much of a cruise man, myself.'

'*I'll* go with Sally, then,' I teased. 'I love to cruise.'

Colonel Greene suddenly shifted on the bench and braced an

arm against the seat, preparing to stand. 'Where are my manners? Would you like a tour, Miss? Miss . . . Sorry. I've already forgotten your name.'

'It's Hannah,' I said. 'Hannah Ives. I would . . .' I started to say, but Naddie interrupted, raising a hand. 'No need, Nate. I'm planning to take Hannah around.'

Colonel Greene had the good manners to look crestfallen. Then he winked michievously. 'Just when I was about to invite Hannah up to look at my etchings.' He jabbed a finger ceiling-ward, in the direction of the mezzanine. 'My apartment's up there. Second floor. Wife and I were going to buy into one of the town homes like Naddie here, but when Adele passed I thought the apartment was a better idea.' He waggled his extraordinary eyebrows. 'I'd be happy to show it to you.'

Naddie and I stood, and she looped her arm through mine. 'Behave yourself, Colonel,' she chided cheerfully. 'Hannah's a married woman.'

He grinned. 'Can't blame an old guy for trying.'

'Come on, Hannah, let's get the keys.'

'Old guys rule,' the colonel said, giving me a big thumbs up. When I caught sight of him again a few minutes later, he stood ramrod straight next to the fireplace, flirting with a well-dressed woman more his own age.

Naddie collected the keys from the receptionist and steered me toward the staircase, giving the lecherous Colonel Greene wide berth. 'We have model apartments set up to show perspective residents, so there's no need to bother Nate.'

I grinned. 'He didn't sound bothered to me.' I paused as a thought occurred to me. 'If Adele is his late wife, who is Sally?'

'His girlfriend,' Naddie said. 'One of several, actually. Stairs, or would you prefer the elevator?'

'Stairs, I think,' I said, aiming myself in that direction.

Naddie paused, resting one hand on the crystal globe that capped the newel post. 'You have to watch out for Nate. He tried it on with me, too. Don't know why he thinks I'm going to fall quivering at the feet of some superannuated dude who refers both to himself and to his, how shall I put this, "equipment," as Easy Rider.'

I stared at my friend for a moment, thinking I'd misheard. Then I started to giggle.

'He fancies himself as Peter Fonda.' She tossed the words over her shoulder as she headed upstairs. 'As if.'

I followed, pausing about halfway to look down, appreciating the broad sweep of the magnificent staircase. 'I keep expecting to meet Scarlet O'Hara. Or Rhett Butler.'

Naddie chuckled. 'It is grand in every sense of the word, isn't it? And check out the view.'

While the windows did not face the bay – the front porch had captured that honor – the landscape architect had more than made up for it. Framed in the Palladian window was a classic rose garden, dominated by a Venetian-style fountain topped by a cherub. Water tumbled cheerfully out of the cherub's tilted urn, cascading over a wedding cake of increasingly larger basins. Just beyond the fountain an opening in a hedge led to another garden, this one more Japanese in style. If I squinted, I could just make out the circular outline of a meditation maze in the far distance. I made a mental note to check it out the next time I felt stressed.

'Getting back to Colonel Greene for a moment,' Naddie commented as we reached the top of the stairs. 'Women at Calvert Colony outnumber the men three to one. While Adele was alive, she kept him on a short leash, but now . . .' She put the thought out there, then let it lie. 'Fortunately, all the ladies seem to love him. He probably thinks he's died and gone to heaven.'

'He's attractive for an older guy. Tall, slim, cleancut.' Colonel Nathan Greene reminded me a little of my father, actually, who had retired from the navy, but not from a lifetime habit of keeping himself perpetually prepared to pass any navy physical fitness assessment. Captain George Alexander, USN, retired, was so fit he put the rest of our family to shame.

'Nate works out every day in the Paradiso fitness center with Norman Salterelli,' Naddie added.

'Ah, Norman!' I mused. 'That trainer with abs from here to eternity. Dangerous.'

Naddie leaned closer and whispered, 'I hear Nate buys Viagra in bulk from a mail-order house in Canada, so I like to keep my distance.'

'Mr Easy Rider's not exactly my type,' I said with a laugh. 'Fabulous etchings or not, and the Viagra information is a little scary.'

We'd reached the balcony. With both hands on the railing, I leaned over and peered down into the aquamarine depths of the aquarium. 'Reminds me of the coral reef off that place we rented in the Bahamas while Paul was on sabbatical,' I said. 'Gorgeous. I could *so* dive in right now.'

'Do it while you can,' Naddie teased. 'The aquarium's another work in progress, I'm afraid. Eventually there'll be a cone-shaped cap over the top. Fancy ornamental ironwork, like the base, with a hinged panel so the divers can get in and out. It's being manufactured by some company out in Las Vegas. The first one they sent out didn't fit.'

'Alas, I forgot my mask and snorkel,' I said, leaning closer. 'Who on earth maintains the tank? It's not like you can just toss in a bucket of water and make a few sweeps around the inside of the glass with an algae pad now and again.'

'We have an arrangement with the National Aquarium in Baltimore,' Naddie explained.

We passed through another comfortably furnished seating area and strolled down a corridor where original oils and watercolors hung on both sides. When I stopped to admire one, Naddie said, 'We encourage residents to bring their art work with them when they move in. If there isn't room in their apartment, the decorator hangs the work up in one of the lounges or in the hallway.' She tugged on the frame of a still life with fruit and dead, drooping ducks. It didn't budge. 'Although security is pretty tight, it's best to be safe.'

As we moved along the hallway, I thought I recognized a Dürer etching, a Dali print – melting pocket watches, who else could it be? – and what I was certain was a Miro lithograph, although it could have been a copy.

Naddie paused in front of a door with a doorknocker shaped like the Naval Academy mascot – a goat – and a brass plate engraved with *204*. 'This is a one-bedroom model,' she told me as she turned the key and pushed open the door. She moved aside to let me pass by.

Although the floor plan was pretty much as I expected – a pocket kitchen with granite countertops and stainless-steel appliances, a living room/dining room combination leading into a bedroom with ensuite bathroom – what I didn't expect was the décor. Move over *Better Homes and Gardens*! This was *Luxe* magazine meets *Architectural Digest*. It was what a small apartment would look like if George Clooney lived there, or maybe George's mother. Both the living and bedroom windows framed the Chesapeake Bay; Mrs Clooney would like that, I was sure. So did I.

Standing at the foot of the beautifully duveted and accessorized bed, Naddie said, 'The two-bedroom unit has a room similar to this on the kitchen side, complete with a second bath.'

'Nice,' I said, fingering the fine brocade fabric of the drapes.

'You could use it for a guest room, Hannah, or even an office.'

'Not quite ready for that yet.' I smiled, thinking about the home Paul and I shared on Prince George Street in the historic district of Annapolis. 'We've got four bedrooms. No way could I downsize to this extent.'

'I think you'll like the town homes, though. I'll show you mine in a couple of days, as soon as the decorator's finished. We're hanging wallpaper.'

'Not ready for a town home, either, Naddie.' I opened the closet and poked my head in. Built-in shoe cubbies, for heaven's sake. 'We still need space for the grandkids to run around.'

Naddie frowned. 'Children aren't allowed at Calvert Colony.'

My head snapped around. 'Seriously?'

'Fifty-five and older. The covenant is strict about that.' Her face softened. 'The grands and great-grands can visit, of course, for up to thirty days each year. That's enough time for most old folks! But nobody with children can actually live here year round.'

'What if the parents died and the grandparents had to take the kids in?'

She shrugged. 'They'd have to move out, of course.'

I stared hard at my friend, who I knew had grandchildren of her own. 'That's harsh,' I said cooly.

Naddie smiled. 'Don't get me wrong, Hannah. I'm as besotted as the next granny with my grandbabies, but there's a reason Mother Nature cuts us off while we're still in our forties. Women of a certain age aren't designed to pack lunches, run carpools and change two poopy diapers before six a.m.'

I laughed out loud.

'Seriously,' she continued as she led me into the hallway and pulled the apartment door firmly shut behind us, 'they come, they visit, then their parents take them home again. Works for me.' She touched my arm. 'Want to see the two-bedroom suite?'

I shook my head. 'I'm sure it's lovely.' I paused, then took a breath. 'Are you trying to twist my arm by any chance?'

She blushed, all wide-eyed innocence. 'Who, me?'

As we swept down the staircase like teenage girls on prom night, Naddie explained that the wing we had just visited was for independent living. 'The residents in the opposite wing require various levels of physical and mental assistance, although it's colony policy to integrate the differently abled populations, even those residents suffering from mild dementia. Everyone generally dines together,' she added, 'at least until they start spilling soup down their shirts or shouting obscenities. Come, let me show you.'

On our way to the dining hall we passed a library, a room filled with computers and a lounge dominated by a giant, flat-screen television. Two women were gyrating in front of the screen, giving their hand controls a workout. 'Wii,' Naddie prompted when I paused in front of the open door.

'Bowling?' I said.

She nodded. 'Baseball and tennis, too. Good for hand-eye coordination.'

One of the ladies had evidently made a strike as she began jumping up and down, squealing with delight, while her companion drummed out a two-fisted congratulations on her back. We moved on, past a bank where nobody was doing any business and an ice-cream parlor where everybody was. Half-a-dozen people sat on vintage heart-backed soda fountain chairs at small round tables enjoying make-your-own sundaes under a sign shaped like a giant waffle cone that said 'Sweet Tooth.'

Although I distinctly heard a tub of rum-and-raisin ice cream calling my name, I scurried along after Naddie, who was waiting for me at the door to the dining room. She pushed it open. 'We're between lunch and dinner. Doesn't it look nice?'

Tables for two, four or six diners had already been set with white linen tablecloths and napkins, quality china, proper silver and glassware. 'Wine glasses,' I noted, nodding my approval.

'Of course,' Naddie said. 'There's a private dining room

adjoining this one that seats twelve, in case you want to invite your family to join you for special occasions. And we have a full-service bar, too, called The Tidewater.' She yoo-hooed to an attractive blonde dressed in a navy blue suit and a crisp white blouse who was seated at a table near the kitchen door, poring over some papers. The woman glanced up from the ledger she was working on, grinned and walked over to us. When she got closer, I saw she was in her early thirties, about my daughter, Emily's age. Her hair was rolled into a twist at the top of her head and secured with a tortoiseshell claw.

'Hello, Mrs Gray.'

'We're just passing through, Filomena. This is an old friend of mine, Hannah Ives. Hannah, I'd like you to meet Filomena Buccho. She's the catering manager.'

I extended my hand and Filomena took it in her small, cold one, squeezing gently. She considered me with cool blue eyes. 'Pleased to meet you, Mrs Ives. Will you be joining us for dinner?'

'No, thank you,' I smiled. 'Perhaps another time.'

'Accent?' I asked Naddie after we'd bid Filomena goodbye and were breezing through the well-appointed, wood-paneled bar, out of earshot.

'Spanish, from Argentina. Buenos Aires, as I recall. Her younger brother, Raniero, is our chef.'

'How fortunate to have a matched set,' I teased.

'Well, exactly. I only hope we can hold on to them. Raniero is fantastic! I know you're busy today but won't you come to lunch tomorrow? See for yourself?'

I consulted my mental calendar. Other than a trip to Wegman's – The bakery! The buffet! The sushi! – my days were embarrassingly free. Paul would be leaving shortly on a summer sailing trip with the Naval Academy midshipman, so I would be more or less on my own.

'I'd be delighted,' I told her.

'Good. Now, here's the library.'

A woman I took to be a librarian was seated in an upholstered armchair behind an elegant Hepplewhite writing desk reading a Kindle. After we were introduced she gave us a quick tour of the shelves which were arranged broadly by topic – romance, mystery, history and biography – in alphabetical order by author.

'We keep the collection fresh and up to date by using a subscription service,' the librarian told us. 'Our residents have access to all the recent bestsellers that way, although I have to say that the self-help books are our most popular items. And large print, too, of course, although some of our residents have graduated to e-readers so they can make the font as big as they want.' She pointed to the Kindle on her desk. 'In fact, I was downloading a book for one of them when you came in.

'And this,' she said with a slight dramatic bow, 'is our *pièce de résistance*.' She pushed through a swinging door that led into an adjoining room. 'Behold! The computer room!'

Eight iMac desktop machines sat on tabletops, two of which were high enough to accommodate wheelchairs. 'Calvert Colony is totally wireless, of course,' the librarian explained, 'and some of our residents have laptops in their rooms, but even then, they sometimes need a bit of assistance when it comes to email and Skyping. And when tax time rolls around, volunteers are kept super busy down here helping out with TurboTax, as you can imagine.'

Two residents who had been typing, one slowly, the other more proficiently, looked up curiously, then went back to tapping the keyboards.

At the far end of the room, a woman dressed in black slacks and a bulky red sweater, presumably to ward off the chill of the air conditioning, seemed to be carrying on a conversation with someone on the screen; her son, I gathered when I wandered over and leaned in casually for a closer look. The guy was in his thirties, wearing a gray T-shirt and a baseball cap turned backwards. The woman, who had combs shoved haphazardly into her spare, improbably orange hair, was rattling on about her dog, Winkle, who had been a very good poochie-woochie while having his toenails trimmed earlier in the day. As I eavesdropped, the son nodded indulgently.

'Residents can have pets?' I inquired.

'Of course.' The librarian smiled. 'They're family members, too. To say you can't bring a family member with you . . . well, that would be cruel. We even have a vet on call twenty-four seven.'

I was mulling that over, thinking sourly that grandchildren were family members, too, when a new voice trilled, 'Hannah!'

It belonged to an old friend, Angela McSpadden, one of my on-again, off-again jogging buddies. I hadn't seen her since we ran together in the Ocean City Komen Race for the Cure to raise money for breast cancer research the previous April. 'Angie! What are you doing here?'

Angie, I knew, had only recently achieved the Big Five-Oh, so unless she'd divorced Bill McSpadden and married an aging sugar daddy she wouldn't yet qualify to live in the colony.

'Visiting Mom.' She nodded in the direction of the woman wearing the red sweater who had moved on from a dissertation on poodle manicures to a spirited discussion of the previous evening's broadcast of *American's Got Talent*. 'Hi, Mom,' Angie trilled, waggling her fingers in her mother's direction.

Her mother frowned, deepening the already prominent lines that furrowed her brow. 'Go away and leave me alone! Can't you see I'm busy?'

Angie must have been used to such shabby treatment because she merely smiled and said, 'Oh, dear. Somebody got up out of the wrong side of the bed this morning.' She took a deep breath then let it out slowly. 'Christie's my mother-in-law, actually. She tries my patience! Honestly, I don't know what I'm going to do with her. She spends hours and *hours* talking to that, that . . .' She paused, searching for the appropriate word.

Naddie saved Angie the trouble, cutting in before she could complete the sentence. 'Have you discussed the situation with her social worker?'

'Yes. She seems to think it's harmless enough.'

I'd completely lost the plot. 'Seems to me that Skyping is a *good* way to keep in touch with your family,' I cut in.

'If only . . .' Angie sighed. 'But that guy isn't family.'

'Then who . . .?' I asked.

'She says he's her boyfriend.'

I was struck momentarily dumb while I processed that information. A woman, eighty years old at least. A young man, clearly on the low side of thirty. 'But . . .' I began.

Angie waved my sentence away. 'Exactly. Mother says I'm just jealous.' She rolled her eyes. 'As if.'

'I can *hear* you, Angela!' her mother-in-law screeched. She flopped back in her chair. 'Now you've done it! I've lost the connection.'

Angie lowered her voice to a whisper. 'They met on Match dot.com. What does that tell you about the website's screening process?'

'Maybe the guy lied,' I suggested. 'Claimed to be older. It's been known to happen.'

'The guy's a dickwad,' she snarled.

'Richard! His name is Richard. Richard Kent.' Christie blushed to her white roots. 'But he prefers that I call him Dickie.' She scowled darkly and began tapping keys, but, judging from the mumbled curses, without much success at restoring the connection.

'I'll bet he does,' Angela muttered under her breath, just loud enough, I calculated, for her mother-in-law to hear. 'Little Dickie Dickhead.'

Christie bristled. 'You wouldn't know true love if it came up and bit you on the butt, Miss Smarty Pants.' She gestured at the monitor where a beefcake photo of her true love shirtless and flexing his tats was displayed, as big as a screensaver. A blue angel wrapped its wings around Dickie's right bicep and rays of light shot toward his shoulder where gothic letters spelled out, 'St Michael the Archangle Defend Me in Battle.'

Angie frowned at the screen. 'Where is spellcheck when you really need it?'

I stifled a laugh.

'You just don't believe that somebody this handsome could want me,' Christie said.

I suspected Angie's mother-in-law didn't have both oars in the water. 'What do you suppose he *does* see in her?' I whispered. 'Not to cast aspersions on Bill's Mom, Angie, but she's got to be fifty years that's guy's senior.'

'And she keeps her teeth in a glass of water by the bed.' Angie sighed. 'May–December romance, my foot!' she hooted. 'January–December is more like it.'

'Nobody thought anything of it when Anna Nicole Smith married that oil baron,' her mother-in-law chimed in. 'And *he* was in his nineties. You're a sexist, Angela, pure and simple.'

'And look how well that relationship worked out,' Naddie

reminded us. 'There hadn't been so much gold digging since 1849. And, in case you've forgotten, everyone ended up dead.'

'The French have a good rule for judging appropriate relationships,' I said, dredging up from the spot in my brain where arcane facts were stored. 'Half your age plus seven.'

Angie furrowed her brow, working it out. 'Mom's eighty-four and Dickie-boy is thirty-two. So half her age is forty-two, add seven and you get forty-nine. In seventeen years, he'll be forty-nine, at which time Mom will be one-hundred-and-eleven.' She rolled her eyes.

Higher math had never been my friend. Just trying to follow along with Angie's lightning-speed calculations made my head explode. 'I'll take your word for it,' I told her with a grin.

'And it's none of your beeswax, anyway,' Angie's mother-in-law grumbled, pounding on the keyboard with a balled fist as if trying to beat it into submission.

I drew Angie aside, leaned close to her ear and whispered, 'Dickie can't get into your mother-in-law's bank account, can he?'

'No, thank God. We sold the house and invested the proceeds. She has life interest in a trust which amounts to about a thousand dollars a month. She gets a bit of spending money for bingo, movies, trips to the museum, things like that, but her capital is all sewn up. There's no way Dickie could clean her out.'

'That's a relief.' I had a sudden thought. 'Where's Dickie Skyping from, anyway?'

'He *says* he's in Afghanistan.'

'You're joking.'

'He *claims* he's an army vet, working for a government contractor, but who knows. I can see that he's Skyping from an office – a room with bookshelves, anyway – but he could be anywhere, really.' Angie clutched her lightweight sweater, drew it more closely around her and shivered. 'I hope he's telling the truth about being in Kandahar,' she said. 'That's far enough away for comfort. But what if he's not? What if he comes calling? I have nightmares about that.'

'Is he an American?' Naddie wanted to know.

Lips slightly parted, Angie stared. 'Except for the atrocious grammar in his emails, his English is perfect. I sort of assumed he was. Why?'

I knew where Naddie was headed. 'What if he's after a green card?' I said.

Angie's eyes grew wide, then narrowed. 'Thanks, Hannah. Dickie-boy as my father-in-law, grandfather to my children. I know I shall sleep more soundly just thinking about that.'

I snaked an arm around her shoulders, pulling her close. 'Sorry, Angie. I didn't mean to upset you.'

Angie stared daggers at her mother-in-law. 'The way I feel right now, Dickie's welcome to her. False teeth, Depends, and that horrible little dog, too.'

FOUR

'"*Most people think that senior food is like cafeteria dining,*" *said Filomena Buccho, catering services manager at Calvert Colony, Anne Arundel County's new fifty million dollar waterfront retirement community. 'We give our residents a true four-star dining experience. We offer menus to suit every taste, from steak and potatoes to carpaccio of smoked beef with marinated aubergine, prepared by Raniero, our master chef, who received his training at the Culinary Institute of America.'"*'
Annapolis Gazette, July 5, 2013, Section B, p. 1.

In the days of tall ships and iron men, sailors went off to sea carrying hardtack and a jug of rum. When I deposited Paul at the Naval Academy sailing center on Wednesday he had a carton of power bars and two six-packs of designer water crammed into his sea bag. But farewell kisses hadn't changed much over the centuries. Like wives and sweethearts long years before me, I planted a good one on my husband, holding him close and making it last, until we both had to come up for air.

'Keep your phone on?' I said as he hugged me one more time.
'Promise.'

'Don't forget the cooler,' I nagged cheerfully. 'I didn't spend a week freezing casseroles for the mids just to have you leave them thawing on the dock.'

'Plebe detail!' he called, waving to a firstie who seemed to be in charge. Seconds later the cooler had been whisked away by an underclassman, vanishing below decks.

As one of the coaches for the Naval Academy's varsity offshore sailing team, Paul was heading up to New York City aboard *Resolute*, one of the *Navy 44*s participating in the annual Around Long Island Regatta. 'Take care, you,' I said as he stepped aboard the sailboat.

'You, too, Hannah. And no dead bodies, OK?'

I shrugged. 'Naddie is threatening to rope me into volunteering at Blackwalnut Hall. That should keep me out of trouble and off the streets.'

'Hah! The last time you two were together . . .' He let the thought go. 'Two peas in a pod, if you ask me, but give her my love,' Paul said as the midshipmen began to untie the lines that secured the vessel to the dock.

I stood by as *Resolute* eased out of her slip under power and turned, heading east down the Severn River. The crew hoisted the main and sailed from the mouth of the river and into the bay. Depending on the weather, I might not see Paul again for weeks.

He was right about Naddie and me, I thought with some amusement as I watched the young sailors haul up and set the jib, the grinders and tailers working the winches like madmen in the brisk breeze. Before our last little adventure was over, I'd managed to get myself and Naddie locked up in a posh wine cellar by a couple of thugs. Paul had been off sailing when that caper began, too. No wonder he worried.

Resolute's enormous sails gradually receded into the distance. I waited until they were a speck of white on the horizon before returning to the parking lot where I'd left my car.

I'd arranged to meet my erstwhile partner in crime for an early lunch at Blackwalnut Hall. When I arrived, the lounge was hopping. I'd clearly walked into the middle of a book club discussion. Six women sat in a conversational grouping around a square table littered with coffee cups and plates – licked clean of all but telltale crumbs – three well-thumbed paperback copies of McHenry's *The Kitchen Daughter* and two Kindles. A chess game was in progress at a table set into a window nook, and another pair of residents sat in overstuffed chairs that flanked the fireplace, that – in deference to summer – had been filled, not with firewood, but with a pyramid of colorful glass balls.

An elderly couple cuddled on a sofa, a walker parked close by. As I passed, the woman kissed her companion's cheek. He captured and squeezed her hand, causing the cartoonish Seabee tattooed on his upper arm to flex its wings.

Naddie wasn't in the lobby, and when I asked, the receptionist hadn't seen her. I settled into an empty chair between a dozing man and a woman reading the Bible and prepared to wait. I selected an issue of *People* magazine from the fanned-out array on the coffee table that separated me from the two young lovers. How could I not? 'Royal Baby Joy!' screamed the headline, but the article inside was disappointingly slim on facts about the newly arrived successor to the British throne.

Across from me the elderly woman giggled, and I looked up from the Royal Baby Gift Guide I'd been perusing. 'You go first,' she said.

'No, you go,' the man replied.

Her elbow nudged him playfully in the ribs. 'If you go, I'll go.'

He took his time considering the offer. A full minute passed before he said, 'OK.' He stood, pulled her to her feet and together they wandered over to the piano bench and sat down.

I watched, an amused smile on my lips, as she rested her fingers lightly on the keys. 'What do you want me to play?' she asked her companion.

He shrugged. 'I dunno.'

'You choose.'

A shoulder bump. 'No, you.'

At this rate, any concert was going to be a long time coming.

'OK,' the woman said at last, and began to play, singing in a slow, but slightly wobbly soprano: '"*The sun shines bright on my old Kentucky home, 'Tis summer, the darkies are gay; The corn-top's ripe and the meadow's in the bloom, While the birds make music all the day.*"'

'I can't believe it,' the woman on my left muttered, laying the Bible down on the crocheted afghan that covered her knees. 'That word's so offensive!'

'Darkie, you mean?' I said, although I knew quite well the word to which she was referring.

The singer began the second verse, singing from memory, her voice growing sweeter, stronger and more confident as she went along.

The woman holding the Bible leaned in closer and whispered, 'It's racist.'

'Well, to be fair,' I whispered back, 'it's been over one hundred and fifty years since Stephen Foster wrote "My Old Kentucky Home," so we should probably cut the man a little slack.'

'They should change it,' she insisted.

'They did,' I told her. 'In Kentucky nowadays, it's summer and the *people* are gay.'

'Really?' she said. 'The people are *gay*? Doesn't sound like much of an improvement to me.'

The gentleman on my right had apparently overheard our conversation. Just as the singer launched into the chorus, joined by practically everyone in our vicinity, some singing in harmony, he leaned across me. 'Well, *I'm* gay, Edith, so stop whining.'

I suppressed a laugh, gave the old guy a mental high five and, in my passable alto, joined in with him and the others: '"*Weep no more, my lady. Oh, weep no more today. We will sing one song for my old Kentucky home, for my old Kentucky home far away."*'

As the last notes of the hauntingly beautiful and melancholy tune died away the guy leaned over, extended his hand and introduced himself. 'I'm Chuck,' he said. 'I live upstairs.'

'Hannah,' I replied.

'Family?' he asked, indicating Edith, who glowered disapprovingly like my great aunt Gerty.

I grinned. 'No, Edith and I just met. I'm waiting for a friend.'

The pianist had a bottomless stock of Stephen Foster in her repertoire. 'I Dream of Jeannie with the Light Brown Hair,' was followed by 'Beautiful Dreamer' and a sensitive performance of 'Old Black Joe,' at which point Edith harrumphed, gathered up her Bible and stomped out of the lounge, her afghan trailing like a bridal train along the carpet behind her. Whether the singer noticed her departure or not, she seemed to sense that the mood of the audience needed lifting after singing about lost friends calling us up to heaven, so she launched into a spirited rendition of 'Camptown Races.'

Rather than prance around the room like several of the book club women were now doing, I checked my watch. Where the heck was Naddie? Thinking I might have gotten my wires crossed and she could be waiting for me in the dining room, I excused myself and headed off to search for her.

Except for the tables and chairs, the dining room was empty.

At the far end, a pair of doors labeled IN and OUT led, I presumed, to the kitchen. The doors were substantial, but not sufficiently padded to muffle the clang of pots, the clink of utensils and the sound of raised voices coming from the kitchen behind them.

'Idiota! Debo hacer todo yo mismo?' Something metal clanged to the floor, followed by a string of words so vile that if I'd uttered even one of them my mother would have washed my mouth out with soap and grounded me for a week. Then:

'Idiota! Tarado! Pelotudo!'

Idiota, I got. But I'd majored in French, so the rest was lost on me, not that they'd teach words like that in Spanish 101 anyway. I didn't need a translator to know that whoever was on the receiving end of the string of expletive deleteds wafting out of the kitchen like the aroma of sautéed bacon and onions was probably hiding in a cupboard or cowering in a corner, protecting his head with his arms.

I decided to get out while the going was good, but I ran into Naddie coming the other way. She paused, cocked her head and listened. 'Gosh, I wonder how he *really* feels?'

'Raniero?' I guessed.

Naddie nodded. 'No doubt. Looks like an angel but has a devil of a temper. Save us from perfectionists with short fuses.' She glanced at the antique Regulator hanging on the wall behind the hostess station. 'We're a bit early, Hannah. Would you like to see my town home before lunch?'

I was about to reply when Raniero yelled, 'Go! Jump in the oven! Make my life easier!' followed by the bright, sharp sound of shattering glass.

As if on cue Filomena erupted from the Tidewater Bar into the dining room, linked her arms through both of ours and urged us gently back toward the lounge, safely away from whatever disaster was noisily brewing in the kitchen. 'The chef, he is temperamental, you know? Have you seen the show on television, *Kitchen Nightmares*? Raniero, he is like that Gordon Ramsay. Everything must be just so. You wait here. I'll go see what's the matter.'

I could think of several television chefs who would be better role models for Raniero than the foul-mouthed Gordon Ramsay – Jamie Oliver, for instance, or Bobby Flay – but decided the suggestion wouldn't be appreciated.

There was a deafening crash of crockery. Filomena winced. 'It's that stupid Korean girl again. We have two kitchens at the colony,' she explained. 'One we must keep kosher for our Jewish residents. This girl, she doesn't understand that the meat dishes and the dairy dishes must be washed separately. There are always mixups.'

'Once they come out of the dishwasher, how would anybody know the difference?' I wondered aloud.

Filomena stared, wide-eyed, as if I'd suggested she cut the grated parmesan with sawdust. 'Raniero would!'

My eyes made a sweep of the dining room. I estimated it could seat one hundred and fifty, maybe two hundred diners. 'How many Jewish residents do you have?'

'Around twenty,' Filomena said.

'There'll be several more in a month or two,' Naddie added. 'Having a kosher kitchen is a big selling point for Orthodox Jewish seniors. We're also one of the very few communities of this type that caters to the dietary requirements of Muslims.'

'And vegetarians,' Filomena cut in. 'Low salt, low fat, dairy-free, gluten-free – we do whatever our residents require.'

Just thinking about a day in the life of the resident dietician made my head spin. It would be worse than planning the menu when Emily brought friends home from college for Thanksgiving, but I wasn't nearly so accommodating as Calvert Colony appeared to be. I drew the line at serving Tofurkys or vegan pumpkin pie made with tofu instead of eggs.

'What do Muslims require?' I asked, genuinely curious.

'Food must be certified halal,' Filomena said. 'This means "lawful" or "permissible." Pork is a no-no, just like it is for the

Jews. In general, what is kosher is also halal, as long as the correct words are said over it at the time the animal is slaughtered.'

'We're very careful about the Circle U and the Crescent M at Calvert Colony,' Naddie explained.

Filomena nodded. 'There are other symbols for kosher and for halal, but those two are the most common.'

'Tomorrow is Italian night,' Naddie said, changing the subject. She snagged a menu from a wooden rack near the hostess station and handed it to me. 'Why don't you join me? You won't be disappointed.'

I quickly scanned the page – *Antipasto, Il Primo, Il Secondo, Contorno.* 'Very proper,' I said with a smile. 'You'd think you were in Rome.'

'The Bucchos come from a long line of restaurateurs,' Naddie informed me. 'Raniero brought a great deal of experience with him from Argentina.'

Filomena beamed. 'My brother and I, it is our dream to have a restaurant one day. It will be *asado*, how do you say? Steak house.'

'*Asado?* Is that anything like *churrascaria?* Where they bring grilled meat to your table on skewers?'

Filomena nodded. 'Exactly. Twelve different kinds. And a salad bar, very fancy.'

I glanced back at the menu again, puzzled. *Bruschetta alla Napoletana. Tortellini alla panna. Capelli d'Angelo alla chef.* It didn't sound Spanish to me. Paul and I often dined at Jaleo, a tapas restaurant in D.C. *Setas al ajilio con la serena. Camarones en salsa verde. Arroz con pollo.* Now *that* was Spanish.

'This menu is so Italian,' I observed as I slipped it back into its holder. 'And you're from Argentina. I was expecting Spanish, I guess.'

'My brother and I, we are *Italo-Argentino*,' Filomena explained. 'During the Second World War, many of our countrymen went to Argentina. Our grandfather, too. In Italy, he was *avvocato*, a lawyer, but he dreamed always to own a restaurant. Argentina was, how do you say, land of opportunity?'

I was quiet for a moment, letting that information sink in.

As if reading my thoughts, Filomena raised a hand and said, 'I know! Nazis. You are thinking Nazis.' She shook her head so vigorously that I thought the pearl studs might drop off her earlobes. '*Nonno*, he was not Nazi. After the war, Italy was all ruins. Foreign armies taking over everywhere. There was no work, so he goes to Argentina like so many people.'

'I read somewhere that Italians began immigrating to Argentina in the middle of the nineteenth century,' Naddie explained. 'Today, sixty percent of the Argentinian population has Italian roots.'

Filomena was nodding. '*Si, si.* If you want a good Italian meal you go to Buenos Aires.'

'Where do you come up with those statistics, Naddie?' I asked, impressed, as always, with her seemingly bottomless reservoir of obscure facts.

My friend shrugged. 'Jorge Mario Bergoglio?'

I blanked. 'Who?'

Naddie punched my arm. 'The new Pope, silly. Don't you read the newspapers? Until becoming Pope Francis, he was the archbishop of Buenos Aires. Born and raised in Argentina but his parents were Italian.'

'*Exactamente!*' Filomena's eyes sparkled with pride, I imagined, for the incredible success of one of her countrymen.

'Go, now,' she said after a moment, making shooing motions with her hands. 'Lunch in twenty minutes. You come back then. I'll save the best dessert for you – crème brûlée.'

'Ah . . .' I breathed as Naddie and I left the dining room together with the sound of smashing crockery still ringing in our ears. 'Filomena said the C.B. words. I will be putty in that young woman's hands.'

'Yes,' Naddie replied. 'But if Raniero can't get it together in the kitchen, they'll be serving it to you on a paper plate.'

FIVE

*'Mark well that in the Catholic Mass, Abraham is our
Patriarch and forefather. Anti-Semitism is incompatible with
the lofty thought which that fact expresses. It is a movement
with which we Christians can have nothing to do. No, no, I
say to you it is impossible for a Christian to take part in
anti-Semitism. It is inadmissible. Through Christ and in Christ
we are the spiritual progeny of Abraham. Spiritually we are
all Semites.'*

Pope Pius XI, Speech to Belgian pilgrims,
September 6, 1938.

Although Naddie's town home was only steps away we
drove there in her golf cart, a souped-up Club Car that
had been tricked out like a powder blue 1957 Buick
Electra, with tailfins so extreme that they reached your destina-
tion a week after you did.

Situated in the middle of a block of eight semi-detached homes,
each with a distinctive façade, Naddie's new residence wasn't all
that much bigger than her double-sized apartment at Ginger Cove,
but it had a superior layout, at least for her purposes. In her so-called
retirement Naddie had become an accomplished watercolorist; her
work was shown at local galleries, where it sold well. To accommodate her passion she had converted the town home's master
bedroom into a studio where finished paintings mounted on boards
were either hung or propped up against the walls, some protected
by glass. An easel held a half-completed study of the Chesapeake
Bay Bridge at sunrise as seen from her window. A photograph of
the same view was clipped to one of the cross pieces.

'Why are these in the trash?' I asked as I bent down and
retrieved a handful of paintings from under a takeaway clamshell
in an oversized plastic tub.

'Watercolor's an exacting medium,' Naddie explained. 'You
have to get it right the first time.'

I ruffled through the rejects: bayscapes, garden scenes. 'These are lovely.'

Naddie snatched the paintings out of my hand and tossed them back in the trash tub. 'Not my best work,' she said, and that was that.

We were sitting side-by-side on the living room sofa, leafing through a portfolio of her recent work – currently on display at a gallery in Baltimore's historic Fells Point – when the doorbell rang. Naddie slid the portfolio onto my lap and got up to answer the door.

'Izzy, do come in,' I heard her say.

'I was passing by and saw your golf cart in the drive, so I thought I'd see if you wanted to come out and play,' a gentle voice said.

'I have company, but it's somebody I'd like you to meet. Don't just stand there on the doorstep. Come on in.'

Izzy was about Naddie's age, but I found it impossible to guess any closer than that. She wore white Nikes, cropped pink exercise pants and a pink-and-black-striped Ralph Lauren hoodie. Abundant snow-white hair was piled into a bun high on her head in an old-fashioned, Gibson Girl sort of way, yet somehow she managed to look incredibly modern.

I stood and extended my hand. 'I'm Hannah Ives. Naddie and I go way back.'

Izzy beamed. 'I'm Ysabelle Milanesi, but everyone calls me Izzy.'

'Hannah and I are having lunch at the hall today,' Naddie said. 'Would you like to join us?'

'I'd be delighted. The only thing in my refrigerator right now is half a tuna salad sandwich left over from yesterday.'

Although Naddie's golf cart could accommodate four, we decided to walk the short distance back to Blackwalnut Hall. Izzy, I learned along the way, had moved to Annapolis from Pottstown, Pennsylvania, after the death of her husband so that she could be closer to her daughter's family. When the daughter and her navy husband got posted to Hawaii, she decided not to join them. Calvert Colony was ready to open, her house in Pennsylvania had just sold, so she decided it was a sign from

God that she should buy in. 'I decided to get rid of *all* the men in my life,' Izzy told me with a laugh. 'The pool man, the plumber, the lawn guy and the exterminator. I want *no* maintenance issues. I have a town home in the block that backs up on the golf course,' Izzy continued after Filomena had shown us to a table near the bar and supplied us with menus. 'Or what will be the golf course once the permits go through.'

'Do you play golf, Izzy?'

'Never. To me, it's about as exciting as watching bread rise. My late husband did, though. That's one of the reasons we were attracted to Pottstown. After my husband retired from the army he taught history at Valley Forge Military Academy. When he retired for the second time . . .' She shrugged. 'We just liked the area, I guess.'

A server appeared at my elbow. She wore a laminated name badge embossed with her name: Susanna. 'Are you ready to order?'

I took another quick look at the menu. I'd been so engrossed in our conversation that I hadn't made any selections. 'The crab salad, I think, Susanna. And iced tea, unsweetened, with extra lemon.'

We were enjoying our entrées when a murmur of excitement washed over the diners. Something was happening at the other end of the room. My tablemates were staring past me, so I swiveled around in my chair.

One of the most beautiful young men I'd ever seen stood chatting with the diners at a table for four near the French doors. He was Tab Hunter in *The Burning Hills*; Michael York in *The Three Musketeers*; Leonardo DiCaprio in *Titanic*. Tall and tanned, his neatly trimmed blond hair curling out just so from under the brim of his white pleated toque. He wore a white chef's jacket, spotless, with a double row of buttons marching up the front and black-and-white houndstooth pants. As he talked he gestured with his hands so gracefully that he might well have been conducting a symphony orchestra.

His jacket was embroidered in red script: Raniero Buccho, Chef.

'"Tall and tan and young and lovely, the boy from Ipanema goes walking . . ."' I sang *sotto voce*.

'Behave yourself, Hannah!' Naddie swatted me playfully with her napkin.

Izzy looked up from her minestrone and smiled indulgently. 'I used to be in love with Frank Sinatra, back in the day. Whenever he sang, "All the Things That You Are" I melted into a little pool of tiger butter puddled around his feet.'

'I felt the same way about Anthony Andrews when I first saw him in *Danger UXB*, Izzy.' I fanned my face with my hand. 'Sorry, I lost control there for a moment.'

'Ipanema is in Brazil, not Argentina,' Naddie scolded.

I set my fork down on my plate and sighed dramatically. 'But he is absolutely gorgeous, isn't he?'

The beautiful boy was making the rounds, working the crowd. Smiling here, bowing modestly there, gradually heading our way. I couldn't take my eyes off him. When he reached our table he rested a hand on the back of Izzy's chair and drawled, *Buenos días*, ladies. Everything is to your satisfaction, yes?'

'I'm looking forward to the crème brulée,' I stammered.

He turned his neon-blue eyes on me. 'Ah, madame, it will be *delicioso*! My pastry chef, Michelle, I have chosen her myself. She is magic with the *dolce*.'

Izzy had just polished off her *calamari vinagreta*. She kissed the tips of her fingers and saluted the chef. 'You are a genius!'

Beneath his tan Raniero flushed becomingly, then turned to me. 'You are new here?'

'Just a guest,' I told him.

'Ah. Well, you tell Mrs Milanesi . . .' a big wink in Izzy's direction, 'to invite you for dinner tomorrow night. We have *Pasta e Fagioli. Ossobucco. Polipo alla Luciana. Melanzane*.'

He paused to let the awesomeness of the menu sink in, which in my case – French major! – wasn't very far. '*Polipo?*' I asked.

'Octopus,' Izzy replied, 'in a tomato sauce with olives and garlic.'

Yuck, I thought. 'Yummy,' I said, smiling toothily.

Raniero picked up Izzy's hand and touched it to his lips. '*A domani, nonna*.' Then, in a wave of aftershave mingled with garlic, he moved on.

'He's flirting with you!' I teased after Raniero had returned to his kitchen.

Izzy flushed and slipped the tip of her spoon into the tiramisu that Susanna had just placed in front of her. 'Nonsense. He's just happy to have somebody he can speak Italian with, other than his sister.'

I smacked my forehead with the palm of my hand. 'Duh. With a name like Ysabelle Milanesi, how could you be anything *but* Italian! Is Milanesi your maiden name?'

'My husband was Italian, too, but he came from the North End of Boston. Second generation. His parents owned a market on Salem Street.'

'Izzy was a war bride,' Naddie explained.

Izzy polished off the last of her tiramisu, shoved the dish toward the center of the table, then rested her forearms on the tablecloth. 'That's true, Hannah, but I spent most of the Second World War in a convent outside of Rome.'

'You were a nun?' I asked.

Izzy shook her head. 'No, I was a fourteen-year-old Jewish girl.'

I sat in stunned silence for what seemed like an eternity but was probably only a few seconds as I struggled to form the words to the questions that were ricocheting around my brain.

Izzy came to my rescue. 'It is a long story, and a sad one.'

Was she dismissing me, or did she really want to talk about it? 'If it's not too difficult for you,' I encouraged, 'I'd really like to hear it.'

Residents at the tables around us had finished their meals and begun to trickle out of the dining room. I stole a quick look at Naddie, who nodded almost imperceptibly, then raised a hand, summoning Susanna over from a table she'd been busily clearing nearby.

'Coffee all around, I think, Susanna.'

'Yes ma'am.'

'Do you mind if we sit here chatting for a while? We're finished with these dishes so you can clear them away.'

'No trouble at all, Mrs Gray. I'll be back in a minute with your coffee.'

Izzy took a deep breath then let it out slowly. 'So, where do I begin?'

SIX

'The Italians are extremely lax in their treatment of Jews. They protect Italian Jews both in Tunis and in occupied France and won't permit their being drafted for work or compelled to wear the Star of David.'
Joseph Goebbels, *The Goebbels Diaries*,
December 13, 1942.

'In the years before the war, my family and I lived comfortably in Rome, in Trastavere,' Izzy began, stirring a generous portion of cream into her coffee.

'Trastavere! I know it. The old Jewish quarter, right?'

When Izzy nodded, I told her, 'Paul and I vacationed in Rome a couple of years ago and we stayed in Borgo, near the Vatican. Several evenings we strolled along the Tiber to Trastavere for dinner. There are some wonderful restaurants there. I remember, oh, what was it? This marvelous fried artichoke dish; it looked like an exploded sunflower.' I demonstrated with my hands.

'*Carciofi alla giudia*,' Izzy supplied. 'Artichoke in the Jewish style.'

'Yes, that's it. Crisp, nutty. Totally delicious.'

Naddie passed me the sugar. 'We should put it on Raniero's list.'

'Absolutely.' I sipped my coffee. 'What did your father do, Izzy?'

'He owned a small art gallery which was popular with local artists, but he made most of his money restoring paintings for larger galleries like the Vatican Museum.'

I set my cup down. 'Wow.'

Izzy smiled sadly. 'I was too young then to be impressed. *Abba* worked primarily in the *Pinacoteca*, specializing in fifteenth-century restorations. When he began, the museum had been open only a few years, and many of the works had been in storage since 1815 when they were returned from Paris, so there was much work to do.'

Paris? Then the penny dropped. 'Napoleon took off with them, I suppose.'

Izzy nodded. 'Years later, when Bruno and I visited the galleries, I found myself looking closely at the paintings. This Fra Angelico, that Raphael, a glorious Bellini . . . searching for any small detail that could be by my father's hand. The halo of a saint, a Pope's ring, a cherub's toe.'

'Bruno was your husband?'

She nodded. 'But Bruno's part of the story comes much later.'

Filomena materialized at my right elbow, creeping up on us so quietly that I was startled. 'Biscotti? We make them here.'

'Yes, thank you, Filomena,' Naddie said as the catering manager set a silver tray carrying an artistically stacked pyramid of biscotti down on the table in front of us.

'In Argentina, we call these cookies *cantuccini*,' Filomena said.

I loomed hungrily over the tray, as if I hadn't just eaten a monster crab salad and a crème brulee. 'That was very thoughtful,' I said, selecting a chocolate-covered *cantuccini* dotted with almonds. 'I hope we're not keeping you?'

Filomena waved away our concerns. 'No worries! Stay as long as you like.' Then she disappeared as quickly as she had come.

Izzy selected a biscotti for herself, dunked it into her coffee and held it there. 'After the war began, my father believed we were safe because he had joined the Fascist Party, and was even active at their meetings.' She bit into the soggy biscotti, chewed, then continued. 'In those days *everybody* in Italy was a Fascist, at least on paper.

'Until the *Manifesto della razza* in 1938, that is. That was when Mussolini's Fascist government forbid Jewish children from attending schools. Mother taught my little brother and me at home, but in the forties the persecutions got worse. My father was forced to sell his business to Aryans at fire-sale prices, and we lost the gallery that had been in our family for three generations.'

The unfairness of it, the cruelty, stung me. 'How awful,' I said.

'I heard about the persecutions in Nazi Germany, of course, but Italy?'

'The racial laws took everyone by surprise,' Izzy continued. 'The Jewish community of Rome goes back to the second century BC when the Roman Empire had an alliance of sorts with Judea under the leadership of Judah Maccabeus.' She shrugged. 'I think the government wanted to prevent people like my father, who had quite a bit of money, from transferring it out of the country. Father continued working for a while – his work at the Vatican offered him some protection – but when the Germans occupied my country in 1943, they came looking for us.'

I'd forgotten my biscotti; my coffee had grown cold. 'Good Lord.'

'My mother spoke five different languages, Hannah. The Nazis *said* they wanted to employ her as a translator but that was a lie. Instead, they sent my parents to Risiera de San Sabba, a rice mill on the outskirts of Trieste, but it was really a concentration camp. From there, they were taken to Auschwitz.'

I swallowed hard and put down the biscotti I'd been nibbling, no longer particularly hungry for it.

Naddie reached out covered Izzy's hand with her own. 'I'm so sorry.'

'That was before the Nazis installed a crematorium at Risiera to save themselves the trouble of shipping undesirables out of the country,' Izzy said bitterly. 'I never saw my parents again. The Nazis took everything from us. Everything.'

I dabbed at my eyes with my napkin, trying to take in the enormity of it all. Like millions before me, I'd had a teary, gut-wrenching visit to the Holocaust Museum in Washington, D.C., but I'd never known anyone who had personally experienced the Holocaust. Those who had survived, like Izzy, were now in their eighties and nineties, and I hoped that testimonies like hers were being recorded before it was too late.

'How did you and your brother escape the Nazis when they came for your parents?' I asked after a few moments of respectful silence.

'When rumors reached Rome that the Germans were coming, my parents sent Umberto and me to live with family friends in the country, the DeLucas, but even there we were not safe. One day, the German soldiers came looking, but the word had gotten around, so the DeLucas hid us under the floorboards under a bed.'

'Someone had turned you in?' Naddie asked.

'Exactly. In those days, it was dangerous to put your trust in anybody. After the soldiers went away, the DeLucas quickly arranged shelter for us in a convent just outside of Rome. My father's connections with the Vatican made that possible. If it weren't for that . . .' She shrugged.

'I wore the habit of a novice,' she continued. 'The Nazis were watching the convent, I know, and soldiers knocked on the gates from time to time, but even the Nazis wouldn't mess with the Reverend Mother Francesca Louise!' She managed a smile. 'Oh, she could be a terror!'

'What was it like, living in the convent?' Naddie asked.

'What I remember most is being hungry. The nuns shared what food they had with us, but we were always hungry. And the flour had weevils in it.'

'Ugh,' I said.

Izzy's mouth twitched. 'Extra protein, Reverend Mother used to say.'

'And your brother? What happened to Umberto?' I asked.

'He got typhus,' she said simply. 'He died.'

'I'm so sorry,' I said, feeling lower than a snake for even bringing it up.

Izzy shrugged. 'When the fever came, the nuns did everything they could for Umberto but there was no food, no medicine. I blame that on the Nazis, too.

'Anyway, you can imagine how happy everyone was when the American soldiers came and Rome was liberated!' She leaned forward over her coffee cup. 'I stayed at the convent, though, because I had no place else to go.'

Filomena had sent a server out from the kitchen with a carafe of fresh coffee. I was already on a caffeine high but asked the young woman for a refill anyway.

'This is where Bruno Milanesi comes into the story,' Izzy said after the server had returned to the kitchen. 'Bruno, he was a corporal with the U.S. 5th Army. The army had taken over a *scuola secondaria* that was near the convent and, even though the war was over, food was still scarce. My Bruno – only he wasn't my Bruno then, of course – comes over with fresh eggs. He says in broken Italian – he didn't speak good Italian at all, being an American boy – that he works in the kitchen, and would we like some eggs?' Izzy rolled her eyes. 'Oh, those were the most delicious eggs I had ever tasted! Bruno brought us eggs and cheese and sometimes apples. Later, when I got to know him better, I found out he was trading the cigarettes in his rations for food. He'd bring us the used coffee grounds, too. So wasteful, the U.S. Army. The nuns could always squeeze some more coffee out of those grounds! "Practically fresh," Reverend Mother used to say.

'One day, Bruno comes to the Reverend Mother and tells her he wants to marry me. There weren't many Italian boys left, and I think the nuns saw it as an opportunity to get rid of me!' For the first time that afternoon, Izzy laughed. 'Bruno and I had fallen in love, of course, but I was only fourteen and too young to marry. Luckily one of the nuns had a brother who got me false papers. He was a printer who had helped hundreds of Jews escape the Germans. I didn't have a passport, but this man provided a birth certificate for me that said I was born in 1928, not 1930. We used the certificate to get a passport saying I was sixteen so that we could get married and I could go back to the United States with Bruno as a war bride. I had to go for blood tests at the Red Cross, and present that certificate and other documentation to his captain in order to get permission to marry.'

'What kind of papers did they want?' Naddie wondered.

'Some of the soldiers had what you would call "a wife in every port." The army wanted to make sure Bruno wasn't already married! But I knew he was an honest boy because he took my picture to send to his mother in Boston so she would know what her new daughter-in-law was going to look like.' She laughed again. 'I often wonder what she thought, Bruno's mother, of Bruno's "Little Bella". I was a tiny speck of a thing back then, you can imagine, after so long with so little to eat. We had rations, like half a pound of bread a day, but if that's all you have to eat it's not much. I weighed ninety-eight pounds.

'Then, we found out that Bruno was being shipped to Germany, and then back to America to be discharged, and the army doesn't give a hoot that he has a fiancée in Italy. So I was thinking I'd never see him again. But, life goes on. I got a job working part-time in an *alimentari*. Then, one day months later, Reverend Mother came with a letter from Bruno. He'd gotten a two-week furlough.' Izzy looked from me to Naddie and back again. 'Everything was destroyed by the war, you understand. Everything. There was no electricity, no telephone, no railroad. It was very cold that winter, but Bruno hitchhiked from Monte Castello, where the army was helping the Brazilians push back the Germans, all the way to Rome! We got married right away. I didn't even have time to rent a wedding dress. The next day we walked to the Red Cross where he signed me up as a GI wife so that I could get benefits, and then he had to leave and I didn't see him again for almost a year. I got his letters, though. Every week he wrote me, although I'd get the letters in batches.

'But then, time passed and I hadn't heard from Bruno for several months. I was worried he'd forgotten about me when the Red Cross sent a letter telling me to go to a certain hotel where I would wait with other GI brides for a boat to take us to America. There were maybe five hundred war brides and over one hundred children all crowded together on that ship. Some of us were seasick for the whole ten days, but all the hardships flew straight out of my mind when we sailed into New York harbor and I saw the Statue of Liberty for the first time. I stood on the deck and bawled my eyes out.'

I scrabbled in my handbag, looking for a tissue. 'Now you've made me cry,' I sniffed, then blew my nose.

'Bruno was there to meet me, and his mother, too. She was a wonderful woman! She'd sent me a dress to wear for my "home-coming." Other than that, I really brought nothing with me.' She paused for a moment. 'Except for . . .'

We waited expectantly, but she didn't finish the sentence. 'Except for what?' Naddie prodded.

'Before *Abba* was forced to sell, he saved one thing. It's a portrait of me, painted when I was around four, holding my kitten, Merlino.'

I was astonished. 'How on earth did you get the painting out of Italy?'

Izzy smiled. '*Abba* carefully removed it from the frame,

wrapped it in a special canvas, and my mother sewed it into the lining of my suitcase. The painting's hanging in my living room now. I'll show it to you sometime.'

'I'd love to see it,' I said.

'It's lovely,' Naddie said. 'I never knew its history. Fascinating.' Turning to Izzy, she asked, 'Is the painting valuable?'

Izzy shrugged. 'It's priceless to me, of course. I remember sitting for the artist, a flamboyant and rather scary woman named Clotilde Padovano. In the early part of the twentieth century, she was very much in demand as a portrait painter to the well-to-do. I don't follow such things closely, but I read in the *Times* that one of her portraits was recently sold at auction in New York for a hundred and twenty thousand dollars.'

I whistled.

'I'll never part with *mine*, of course,' she said.

'Nor would I, if it were mine,' I said. 'Not even if I were reduced to selling umbrellas on street corners.'

Izzy laughed then picked up her handbag, preparing to go. As we got up to join her, I turned to Izzy again. 'Izzy, I have a rude question.'

'Yes?'

'For lunch just now, you had calamari. Isn't squid a non-kosher food, *treif*?'

Izzy laid a hand on my shoulder. 'I learned a long time ago, Hannah, that it is never safe to be Jewish. Maybe it was the years of living on the edge of being found out. Maybe it was the hours of kneeling on the cold floor of the convent at *matins* and *prime*. But, after I married Bruno, I converted. I've been a practicing Catholic ever since.'

I accompanied my friends to the entrance of Blackwalnut Hall, hugged them both goodbye then headed off in the direction of the parking lot to collect my car.

As I rounded the corner of the building I noticed two men squared off on the concrete apron outside the service entrance to the kitchen, looking for all the world like boxing bears. One had to be Raniero Buccho; nobody else at Calvert Colony had hair that impossibly blond. From his black-and-white uniform and the argument I'd overheard earlier, I guessed the other was probably the hapless kitchen staffer. I was too far away to hear what the men were saying, but from the way Raniero's arms were flailing about I could tell he was giving the other guy a sizable piece of his mind. Raniero's adversary stood his ground, his chin thrust forward, unflappably defiant. Curiosity aroused, I briefly considered moving to within earshot of the pair, but when I checked my watch I knew I had to hustle. I was due to pick up my granddaughter, Chloe, from her ballet lesson at three, and if I didn't hurry I'd be late.

It was none of my business anyway, I thought as I climbed into my ancient LeBaron and slotted the key into the ignition. Raniero had a short fuse, no doubt about that. He was as likely to clobber someone over a dropped serving platter or a misplaced twist of lemon peel as he would, say, over a diner's complaint about finding a hair in the *vichyssoise*. Besides, I thought, as I pulled out of the parking lot and into the drive, the other guy seemed to be giving as good as he got. I smiled. Poor Raniero.

SEVEN

'As early as 1998, researchers were reporting that music could serve as an important tool for decreasing aggressive behavior in Alzheimer's sufferers. In 2004, another paper suggested that memory for familiar music might remain intact in some dementia patients. "Music of the right kind," neurologist Oliver Sacks said in a 2007 interview, "can serve to orient and anchor a patient when almost nothing else can. The past, which is not recoverable in any other way, is embedded, as if in amber, in the music, and people can regain a sense of identity."'
Anne Arundel *Health Matters* magazine, Spring, 2012.

Early the following morning I was soaking in a bathtub full of lavender bubbles when Naddie called and made me an offer I couldn't refuse. Become a volunteer in the memory unit and Calvert Colony would provide me with lunch. Free. All

I'd have to do is help some of the residents with their individual iPods, take walks with some and read stories to others.

Since Paul was still in the process of circumnavigating Long Island, the prospect of Raniero's cooking was a lot more appealing than what I'd planned for myself that day, namely sliced tomatoes and a carton of Stouffers macaroni and cheese, which still lay rock solid in the freezer compartment of my fridge.

Besides, it wasn't exactly a hardship. Visiting Blackwalnut Hall was like checking into the Hyatt Regency. In fact, when I reported to the lounge for duty later that morning, an attractive man dressed in high prep – khakis, a navy sports jacket and a button-down oxford shirt with a red tie – sat coaxing sixties and seventies tunes out of the Steinway grand.

While I waited along with Naddie for a woman named Elaine Broering to escort me into the memory unit, I couldn't resist singing along, echoing the responses in 'The Candy Man' along with most of the residents sitting around me. Two of the singers were the pair of lovebirds I'd seen sitting at the piano the previous week, sharing their love of Stephen Foster favorites with the other residents.

Halfway through the next selection, where a couple of members of our intrepid gang of backup singers got irretrievably stuck on 'Sgt Pepper's lonely, Sgt Pepper's lonely, Sgt Pepper's lonely, Sgt Pepper's lonely . . .' with no indication that they'd ever reach the 'Hearts Club Band' part of the song, I noticed a young man pacing nervously in front of the reception desk. He wore a shiny blue suit that stood out like a neon sign among the more casually attired seniors around him. He carried a bouquet of flowers, too, their stems wrapped in the familiar green tissue paper of a local supermarket chain. He also looked vaguely familiar.

'Hold the phone! Isn't that . . .' Naddie began, but for me, the penny had already dropped. The last time I'd seen that dude, he'd been showing off his tats on a video chat with Christie McSpadden.

'Apparently Dickie-boy isn't in Afghanistan anymore,' I said. 'I think I better go telephone Angie.'

I excused myself and slipped out onto the front porch. At first I thought Angie wasn't going to answer. After four rings my call switched over to her answerphone, but she picked up mid-message with a breathless, 'Hello.' Then: 'You got me down in the basement doing laundry,' Angie said after I'd identified myself. 'What's up?'

'Thought you'd want to know that Dickie-boy has come to call.'

Silence stretched out for several long seconds before Angie exploded, 'Shit! He's not in Kandahar. No wonder she's been so concerned over her appearance lately. I should have picked up on that. What should I do, Hannah?'

'Tell you what, I'll keep an eye on him while you get yourself over here.' I watched through the leaded glass on the door while Richard Whatever-his-name-was signed in on the little computer screen at reception. 'Your mother-in-law hasn't shown up yet. But Angie,' I continued, 'the guy's got flowers.'

'Of course he does. And probably a box of chocolate-covered cherries, too.'

'How soon can you get over here?'

'I'm on my way.'

'What if he plans to take Christie out?' I asked.

'Well, we can't stop her. Calvert Colony isn't a prison camp, and she still has a car and a valid driver's license, although I wish like hell she wouldn't drive.'

'I just watched the guy sign in. Would an ax murderer do that?' I paused to collect my thoughts. 'Tell you what,' I volunteered, Nancy Drew to the rescue, 'if they leave, I'll try to follow. We can keep in touch by cell phone, OK?'

Angie agreed and cut the connection.

I rejoined Naddie. We had reached the final verse of 'I Got a Crush on You, Sweetie Pie' when Christie finally appeared, gliding down the grand staircase like Loretta Young. Loretta would have been wearing a designer ball gown and masses of jewels, but Christie looked smart in a surprisingly age-appropriate blue-checked shirtwaist dress and a pair of black-and-white spectator flats. She'd even dug a chunky gold chain necklace out of her jewelry box, with a pair of matching earrings.

Clearly, Richard's visit was no surprise.

He recognized her at once, took several quick steps forward and gave her a chaste kiss on the cheek. The flowers were handed over. I wasn't close enough to hear what the two were saying over the exuberant, off-key singing that was filling the lobby, but their body language was clear enough. Christie pressed her hand against her breast. *For me? How sweet!* Then enveloped him in a hug.

Oh, it's nothing. He accepted the hug a bit stiffly, or so it seemed to me.

Christie handed the bouquet to the receptionist – *would you put these in water for me, please?* – took Richard's arm and dragged him over to a loveseat by the fireplace. Never mind that Edith was already sitting there, reading. With an imperial wave, Christie promptly dispatched the poor woman – afghan, paperback, teacup and all – so that she and Richard could sit down on it.

'I'll be right back,' I whispered to Naddie, and scooted off.

'. . . take a taxi?' Christie was saying to Richard as I crept up casually behind them, feigning fascination with a game of hearts going on at a table in a nearby corner.

'Cab? You've got to be kidding, Christie. I walked the queue, took one look and said no way. Decided to get a rental car. All the cabbies at BWI are Muslims.'

'Surely not!' she chirped.

'It's the same in New York. I'll bet you didn't know that they come to the U.S. to work as cab drivers for a year so they can get enough money to blow themselves up.'

I turned away from the card game in time to see Christie shove Richard's arm playfully with the flat of her hand. 'You!'

'There goes one now,' Richard said. 'Halloween must be coming early this year.'

He was obviously referring to Safa Abaza, wearing a pale blue hijab, who had paused in front of the reception desk to hand an envelope to the receptionist. Richard stared with obvious venom at Safa's back as she disappeared through the doorway of the memory unit.

'Don't be ugly, Dickie,' Christie chided. 'She's really a nice woman. Volunteers with the dementia patients, which is more than most people would do.'

'You can't trust *any* of 'em, not even the children.' His voice broke. After a pause, he cleared his throat and continued, 'Let's just say it's my first amendment right as an American to hate anybody I want, even Muslims.'

One of the hearts players had a gold-knobbed walking stick propped up against his chair. I felt like grabbing the stick and using it to clobber the Islamophobic jerk, but I was saved from a life sentence for murder when Richard reached over and picked up Christie's hand, clasping it in both of his own. 'I was an army medic in Afghanistan, Christie.'

Christie stared at Richard for a moment as the significance of his statement sank in. She withdrew her hand from his and pressed both her palms over her ears. 'Stop. I don't want to hear it.'

Richard ignored her. 'I was in a convoy when it was halted by an IED up ahead. While we waited for our guys to move the wreckage off the road, our Jeep was rushed by a crowd of kids – seven, maybe eight years old – begging for candy. I was tossing out strawberry Pop-Rocks when they swarmed over us, and one of them cut my buddy's neck with a knife. I did everything I could to stop the bleeding, got him on the helicopter and out to the hospital in Bagram . . .' Richard paused and swallowed hard. 'He . . . he didn't make it.'

Christie's hands came down. She'd been listening after all. 'Eight years old?'

Richard nodded. 'If that.'

'Bomb 'em back to the Stone Age,' Christie chirped. 'That's what Colonel Greene always says.'

'We can't,' Richard said. 'They're *living* in the Stone Age.'

I was observing the couple openly now, but they were so engrossed in their own conversation that they didn't seem to notice.

'My skills as a medic went *way* beyond your average Afghan doctor,' Richard said. 'You know what they do for wounds?'

Christie shook her head.

'Slop red dye all over it and hope.'

'Did you have to treat the locals, too?' Christie asked.

'Damn straight. But even when they're shot up or sick you can't be sure they're not wired up with explosives.'

Christie mewled. 'It must be nerve-wracking to risk your life trying to save the life of someone who woke up that morning planning to kill you.'

'That's my point, Christie. The fewer Muslims there are the better it will be for the world.'

'So you're back now?' Christie asked. 'For good, I mean.'

'I'm at Walter Reed,' Richard began, 'in the . . .'

'Hannah? Hannah Ives?'

A pleasingly plump woman wearing a peach-colored suit and a nametag that read 'Elaine Broering, Supervisor, Memory Unit,' appeared at my elbow and introduced herself. 'The receptionist pointed you out.'

My mental gears ground from fast forward into reverse as I tried to push Christie and Richard's conversation out of my mind. 'The man's good,' I said, referring to the pianist who had segued neatly from Perry Como and 'Papa Loves Mambo' into Leslie Gore's 'It's My Party and I'll Cry if I Want To.'

'I agree completely. That's Charlie Robinson. He volunteers here every Thursday afternoon. In his regular life he's a building contractor, although you can sometimes catch his act out at Nordstrom, particularly during the holiday season.'

'Love the tie,' I commented. Robinson had shifted slightly on the piano bench and I could see that the red tie had Scottish terriers on it.

'He has quite a collection,' Elaine told me. 'Last week he showed up wearing a tie that looked like a whole fish. On the Fourth of July it was the Statue of Liberty. The residents love it. The ties entertain them almost as much as his music.'

'I'm getting a kick out of the couple on the sofa,' I said, bobbing my head in their direction. 'She plays the piano rather well, too.'

'Ah, you must mean Jerry and Nancy – two of my favorite people. Hard not to smile when you're around them. Until a month or so ago Nancy was on a walker, in physical therapy every day.' She chuckled. 'Don't know why we bother with the PT now. Jerry seems to be just as effective.'

Charlie Robinson, flashing a Liberace-esque grin, segued into a hopping rendition of 'Boogie Woogie Bugle Boy of Company B.' As we watched, Jerry sprang to his feet with a spryness that surprised me, hitched up his pants, straightened his bow tie, grabbed Nancy by the hand and led her onto the dance floor. Soon they were jiving like arthritic teenagers. When the tune changed to 'Chattanooga Choo Choo' the couple barely paused, continuing a careful, but surprisingly sprightly two-step all around the lobby.

'Aren't you afraid they're going to fall and hurt themselves?' I asked.

'Hah! I can see his obituary now: Jerry Wolcott, age eighty-eight, collapses and dies while doing the boogie woogie at a local retirement home. In lieu of flowers, donations may be sent to the Welfare Fund for Aged Bankers.' She snorted softly. 'Frankly, I hope I go that way.'

'Me, too, but I'd go out discoing to something by the Bee Gees.'

'Chubby Checker, for me,' she said, swiping her bangs out of her eyes. 'Doing the twist.'

While I wondered whether Richard Kent was likely to be at Walter Reed as a patient or if he actually worked there, Elaine took me to her office, where she explained the typical duties of a volunteer, gave me background information on some of the residents, and a consent form to sign that said, basically, that if any of said residents decided to hit me over the head with a bedpan I was shit out of luck, lawsuit-wise. After a trip to Human Resources where I had my picture taken and was given a laminated clip-on name badge that identified me as an official volunteer, I was escorted back to the memory unit and given the combination to the door – 1632, the year Maryland was founded.

The memory unit was smaller and more intimate than the grand expanse of the main lobby, but handsome enough to qualify for its own spread in *House Beautiful*. There was nothing depressing about it. To my right was a small dining area that could seat a dozen diners; to my left, a comfortable lounge where several residents now sat, their backs to me, watching a rerun of *I Love Lucy* on a large, flat-screen TV mounted on the wall. A long corridor extended from where I stood near the entrance of the unit – which was secured with a push-button combination lock – to a double door at the far end. The corridor was carpeted with a short-napped broadloom with a unique design woven into the nap outside each resident's door – flowers, stars and geometric shapes.

As I watched, a man emerged from his room and shuffled down the hallway, talking to himself. He let himself out through the double door at the opposite end.

I tapped Elaine's arm. 'He's going outside.'

'Not to worry. There's a walled garden out there. Residents like to come and go as they please. He can't stray far.'

We poked our heads into the lounge, where Elaine introduced me to one of the uniformed aides who was dressed in pale yellow scrubs stylish enough to have been designed by Ralph Lauren, if only his logo had been embroidered on the pocket. The aide was filling a bowl from a family-sized bag of Hershey's miniatures. 'Help yourself,' she said after formal introductions were over.

I selected two semi-sweet chocolate bars and tucked them into my pocket. 'Thanks.'

The familiar theme song for *Gilligan's Island* drew my attention to the television and I noticed that the couple watching TV was Nancy and Jerry, who'd been tripping the light fantastic in the lounge only a couple of hours before. He kissed her cheek. She giggled.

'Sweet,' I whispered to Elaine. 'I hope Paul and I will be so happily married when we're that age.'

'Oh, they aren't married,' Elaine explained. 'At least, not to each other. Nancy has a husband up in Baltimore, but because of the Alzheimers and all he rarely visits anymore. Damn shame, really. He says, "What's the point?" Tells us he's "moved on with his life."' She drew quote marks in the air with her fingers and snorted her disapproval. 'Jerry's family is more attentive, but then they live right around the corner on East Lake. As I may have mentioned before, Jerry's a retired banker. He's been widowed for years.'

As I watched, feeling like a Peeping Tom, Jerry tipped up Nancy's chin and kissed her full on the lips. 'Doesn't her husband mind?' I asked.

'He knows. Whatever keeps her happy, that's what he tells us. If he doesn't mind, I don't know why anybody else should.' We walked a bit further, heading for the room of a woman named Lillian Blake to whom I was supposed to read. 'In nursing school,' Elaine continued, 'we learned that touch is the first sense to develop in the womb, and the last one to go before death. We can all benefit from a loving touch, no matter how out of it we appear.'

'I saw Jerry and Nancy in the main lounge a couple of days ago, too,' I said. 'She was playing the piano, so I'm quite surprised to find that they live here, in the memory unit, I mean.'

'We like to integrate our resident population,' Elaine said. 'Staff are always out there to keep an eye on them, just in case, but we keep it as unobtrusive as possible, very low key.'

'Aren't you afraid your residents will wander away?'

She smiled. 'We used to, until we got the special shoes. There's a GPS tracking device imbedded in the heel. If patients assigned to the memory unit wander outside the specified area, an alarm goes off. Using the GPS, security can quickly track them down. Unless they take their shoes, off, of course, but that rarely happens. It's usually hard for dementia patients to manage the laces.'

A resident marched crisply down the hall, a stopwatch in his hand. At the end he stopped, clicked the watch and shouted, 'Ninety-two seconds! A new world record!' He paused for a moment, as if to acknowledge silent applause, then headed back in our direction, his eyes glued to the stopwatch like the White Rabbit in *Alice in Wonderland*.

'Good morning,' I said as he breezed past.

'Can't stop now,' he said without looking up, 'or I'll be late for the train.'

'Pete worked for Norfolk Southern.' Elaine grinned at the man's departing back then turned to me, her light brown hair swinging just clear of her shoulders. 'Here we are. This is Lillian Blake's room. It's such a nice day, you might want to sit out in the garden.' She lowered her voice. 'Lillian's practically blind, I'm afraid, and she isn't able to feed herself very well, so she spends almost all her time here in the unit. Getting a little sun will be good for her.'

Lillian's room was the size of your average college dorm room. A double bed stood against the long wall, covered with a hand-made quilt; in the center lay a life-sized plush cat surrounded by more than a dozen other stuffed animals. The headboard, bedside table and dresser were made of matching honey-colored oak. Placed at an angle to the picture window was a loveseat upholstered in green and gold-striped silk; two lipstick-red pillows were plumped up and resting against the armrests. An afghan, neatly folded, was draped over the back.

Lillian waited for me on the loveseat, smiling, her hands folded primly in her lap. She was a sunny, apple dumpling of a woman dressed in a 1950s-style cotton housedress imprinted with white roses on a black background. Her feet were clad in bright red socks and laced up in sensible black oxfords.

Displayed on a coffee table in front of her were several large picture books: Cameron's *Above Washington*, a National Geographic encyclopedia of animals, and *Star Wars: A Galactic Pop-Up Adventure*. I had to laugh, but, hey, you'd have to be dead not to be a *Star Wars* fan.

'Lillian likes poetry,' Elaine said. From a bookshelf next to the dresser she extracted a book and handed it to me: Robert Lewis Stevenson's *A Child's Garden of Verses* with the classic illustrations by Mary Hallock. The cover was worn, and the spine mended with two kinds of plastic tape.

With Lillian clinging loosely to my arm we shuffled down the long hallway, out of the door and into a glorious secret garden. Paved paths wide enough to accommodate a wheelchair meandered among beautifully maintained beds of marigolds and hibiscus. Rows of perennials stood tall along the fence – I recognized rhododendron, yarrow and spiderwort – while ground ivy elsewhere provided a blanket of green. Several wrens and a fat robin were busy at a birdfeeder shaped like a pagoda that was under-planted with ferns and hosta. Somewhere a wind chime tinkled.

After Lillian and I got settled side by side on an old-fashioned glider swing, I opened the book and began to read. '"*In winter I get up at night, And dress by yellow candle-light. In summer, quite the other way, I have to go to bed by day. I have to go to bed and see . . .*"'

Lillian grabbed my wrist and squeezed, hard, harder than I believed possible for anyone so frail. 'They can't make *me* go to bed before dark,' she said, her pale blue eyes fixed so intensely on me that I imagined my cheek starting to burn. 'I'm a grown-up, you know.' After a pause, she said, 'I thought you were going to read.'

So I finished the poem. 'Should I read another one?' I asked, turning the page.

She nodded and began to hum tunelessly.

'"*How do you like to go up in a swing*? *Up in the air so blue* . . ."' I read before the humming stopped and her hand tightened around my wrist again.

'They *make* us go to bed early. But, sometimes I go visiting after dark.' She smiled mysteriously.

I lay the book of poetry, still open to the poem I'd been reading, in my lap.

'Where do you go, Lillian?'

'Oh, out and about. Out and about.'

I doubted if memory unit residents were allowed the same freedom to roam about the premises at night, when staffing was at reduced levels, as they did during the day. 'What is there to do at night?' I asked her, not really expecting an answer.

She pressed an index finger against her lips then poked me with it. 'I look after my babies.'

'Your babies?'

'I have lots of babies,' she told me. '*Lots* of babies!' She began humming again, rocking from side to side to a rhythm only she could perceive. 'Do you have babies?'

'I used to,' I told her. 'One, but she's all grown up now.'

Lillian nodded sagely. 'One, that's good. So much easier. If you have too many babies they squabble all the time.' She paused and looked directly toward a tree whose magnificent branches overhung the wall at the far end of the enclosed garden. 'I hear them, making noises.' She stared at it for a good few seconds then leaned in closer to me and started rocking again. 'Or they're whispering behind your back, cooking up mischief.'

Perhaps because we'd been reading classic children's verses I had to smile, picturing Lillian as the old woman who lived in a shoe, the one who had so many children she didn't know what to do. 'My daughter is named Emily,' I said. 'What did you name your babies?'

Lillian stopped rocking and frowned, as if giving my question serious consideration. 'There's Princess,' she said, touching the tip of one index finger to the other. 'And Spot. And Freckles.' She scowled, her index finger hovering. 'I forget the rest.'

Dogs? Lillian's 'babies' were dogs?

'I don't see very well,' she confided after a bit, 'but I can tell your trousers are red. I like red.'

'I like red, too, Lillian.'

In a seat under an arbor up which tendrils of wisteria had already started to climb, a woman in an orange sweater with an untidy mass of white hair sat in a wheelchair, smoking a cigarette. She inhaled and held the smoke in her lungs for so long that I was having flashbacks to 1967 and the Summer of Love. Then she exhaled slowly with obvious pleasure.

On the opposite side of the garden, under a plexiglass kiosk that looked for all the world like a bus stop, an even older man sat, his bald head encrusted with scabs, legs stretched straight out in front of him, his head thrown back and his mouth open. I worried for a moment that he had died, but then he snorted, started, looked around in confusion, checked his watch, shrugged, and then carried on with his nap. After puzzling over it for a moment I realized the kiosk *was* a bus stop, advertising posters and all. I smiled. All the comforts of home without going anywhere.

Next to me, the humming abruptly ceased. Lillian reached for the book in my lap, quickly flicked forward through the pages, then back, then forward again. She stopped, squinted and tapped the new page. 'Read this one,' she instructed.

As I did so, she leaned her head against the back of the seat and recited the poem along with me from memory, softly, barely moving her lips. '"*A birdie with a yellow bill, Hopped upon the window sill, Cocked his shining eye and said: Ain't you 'shamed, you sleepy-head.*"'

'I like that one, too,' I told her.

'More, please, lovey,' she said.

By the time I'd worked my way through 'Travel' and 'Land of Counterpane' Lillian Blake was sound asleep. I sat there quietly for a few minutes, enjoying the garden, the sun and the soft August breeze.

'The babies are fighting again.' Plump, sausage-like fingers closed around my wrist and squeezed.

I looked up from the page I'd been nodding over, wondering how long I'd been asleep. 'What?'

'*Agg! Argh! No! Arrr!*'

The sounds seemed to hover over the garden wall, encased in cartoon balloons.

'What's on the other side of the wall?' I asked Lillian.

'Dunno, lovey dove. Don't get out much.'

When designing the brick wall, Calvert Colony architects had taken precautions so that memory unit residents couldn't get out – safety measures that defeated me, too. At five foot six inches there was no way I could see over a seven-foot wall. I tried a few experimental jumps, accomplishing nothing but giving Lillian the giggles.

'Don't move,' I told her.

As Lillian observed with a bemused expression on her face, I rested one foot on the armrest of the swing, pulled the other foot after it, teetered for a moment to gain my balance, then stood on tiptoe and peered over the wall.

In a grassy patch on the other side, not far from the *musalla*, a man was on his hands and knees under a large tulip poplar. As I watched he struggled to his feet, dusted off his pants then inspected the front of his shirt, which I noticed was splotched with blood.

'Mr Abaza! Are you all right?'

Masud touched his nose experimentally. 'I believe so.'

'What on earth happened?'

'I was at prayer, and when I left the *musalla*, I caught a man . . .' He paused to take a handkerchief out of his back pocket and use it to clean his hands. 'This evildoer was spray painting graffiti on the wall of the *musalla*.'

I squinted into the distance and saw that Masud was right. *Remember 9/11!!* and *Burn the Kor* had been sprayed in bold black letters, defacing one side of the pretty little building.

'I tackled him before he could finish the job,' Masud said, which explained the 'Kor.'

'Who was it?' I asked. 'Another resident?'

'If it was I didn't recognize him. He was wearing a monkey cap.'

My granddaughter, Chloe, had a winter hat knit up like a sock monkey. Masud must have noticed my puzzlement because he explained, 'A balaclava, like you wear for skiing, with holes for the eyes and mouth. He wore a ball cap, too. Gray, with a blue star on it.' He tucked the handkerchief back into his pocket. 'I kicked the man hard in the uh, uh . . .'

The next word was probably going to be 'balls' but Masud

did a quick vocabulary adjustment and substituted 'thigh.' He waved an arm. 'After that, he ran across the lawn and into the woods over there.'

I scanned the line of trees that bordered the property and, seeing nothing, turned my attention back to Masud. 'Do you need an ambulance, Mr Abaza?'

He shook his head. 'No, no. A bloody nose, a few bruises. It's already stopped bleeding. I'll be fine.'

'Shall I call the police?'

'No, but thank you.' His dark eyes met mine. 'I'd appreciate it if you'd say nothing about this to anyone until I've had an opportunity to take the matter up directly with Mr Bennett.'

'Are you . . .' I began, but he cut me off with a wave.

'Calvert Colony is supposed to be a *secure* facility. Where are the security guards, that's what I want to know. Somebody is not doing their duty.'

Masud bent over, felt about in a bed of *pachysandra* that bordered the wall on his side and came up holding a spray can labeled Krylon. 'I got his paint can,' he said, not bothering to suppress the note of triumph in his voice. 'That man will pay for insulting Islam.'

'Maybe there'll be fingerprints,' I pointed out helpfully.

'Perhaps.' Holding the can gingerly by the rim, he turned to go, paused for a moment then looked up at me. 'Thank you for your concern.'

'No problem.' I watched until he disappeared around the side of the building.

'What's happening?' Lillian asked in a quiet, worried voice.

Too late, I realized that she was standing to my right, next to the wall. Since Lillian's ample bottom had been providing the ballast that kept me more or less securely balanced on the arm of the glider, I found myself suddenly catapulted into the flower bed when the arm dropped out from under me.

I must have cried out as I hit the ground.

'Hey! Everything all right over there?' the orange-sweatered woman wanted to know.

'Fine!' I caroled from a prone position in the zinnias.

'Peachy,' Lillian replied with a conspirational glance in my direction.

'Those men?' Lillian said as I got to my feet, dusted off my red slacks and began to pick cedar chips out of my hair. She bobbed her head, indicating the wall. 'My eyes are no good, but there's nothing wrong with my ears.'

'You heard something interesting, Lillian?'

'Uh huh.'

She was making me work for it, and judging by the sly grin lighting her face, Lillian knew it, too.

'One man said, "I'm going to kill you, you mother fucking son of a bitch."'

'Which one?' I asked, trying hard not to laugh at the poster image of a grandmother standing before me, swearing like a longshoreman.

She shrugged then smiled beatifically. 'Dunno, lovey.'

Which left me wondering whether it really was the graffiti artist who'd threatened to kill Masud. Could it have been the other way around?

EIGHT

'O Prophet! Tell your wives and your daughters and the women of the believers to draw their cloaks (veils) all over their bodies. That will be better, that they should be known (as free respectable women) so as not to be annoyed.'
Quran, 33:59

When I met Naddie for lunch in the dining room half an hour later, as hard as it was not to mention the attack on Masud that I'd come within sixty seconds of witnessing, I kept my promise. My head was spinning with thoughts as to who the balaclava man might have been – sadly, there were a few potential suspects. Naddie was an investor in Calvert Colony so she'd find out about the incident eventually, but I owed Masud the courtesy of allowing him to report it to The Powers That Be himself.

'Who is that?' I asked, as we tucked into our starters.

'Who?' Naddie considered my question over a bowl of *vichyssoise*.

I pointed with my soup spoon. 'That guy talking to Raniero, over by the kitchen door. Light brown hair. Blue suit, yellow tie. He looks like a lawyer.'

She turned her head. 'Oh, I should introduce you. That's Tyson Bennett. He's the executive director of Calvert Colony. A hands-on kind of guy who really seems to care about the residents.'

Ah ha, I thought. The Powers That Be himself.

Naddie waved in Tyson's direction but he was too engrossed in his conversation with the chef to notice. 'Tyson used to be a lawyer but after he won some sort of long-running, high-profile liability case and got a whopping settlement for his client, he decided to retire from practicing law.'

I blew on a spoonful of clam chowder to cool it. 'Must be nice.'

'Everyone thought Tyson was going into politics,' Naddie continued, 'but he disappointed everyone by applying his considerable clout and expertise to community work. After he uncovered Medicare fraud on a massive scale at a national nursing home chain where, basically, the company was giving patients rehab they didn't need and billing the government for it, he found himself on the board of several hospitals, so when the investors were looking for somebody squeaky clean to run Calvert Colony, his name shot to the top of the list.'

'I haven't talked to all the staff, of course, but from what I've heard, I really like Tyson's philosophy.'

She smiled. 'We all do. That's why he's in charge here.'

The server had just delivered our sandwiches – tuna melt for me and a BLT for Naddie – when Tyson Bennett made a pit stop at our table. After Naddie introduced me, he said, 'Ah yes. Mrs Ives. I hear you're volunteering in the memory unit. Thank you for that.'

'No secrets around here, then,' I joked. 'And please, call me Hannah.'

'I believe I know your husband, Paul? We met at the Rotary Club crab feast last week.'

If the annual Annapolis Rotary Club crab feast didn't have a place in the *Guinness Book of World Records* as the largest crab feast in the world, it ought to. For sixty bucks, you, too, could be one of the twenty-five hundred folks who filled the Navy-Marine Corps stadium and chowed down on four-thousand crabs, thirty-four hundred ears of corn, a hundred-and-thirty gallons of crab soup, God only knows how many hot dogs, and barrels and barrels of draft beer. You could buy T-shirts, too, natch. 'Sorry to have missed it this year,' I lied. Picking crabs just wasn't my thing, not even for charity.

Tyson's blue eyes considered me curiously from behind his aviator glasses. 'Paul and I were working the Budweiser truck,' he said. 'Sixty kegs consumed, more or less.'

'Not much left for the ticket holders, then,' I joked.

Tyson laughed. 'Well, can't claim we didn't sample the merchandise, but somebody had to make sure it was potable.'

'A tough job, but somebody has to do it,' Naddie said.

'Will I see you at the board meeting this afternoon, Mrs Gray? Something just came up that we need to discuss.'

'With bells on,' Naddie replied, sounding grim.

'Nice to have met you, Hannah.' Tyson extended his hand.

'Likewise,' I said, shaking it, thinking Masud Abaza hadn't wasted any time taking his complaint straight to the top of the food chain.

After Tyson disappeared into the lounge, Naddie took a bite of her sandwich, chewed thoughtfully, then said, 'To tell you the truth, Hannah, I can't *stand* board meetings. If they simply read what's been sent out with the agenda ahead of time, what the hell is the point? Should be spelled B-O-R-E-D, if you ask me.'

I'd been the records manager for a large accounting firm in Washington, D.C., so I'd attended my share of 'bored' meetings, too. It was another thing I didn't miss about not having a career 'outside the home' – that and the punishing commute.

'I think you'll find there's an item on the agenda that wasn't included in the email,' I said. Over the soup, I gave Naddie a head's up on the vandalized *musalla* and Masud's tussle with Balaclava Man.

Naddie dabbed her lips with her napkin then threw it down on the tablecloth. 'Damn, damn, damn! *Just* what we need.'

'Do you think Tyson will report the incident to the police, Naddie?'

'I'm *sure* of it, Hannah. If it were simply an act of vandalism . . .' She looked thoughtful. '. . . probably not. But you say Masud Abaza was attacked by this guy?'

In spite of the seriousness of the conversation, I smiled. 'According to Masud, it was quite the other way around, Naddie. Masud caught the guy in the act and tackled him. That's when the fist fight broke out.'

After a pause, during which Naddie seemed to be marshalling her thoughts, she said, 'So, other than that, Colonel Custer, how was your first day on the job?'

'Uneventful,' I fibbed. 'At least nobody yelled or threw things, or decided to take off their pants like Paul's great uncle William used to do whenever things at the nursing home didn't go his way.' I slid a homemade potato chip into my mouth, bit down and sighed with pleasure – crunchy, nutty, just a hint of salt. 'Why me, though? Are you short-staffed or something?'

Naddie frowned. 'Not at all, it's just that we've found that the residents benefit from the extra one-on-one attention they receive from somebody not in a uniform. Our volunteers tend to serve as an extended family for the residents, and they look forward to every visit.' She waved a dill pickle spear over her plate. 'It's especially true for the older residents who have outlived most of their family. One of our volunteers brings in her children and the residents treat them like their own grandchildren. It's really heartwarming.'

'How many volunteers are there?'

'It varies but right now, counting you, there's eight.' She folded her napkin and laid it on the tablecloth. 'There's another volunteer over there, in fact, having lunch with her husband, the guy we've just been speaking about.'

I swiveled in my seat. The dining room was full so I wasn't sure to whom she was referring. In addition to several faces I recognized from the sing-alongs in the lounge, I noticed Safa Abaza sitting with Masud at a table for two in an isolated corner of the dining room. A shopping bag from Nordstrom rested on the floor next to her chair and she was showing him a necklace she'd evidently purchased. His face remained blank, bored. He concentrated on his plate, where he seemed to be dissecting a lamb kabob. As I watched, he dragged a cube of lamb through a pile of rice, not seeming to notice either his wife or the necklace with which she seemed so pleased.

'You mean the Abazas.'

'Correct. Safa has been volunteering in the memory unit for several months. She's a quiet, gentle soul and the residents love her.'

'Confession,' I said. 'I've met Safa, too, while I was waiting for you the other day. Since you were so late . . .' I gave her a wink, '. . . we had time for a good chat. Interesting woman.'

Her mouth full of fruit salad, Naddie simply nodded.

Before coming to lunch, Masud had changed into a clean shirt. Safa wore an ankle-length, long-sleeved shapeless black garment, possibly because she'd been out in public, shopping at the mall. A brilliant saffron-colored silk scarf covered her head and neck. 'It's August, for heaven's sake. It must get hot under all those layers,' I mused. 'She must feel like ripping them off and jumping into the swimming pool.'

'From time to time, she does. You should see her burkini,' Naddie said.

'You're kidding me. A burkini?'

'It looks like a full-body wetsuit with a colorful hood to pull over your head. Safa's a modest but thoroughly modern Muslim woman.'

I considered going up to their table and introducing myself to Masud – he'd seen me at least two times, after all, but we'd never been formally introduced. He probably thought I was a member of the staff. Masud looked like such a sourpuss, however, that I decided to put that on the back burner. Besides, I might unwittingly be breaching protocol.

I decided I'd let Safa make the first move in that direction. I'd probably see her again soon enough anyway – if not around Calvert Colony proper, our paths might cross eventually in the memory unit.

It ended up being much sooner than I expected.

NINE

'Regardless of a nursing home resident's age or mental capacity, they need touch and affection. Residents of all U.S. facilities have a right to romance – as long as it's consensual. "We try to keep residents as independent as possible," said Suzanne Garside, executive director of Emeritus at Federal Way. Residents find love and get remarried at the assisted living facility. Caregivers have also walked in on couples by accident, but unless safety is compromised, they let the fireworks continue.'

FederalWayMirror.com, July 3, 2012.

As was quickly becoming our habit, Naddie and I lingered over our coffee for so long that the wait staff had begun to loom like vultures, preparing to pounce on our dishes the instant we finished with them. 'Guess it's time to go,' I said, laying my napkin down and rising from my chair.

Naddie grinned at the bus boy. 'We can take a hint, Michael!'

When Naddie and I entered the lobby a crowd had gathered around the fish tank, so we wandered over to see what all the fuss was about. 'The fishkeeper's here,' Colonel Greene explained when we asked. 'They've added a cownose ray.'

During our years of sailing the Chesapeake Bay on my sister-in-law's sailboat, *Sea Song*, we'd encountered schools of rays from time to time, particularly in the fall when they were migrating south. Brown, kite-shaped creatures, they swam by flapping their 'wings,' often being mistaken for sharks when their triangular wing tips broke the water. I peered into the tank where a woman in full scuba gear – wetsuit, tank, facemask and all – appeared to be adjusting some filtering equipment.

'She's from the National Aquarium,' the colonel added helpfully. 'They do the maintenance.'

'You're kidding.'

'Would I kid you, Little Lady?' he drawled. He favored me with a thousand-watt grin. 'The fish tank was a gift and it came with an endowment. Eventually they'll get around to putting a plaque up about it somewhere.'

As he spoke, the new ray swam into view, and I remembered what Naddie had told me about the arrangement with the National Aquarium. The ray was just a pup, with a wing span of about twelve inches.

'They've taken the stinger out,' the colonel informed us. 'Not that it'd do any more damage than getting stung by a bee.'

'Let's not and say we did,' Naddie muttered.

'There's a contest to name the little guy,' the colonel informed us. 'Drop your suggestion into the box on the reception desk. I just did. What do you think of "Ray"? You can call me Ray, or you can call me Jay, or you can call me RJ . . .'

'Must go,' I told Naddie, feeling a desperate need to blow the joint before the colonel trotted out the whole of his Ray J. Johnson routine. I gave her a hasty kiss on the cheek. 'See you tomorrow? I'm scheduled to be with Nancy in the morning. Jerry has some medical appointments so she'll be on her own. She's made so much progress lately and they want to keep her engaged.'

Naddie gave my arm a gentle squeeze. 'I hope you're enjoying your time here, Hannah. Maybe I'm just being selfish, but I'm glad of the excuse to be back in touch with you.'

'The feeling is mutual,' I said and, with a nod of farewell to the colonel, who was still muttering to himself, I aimed myself in the direction of the door.

I paused on the porch to check my iPhone for messages – Emily wanted me to run the soccer carpool for my grandson, Jake, that afternoon. I texted back that I would, then headed to the parking lot where I'd left my car. As I rounded the corner of the building I heard raised voices. Déjà vu all over again, I thought. This time, though, there were three people clustered outside the service entrance door. One of them was Safa, a standout even from a distance in her black outfit and brilliant saffron-colored hijab.

Sue me, but curiosity took over. Keeping as much of the ornamental hedge as I could between me and the kitchen door, I eased as close as I dared.

When I was about thirty feet away I separated the branches a bit and peeked through. Masud loomed tall, leaning forward, inches from Safa's face. 'What are you doing to incite him, Safa?'

Safa shrank back, her lower lip quivered. 'Nothing, Masud.' She extended her arms, palms up. 'I am as you see me.'

Masud threw his arm back, his palm flat and stiff, while Safa flinched and covered her face protectively with her hands.

'Sir!' Raniero took a step toward the couple.

As if suddenly realizing where he was and what he was about to do, Masud let his arm fall to his side. 'Go home, wife. I will have a few words with the chef.'

Safa bowed her head, backed up a few steps then spun and fled down the sidewalk, rapidly closing the distance between us. When she got even with me I reached out and pulled her into the shrubbery.

Safa sucked in air. 'What are you *doing*, Hannah?'

I kept my voice low. 'Are you OK?'

Safa brushed imaginary dust off her clothing and her face stiffened. 'Of *course* I'm OK! Masud is having a little discussion with Raniero, that's all.'

'So I see.'

'I need to go.'

'Shhhh,' I said, still keeping a light hold on her arm, as the two men raised their voices.

'I must speak to you,' Masud snarled. 'You have been disrespectful to my wife.'

Raniero wiped a hand down the front of his white jacket. He looked genuinely perplexed. 'Sir, you are mistaken.'

'I am not. You are too friendly.'

'I am friendly to *all* of the residents,' Raniero countered. 'It is my nature to be friendly. It is my *job* to be so.'

'You talk, you laugh, you touch her arm. This is not showing respect to a devout Muslim woman.'

'Your wife is a beautiful woman, Mr Abaza. Only a dead man would not notice. I meant no disrespect, I assure you, and I'm sorry if my friendliness is being misinterpreted.'

'I have spoken to you about this before, Mr Buccho. Perhaps I did not make myself clear at that time. You must cease this unacceptable behavior.' His hands began to tremble. Was it from rage, or his Parkinsons?

Raniero stood his ground. 'I'll keep my distance in future, sir.

But you should know that in America, touching another person in a friendly way is not considered unacceptable. No court of law . . .' he began, but Masud stiffened, silencing the chef with a laser gaze that could have sliced through steel.

'I don't care how well you cook, Mr Buccho, I can see to it that you lose your job.'

'Sharia is not the law of *this* land, sir,' Raniero continued, taking a brave step forward. 'You choose to live here.'

Next to me, Safa tensed. 'I have *got* to go! A jealous husband is a problem, but a jealous *Muslim* husband . . .'

Before I could stop her, she fled.

I started to follow, but decided it might only exacerbate the situation if Masud found me in their home when he returned. Instead, I hung back and waited to see what would happen next.

Suddenly, it hit me. I realized that it had been Masud I'd seen arguing with Raniero in the same spot the previous day. In his white shirt and black pants I'd mistaken Masud for one of the wait staff. And, clearly, the disagreement between the two men was far from resolved. Masud made a fist then drew his right arm back, while Raniero raised his own fists protectively. Still cowering in the bushes, I waited, wincing, expecting the inevitable.

Masud didn't disappoint. His fist shot out, catching Raniero on the chin. Raniero staggered, momentarily stunned. He shook his head as if to clear it, then drew his own arm back and landed a solid blow to the older man's midsection.

Masud doubled over. Raniero watched him heave for a few seconds, then spun on his heel and stalked off toward the loading dock.

Quickly, I scurried in the opposite direction, not stopping to breathe until I was safely in the driver's seat of my car in the visitor's parking lot with the door locked. Raniero's goose is cooked, I thought as I started the car and peeled out of the parking lot, tires squealing. What were the chances of Masud not reporting the wayward chef to Tyson Bennett?

Slim to none.

As I waited in a long line of cars for a cluster of sailboats to pass under the Eastport drawbridge, I was mentally bidding farewell to Raniero's amazing bruschetta with sautéed mushrooms and mourning the loss of his sweet peas with prosciutto. I prayed it wouldn't come to that.

Happily, I ran into Safa the following day when we both reported for duty at the memory unit. She was bent over, squinting at the lock, punching in the combination when I came up behind her.

'Safa! I'm so glad to see you. Is everything all right?'

Safa straightened and smiled. 'Of course. Why wouldn't it be?'

Was the woman in denial? I was far from convinced that all was well in the Abaza household. I stood in silence for a moment, my head cocked, checking my friend out for red marks or bruises, but it was an exercise in futility. Any signs of physical abuse would have been well-hidden beneath the clothing she wore.

'After yesterday . . .' I shrugged. 'I was worried, that's all.'

This time Safa's smile seemed to genuinely light up her face. 'No need, Hannah. Masud overreacted, that's all. He's already apologized to Raniero, so the matter is settled.'

'Good,' I said, doing a mental fist pump and awash with relief. I wouldn't have to live without the mushroom bruschetta after all.

We stepped into the memory unit and closed the door firmly behind us. 'I'm supposed to be walking with Nancy today,' I said. 'What are you doing?'

'They asked me to set up a playlist for the iPods. Big band music, mostly, folk songs, spirituals, a bit of Mozart.'

'*Eine Kleine Nachtmusik* is always soothing, or Bach's *Goldberg Variations*,' I suggested. 'Sounds like fun. Catch you later, then.'

Safa slipped through the door that led to Elaine Broering's office and the cabinets where the technical equipment was stored while I headed down the hallway to keep my date with Nancy.

Nancy's door was slightly ajar. Through the crack I could see the brilliant plaid of her bedspread on the floor. Although it was only ten in the morning, I wondered if she were napping.

Then I heard moans. *Oh, uh, ah.*

Worried that Nancy had fallen and couldn't get up, I pushed the door open and barreled on in.

Nancy wasn't lying on the floor. She was on her bed, her arms outstretched, grasping the top of the headboard with both hands. 'Oh, Frank,' she moaned. 'Oh, oh!'

Lying on top of her, with only the soles of his feet and naked butt visible, was a man doing pushups. Jerry. I recognized the tattoo on the forearm that propelled him up and down on the mattress.

As I stood there, gaping, rendered speechless, Nancy arched her back and cried, 'Yes! Yes! Yes! Yes!'

Jerry collapsed on top of her, spent, his cheek resting against her naked breasts. Nancy wrapped her arms around him and began to giggle, as breathless and giddy as a schoolgirl. 'Darling, Frank,' she cooed, running her fingers through Jerry's silver curls. 'You are a tiger! My little furry tiger!'

Apparently the 'furry little tiger' hadn't gone to the doctor's office after all.

Feeling like a creepy voyeur, I took a step backwards, preparing to sneak quietly away before the couple noticed me. I took a second cautious step and backed into someone.

'*Ya Allah!*' It had to be Safa.

I spun around to face her.

'I came to fetch Nancy's iPod,' Safa stammered.

I grabbed my friend's arm and dragged her into the hallway, closing Nancy's door quietly behind us.

Safa flattened herself against the chair rail, looked left and right down the hallway, then whispered, 'What do we *do*?'

'Do? Nothing. Give them a little privacy, I suppose.'

'Privacy? Are you nuts, Hannah? That man was *raping* her!'

I gaped. 'That man is Jerry, Safa, and I've never seen two people more crazy for one another. Rape? No way. What we saw going on in there wasn't rape. Nancy and Jerry were making love.'

Safa shook her arm free. 'We have to report this.'

'Why? Haven't you seen the two of them in the lounge? They're like teenagers. Boyfriend and girlfriend, totally besotted with one another. Who are we to deny them a little pleasure?'

Safa's eyes grew wide. 'But they aren't married!'

'I know that, but . . .'

Safa didn't let me finish. 'And who on earth is "Frank?"'

'Frank is Nancy's husband.'

'So, she's *married*?'

I nodded. 'But she has dementia, Safa. She's completely forgotten who Frank is. As far as Nancy's concerned, Jerry *is* Frank.'

'So, she just *thinks* that Jerry's her husband. But he's not!'

'No, but . . .'

Safa flapped her hands in front of her face. 'This is too much. I can't take it all in.'

'It's complicated, I know, but Elaine Broering told me that Nancy's husband is aware of the friendship his wife has with Jerry and he's OK with it.'

'Friendship is one thing, but that . . . that . . .' She gestured at the closed door then dropped her hand to her side. 'We *must* report this, Hannah.'

As we stood there, staring each other down, Jerry's rich laugh rolled out into the hallway. It broke my heart to turn the lovebirds in, but I had to admit that Safa was right. The unit staff needed to know that Nancy and Jerry's 'friendship' had matured into something a little more serious than holding hands and cuddling, assuming that they weren't aware of the situation already and were turning a blind eye, as I would have done.

I caved. 'OK. We need to let the nurse on duty know. Then it'll be up to the memory unit staff to decide what needs to be done.'

Safa puffed air out through her lips. 'Thank you.'

I waited while Safa straightened her hijab. During all the excitement it had slipped to one side, just enough so I could see she was a strawberry blonde. Together we walked to the glassed-in cubicle near the entrance where a nurse named Heather was on duty, tapping something into an iPad using a stylus.

'Nancy and Jerry are having sex in her room,' Safa blurted before I had a chance to say anything.

Heather glanced up from the screen, one eyebrow raised. 'Intercourse?'

'Well, yes!'

'Thanks for letting us know, Safa.'

When Heather made no move to put down her stylus, Safa raised her voice. 'Aren't you going to *do* something? He's still in there!'

Clearly, the fact that Nancy and Jerry were engaged in a little chitty-chitty-bang-bang wasn't news to Heather. 'Jerry isn't hurting Nancy,' she explained. 'Sex is a basic human need, staff feels, no matter how old one might happen to be. I'm sure you've noticed how much pleasure they derive out of one another's company.'

'But it's just plain wrong!' Safa insisted. 'The Quran teaches that extramarital sex is an outrage, an evil path.' She paused, then drew a quick breath. 'Even your *Bible* says it's wrong. "Let marriage be held in honor among all, and let the marriage bed be undefiled; for God will judge the immoral and adulterous." That's from the book of Hebrews.'

From the look on her face, I figured Heather was thinking that God should be the judge of it then, and not Safa Abaza, but it must have occurred to her that arguing with Safa would be counterproductive. With elaborate patience, she smiled, pocketed her stylus, hopped off her stool and said, 'I'll go down and make sure Nancy's all right, OK? Then I'll see to it that Jerry gets back to his own room.'

'Do you need help?' I asked.

Safa shot daggers at me.

'No, no, that's not in your job description! Elaine and I can handle it.' Heather slipped a cell phone out of the holster attached to her belt and tapped a few keys. 'Why don't you two call it a day? Come back tomorrow.'

'What a good idea!' I said, laying a hand on Safa's back and gently propelling her toward the door that led into the lobby.

'Rape must be reported!' Safa hissed as I punched in the combination that would open the security door that led out into the lobby.

'We just did,' I said as the door shushed shut behind us. 'It's in capable hands.'

'Just the sight of that wrinkly, hairy butt . . . oh, Hannah, I am going to have *nightmares*!'

I didn't know how I'd ever unsee that either. I decided the best course of action was to distract her. 'Let's go for a walk,' I suggested. 'It's a beautiful day. It might take your mind off things.'

'You know what I'd really like?' Safa said as we wandered

past the beauty parlor where two women were installed under hair dryers, one smiling beatifically, the other dozing.

'Just name it, and I'll see how I can help.'

She stopped in her tracks. 'An ice-cream sundae. I haven't had a sundae in ages.'

'And I know just the place,' I said, turning into the Sweet Tooth. 'Häagen-dazs. Pure. Absolutely no additives.'

When Safa seemed to hesitate, I said, 'Chocolate ice cream with caramel sauce has been known to cure cancer.'

'But only with sprinkles,' she said, following me in.

TEN

'LORD ILLINGWORTH: The Book of Life begins with a man and a woman in a garden.
MRS ALLONBY: It ends with Revelations.'
Oscar Wilde, *A Woman of No Importance*, Act I, 1893.

I'd been so busy at Calvert Colony over the previous few days that I hadn't bothered to check our mail. When I remembered it after breakfast early the following morning I found three days' worth of catalogs, grocery store flyers, unsolicited mail and bills lying in a jumble on the threshold of my front door. A particularly fat catalog from West Marine clogged the mail slot. I pulled it out, set it aside for Paul, and took the rest of the pile directly to the kitchen trash can for sorting.

Time shares in North Carolina? Buh-bye. Ditto a free dinner at Ruth's Chris Steak House, if only I agreed to sit through a retirement seminar sponsored by a local investment counselor. Coupons for Wegmans and Safeway I'd keep, although Paul's definition of 'coupon' was something Hannah stuck to her refrigerator door with a magnet and kept until after the expiration date had passed.

There was a course catalog for Anne Arundel Community College which I tossed away, and an 'urgent' message from my congressman, which wasn't. I was mechanically pitching catalogs into the bin – Christmas, already? No, thanks! – when a trifold brochure caught my eye. It featured a painting of a chubby toddler dressed in blue, blowing bubbles. I grinned. The subject looked a bit like my grandson, Timmy, at that age.

La Bolla di Sapone by Cagnaccio di San Pietro would be one of sixty paintings on display at the Baltimore Art Gallery this weekend as part of a new exhibit entitled, 'Art in Italy Between the World Wars.' Immediately I thought of Ysabelle Milanesi. Would she like to go? Although tickets cost fifteen dollars, even for seniors, I was a gallery member and could bring several guests along with me for free. I set the brochure aside, already planning the outing in my head: drive to Baltimore, tour the museum, have a late lunch at the crêpe place next door to the Charles Theater – Apple Crisp! S'mores! Nutella and Banana! 'Nuff said.

When I arrived at Calvert Colony later that morning, though, Izzy was not at home. Naddie was supervising an art class, but when I reached her via her cell phone she agreed to the museum trip at once, and informed me I'd find Izzy in the beauty parlor getting a manicure. 'Filomena is looking for you, by the way.'

'Filomena? Why?'

'One of the residents is about to start chemotherapy. I told Filomena you might have some practical tips about diet.'

'It's been a while.' I winced, remembering. 'Goldfish crackers and tea. Not a particular challenge, culinary-wise.'

'Ha!' Naddie said and hung up.

I trotted over to Blackwalnut Hall. Izzy, fingernails freshly painted with Tutti Fruiti Tonga, was game for the museum trip, too, so it was definitely afoot. We decided on Thursday.

Next stop: Filomena.

As I entered the dining room, the kitchen door swun open and Safa emerged, straightening her hijab.

Framed by the doorway, behind a long, stainless steel prep table, stood Raniero.

Safa braked and pressed a hand to her chest. 'Gosh, Hannah! You startled me!'

'I'm looking for Filomena, Safa, have you seen her?'

Safa shot a glance, all wide-eyed innocence, over her shoulder. 'The *panzanella* will be fine! Thank you very much, Raniero.'

As for Raniero, he seemed to be doing some fancy footwork

of his own, chopping away vigorously on a defenseless head of romaine. The door swung slowly shut on his reddened face, whether flushed with embarrassment or the heat of the kitchen it would be hard to say.

To me, Safa said, 'Raniero wanted to consult about the menu for tonight. There's been a delay in the halal meat delivery so he's having to improvise with vegetables.'

'Uh huh.'

'He could have asked Masud, of course,' she babbled on. 'But he's at prayer.'

'Are you playing hooky, then?' I teased.

Safa flushed. 'Sometimes I skip *asr salat*. It is permitted.'

'Have you seen Filomena?' I asked again, in case she'd forgotten.

'What? Oh, no. Sorry. I haven't.' She fell into step next to me. 'Is it important?'

'Not really.'

As we left the dining room I checked the clock on the wall. Had it really been an innocent consultation with the chef or was Masud justified in his concerns about his wife? Had Safa waited until her husband was busy at prayer before sneaking off to meet up with Raniero? It was a dangerous business, considering the bad blood between the two men.

'I'm visiting Nancy today,' I told Safa. 'Do you still need her iPod?'

Taking my arm, Safa drew me gently into an alcove. 'No, thank you, Hannah. I shouldn't have anything more to do with that woman.'

I stared, stunned. 'What possible reason . . .?' I began, but then it dawned on me. 'The woman has *dementia*, Safa. You can't judge her based on what she was *before* she lost her marbles. As far as Nancy is concerned, Jerry *is* Frank.'

Safa frowned. 'I wish I hadn't seen what I saw, but I did, so there's nothing to be done. I can't rewind that tape.'

'You could try.'

'Impossible,' she said. 'Especially since somebody called our home from the Maryland Office of Health Care Quality asking for me.'

'What?'

'I'm supposed to report to the conference room for an interview sometime next week. Masud is *not* happy about that.'

I was wondering what on earth Masud had to be unhappy about. He wasn't the person who accidently stumbled across two old folks having wild and wooly sex. But mostly I wondered who had tattled to the health care authorities about the relationship between Nancy and Jerry.

'It's so embarrassing,' Safa continued. 'Masud will have to come along while I talk to those men. I can't be in a room alone with them.'

I thought about the glass-enclosed conference room situated just off the lobby with its inlaid walnut table, comfortable upholstered chairs, and gas log fireplace. 'But you wouldn't exactly be *alone*. Anyone passing by would be able to see what was going on inside,' I pointed out. 'What could be the harm in that?'

'"Being alone with,"' she drew quote marks in the air, 'also includes situations where a man is conversing with a woman, even out in the open where they can be seen by other people, if their words cannot be heard.'

I silently counted to three, suppressing an exasperated sigh. Why did converts always seem so zealous, more zealous even than those born into the faith? 'The interviewer is just as likely to be a woman,' I said gently. 'But in case it isn't, would it be acceptable if a woman came along instead of your husband? If so, I will be happy to do it.'

Her face brightened. 'Would you?'

'Of course.'

'I'm surprised they haven't called you, too, Hannah.'

I shrugged. 'It's possible someone did, but I was out late babysitting my grandkids last night, so when I got home I fell right into bed without checking my messages.' I patted my handbag. 'Hold on.'

I scrabbled around in the murky depths of my bag until I found my iPhone. I switched it on and studied the display. 'Darn, there *is* a message.'

'You have the ringer turned off,' Safa pointed out helpfully.

With an exasperated sigh, I switched the ringer back on, tapped the messages icon, put the phone to my ear and listened.

'I'm to pop in for a chat with them, too,' I told her after the message ended. 'At my convenience, of course, but would tomorrow at one-thirty be OK? I'm to let the director know.'

'I'm sure they'll want to interview us separately,' Safa said. She clouded up. 'I guess I'll need to find somebody else to accompany me.'

'As if we're going to put our heads together on a story,' I huffed. Safa looked crestfallen so I added, thinking quickly, 'I'll ask my friend, Nadine. I'm sure she'll be happy to do it.'

Since I had my cell phone in my hand, I called Naddie. She answered on the first ring. 'No, no, not doing anything special, Hannah, just . . . Hate to confess that I'm wasting the morning watching a rerun of *Masterchef*.'

When Naddie readily agreed to chaperone Safa for her interview, if it came to that, I gave Safa a thumb's up. Still, she didn't smile.

'Look,' I said a few minutes later, taking pity. 'Naddie, Izzy and I have a trip planned to the Baltimore Art Gallery this Thursday, then lunch at a little place around the corner afterwards. Would you like to come?'

Her remarkable eyes lit up. 'Oh, yes! Can I let you know?'

I figured she'd have to ask Masud for permission, but what could go wrong with three women acting as chaperones? 'Of course,' I said. 'Just call when you can.'

Safa had taken three steps down the hallway when I stopped her. 'Safa?'

'Yes?'

'Did *you* report the incident with Nancy and Jerry to the Office of Health Care Quality?'

She shook her head. 'No. Why?'

'Did you tell anyone else?'

'Yes, Masud, of course. Didn't you tell your husband?'

I had to confess that I had, via cell phone when he telephoned the previous evening from somewhere off the coast of Long Island. Paul had laughed it off, though, so I knew *he* hadn't spilled the beans to the authorities. I wasn't so sure about Masud . . .

Still, it was more than likely that Elaine had decided to play it safe and report the incident to Tyson Bennett, who would have had no choice but to take it up the chain of command. Rules were rules, I thought sourly. And sometimes, if you didn't follow the rules, there were consequences.

Save us from intransigent bureaucrats, I thought as I waved Safa goodbye.

In the memory unit office I learned from Elaine Broening that Nancy Harper was in the art studio. 'You should visit,' she suggested. 'There's nothing childlike or primitive about Nancy's work. It's as if her fingers remember what her failing brain cannot.'

The art studio, I knew, was several doors down from the library, on the opposite side of the hallway. When I got there, the instructor welcomed me, introduced herself – an unnecessary formality since her nametag said 'Mindy' in black capital letters at least two inches high.

'I'm assigned to Nancy today,' I told her.

'She's at the table over by the window.' Mindy pointed with clay-caked hands. 'We're working with clay,' she told me unnecessarily. 'Sculpting things from memory.'

Half-a-dozen seniors were hunched over lumps of clay at two long tables in the bright, cheerful room. The walls were decorated with residents' art. On the worktable nearest me, a dog – or perhaps it was a cat – was emerging out of the shapeless lump in front of Chuck, the mustachioed guy who'd sat next to me at the lobby singfest. Next to Chuck sat Lillian, who I hadn't seen since our adventure in the garden several days earlier.

I touched her shoulder. 'Hello, Lillian.'

She looked up at me with no sign of recognition. 'Hello. Is it time for lunch?'

'Not yet,' I told her. I indicated the block of clay she was pounding into submission with a loosely-balled fist. 'That's nice. What are you making?'

'It's Banjo,' Lillian said, which didn't exactly answer the question.

'Who's Banjo?' I asked.

'One of my babies. I have *lots* of babies.'

I figured I'd have to wait until all the clay that wasn't Banjo was excised from the lump before I'd be able to determine what kind of baby Banjo was. 'That's nice,' I said stupidly.

At the sound of my voice, Nancy looked up from her project and waved. An obelisk rose straight and true from the mound of white modeling clay in front of her.

'Oh, look,' I said, taking a few steps in her direction. 'It's the Washington Monu—' I paused and caught my breath. Nancy had sculpted a fully erect penis, so perfectly rendered that it could have been cast from a mold. What I had taken for shrubbery at the base of the famous Washington landmark was, in fact, an equally perfectly sculptured scrotum.

Nancy beamed then spread her clay-caked hands. 'Tah dah!'

'It's, uh, very good,' I said truthfully, thinking how fortunate it was that Safa Abaza hadn't been assigned to work with Nancy today. 'I didn't realize what an artist you are.'

'I like to draw, too,' Nancy said, pinching a bit of clay off one side of her project and adding it to the other. She leaned back, closed an eye and considered the effect.

I felt my face flush. 'That's extraordinary,' I said to Mindy, meaning it. 'The detail!'

'Indeed. It's amazing what's stored in the brain of even the most advanced dementia patient. An incredible wealth of memories can be unlocked with music or with art.'

'Nancy's certainly enjoying herself,' I said. 'Should I come back later?'

'We'll have her back in her room at around two.'

'What are you going to do with Nancy's sculpture?' I whispered. I couldn't imagine it would be going on display on the credenza in Tyson Bennett's office or in the Calvert Colony gallery along with other examples of resident art.

'We'll dump the clay back in the tub,' Mindy said. 'By tomorrow she'll have forgotten all about it.'

'Damn shame,' I said. 'She's extraordinarily talented.'

Mindy shrugged. 'Yeah, well . . . what can you do?' She wiped her hands on her apron. 'You should see her drawings, Hannah. Trees, leaves, flowers . . . absolutely perfect, too, like illustrations in those old botanical textbooks. We hold on to those, however,' she assured me with a smile. 'You'll probably find the folder in her room.'

I eased toward the door and paused for a final look. Chuck's sculpture was definitely a cat, while Lillian's Banjo was still a mystery. As I watched, Nancy moistened her fingers then moved them up and down along the shaft of her 'monument,' smiling, stroking, smoothing – making it perfect.

Several hours later, with quiet poise and grace, Nancy showed me around her room. She could have been Marjorie Merryweather Post giving me a personal tour of her beloved Hillwood, if Marjorie had completely forgotten what her collections of Wedgwood, Bleu Celeste, and Fabergé Easter eggs were all about, that is.

In the comfortably furnished room, Nancy was surrounded by relics of her past – not souvenirs or mementoes as those words imply a memory, but by keepsakes that had lost all meaning for her. I noticed a photograph of a German shepherd, head cocked, tongue lolling; a sampler, cross-stitched with flowers and the words, 'Home is where the heart is,' and a stuffed giraffe, three feet tall.

'These are my favorites,' Nancy said, running her fingers along the spines of a shelf of classic novels – *Anna Karenina, Madame Bovary, Jane Eyre, Pride and Prejudice, Rebecca, To Kill a Mockingbird, The Diary of a Young Girl* – but I had the feeling that if I were to ask Nancy who Anne Frank was she would have drawn a blank.

I wondered if I should be reading to her from one of these classics, but just as I reached up for DuMaurier's *Rebecca*, Nancy said, 'Please sit down.' She indicated one of two Queen Anne chairs that flanked a picture window, facing out. 'I like my garden,' Nancy told me as she took the opposite chair.

Like all the rooms on the south side of Blackwalnut Hall, Nancy's overlooked the fabulous and appropriately named Tranquility Garden. It wasn't walled like the 'secret' garden at the far end of the memory unit's hallway, but much larger, laid out behind the building Japanese-style, where residents could meditate, relax, rest or even recline on one of the wooden benches.

A dense bamboo hedge separated the garden from the parking lot on one side, while the other side was open to a field that would someday turn into a golf course. From this elevation it was easy to pick out the vine arbors and pergolas that were spaced at irregular intervals along the serpentine paths. Several varieties of fern grew in clumps near a foot bridge that arched over a miniature stream which ended in a pond, covered with water lilies. Here and there, sculptures peeked out from nooks and crannies in the foliage, and at the far end stood an enclosed pavilion where residents could seek shelter should there be a sudden shower.

I knew at once where I would like to take Nancy: the meditation labyrinth, marked out in stone pavers in a circle not far from the lily pond. But she seemed to be having a more lucid day, so I decided to consult her about it. 'What would you like to do today, Nancy?'

'Where's Frank?' she asked.

'He went to the doctor,' I told her. I saw her face start to crumple so I quickly added, 'He's fine, he just needs a checkup,' although I had absolutely no idea why the doctor needed to see him.

'OK,' she said, as if she had actually taken it in. 'I'd like to walk, then. Out there.' She stabbed her finger at the window. 'In the garden.'

If was a perfect day, unusual for Annapolis in August, when the sun could be so brutal that if the temperature dropped below ninety-five degrees, it felt a bit chilly.

I accompanied Nancy through the lobby, out of the double doors and onto the brick path that led to the Tranquility Garden. Although Nancy had forgotten she had a husband, when it came to flowers her mind was a steel trap. Sunflowers, hibiscus and pansies; mums wearing their fall colors of red, orange and gold. She pointed them out to me by their scientific names: *Helianthus annuus, Viola tricolor hortensis.*

'Chrysanthemum comes from the Greek,' she said. 'Did you know that? It means "golden flower."'

I was marveling at the intricacies of the human brain as I led her over the foot bridge, where I stopped so quickly that she barged into me. '*Do* watch where you're going!' she snapped.

I took her hand. 'Look, Nancy!'

Nestled in a clump of cattails at the edge of the pond, turned slightly on its side, was a weather-worn rowboat filled with multi-colored glass balls of varying sizes: exercise balls, beach balls, soccer and tennis balls. There were hundreds of them. To our right, a patch of purple reeds made entirely of blown glass shot like enormous needles from a driftwood log covered with moss. Further along, hand-blown flowers edged the walk, each reflecting the other in a shimmery mix of tendrils, buds and fronds. Shells and sea stars were strewn along the ground at their glassy roots. From a branch overhead hung clusters of glass icicles, tinkling in the gentle breeze like temple bells. Dale Chihuly, I thought, or an artist very much like him. Paul had been right when he said that Calvert Colony had deep pockets.

'An exotic species,' Nancy commented, bending at the waist for a closer look at an orange glass flower, its petals as abundant and twisted as a Medusa.

She'd made a joke! I stared for a moment in surprise.

'You're looking at me like I live here,' she said.

Oh, dear, I thought. One step forward and two steps back.

We made a complete circuit of the garden then paused to rest on a stone bench in a cherry tree grove that would, come spring, blossom in pink, heart-stopping splendor. The marble felt deliciously cool under the thin cloth of my slacks. I leaned back and said, 'Ah . . . I could sit here all day.'

Nancy fussed with the buttons on her blouse and looked from side to side as if she were expecting somebody. 'People do,' she said.

'Do what?' I asked. 'Sit here all day?'

'Yes. I see them from my window.'

I turned to look at Blackwalnut Hall. Banks of picture windows winked at me like two dozen eyes. 'Who do you see?'

She smiled slyly. 'Frank. And me.'

'That's nice,' I said.

'Where is Frank?' she asked again, and once again I explained about the doctor.

'OK,' she said, then screwed her face into a frown. 'Can we go for a walk now? You *said* we were going for a walk.'

ELEVEN

*'I declare that it is far from my idea to encourage anything
like a state art. Art belongs to the domain of the individual.
The state has only one duty: not to undermine art, to provide
humane conditions for artists, to encourage them from the
artistic and national point of view.'*
Benedito Mussolini, Speech at the Opening Exhibit of
Il Novecento Italiano, Milan, 1923.

'**B**AG' read the blue-and-white buttons we pinned on our
lapels. Someone had not been thinking ahead when they
named it the Baltimore Art Gallery.

The eclectic collection was housed in a former high school on
Guilford Avenue, not far from Penn Station, in an area called
Greenmount West that was emerging, slowly but steadily, from
the rubble of the Baltimore riots of 1968. Did you watch the HBO
drama, *The Wire*? Then you've been to Greenmount West.

Recently designated as a Maryland Arts and Entertainment District,
the area had experienced a renaissance of theaters, cafes, and restaurants
as well as an explosion of space for artists to live and work in
the sprawling former Crown Cork and Seal factory. Nevertheless, the
streets could be a bit dicey, so I was glad I had my posse with me.

'Elevator or stairs?' I asked my friends as we entered the spacious
lobby of the museum and showed our passes to the attendant.

'Oh, stairs,' Izzy said. 'I need the exercise.'

'"The new Italian Renaissance,"' I read aloud from the exhibit
brochure as we climbed the marble staircase to the gallery, '"was
described by Margherita Sarfatti as a *ritorno al mestiere*, or a
return to craft."'

'Sarfatti was Mussolini's mistress,' Izzy informed us. 'Awkward
for him, because she was Jewish. She ended up fleeing to
Argentina, but she returned to Italy sometime after the war and
became an influential art critic.'

'Susan Sarandon played her in the movie,' Naddie added.

'What movie?' Safa wanted to know.

'*Cradle Will Rock.*'

I paused on the landing. 'When I die, please note I want Susan Sarandon to play *me* in the movie.'

I started up the next flight. 'Where was I? Uh . . . "This classicizing moment gave birth to renewed interest in Italian Renaissance painters such as Fra Angelico and Piero della Francesca" blah blah blah . . . "and demonstrates the power of the neoclassical paradigm for postwar Italian modernists" . . . and so on and so on.' I closed the brochure and used it to fan myself. 'Whenever I get to the word "paradigm" my brain shuts down.'

'"Hegemony" does it for me,' Naddie confessed. 'Best to let the works speak for themselves, I always say.'

At the head of the stairs, a huge banner hung from the ceiling – identical to the cover of the brochure – which indicated where the exhibit began. Sixty artists were represented, according to the banner, comprising painting, sculpture, photography, architecture, film, fashion and the decorative arts, on loan from museums all over the world.

'I don't think much of de Chirico's paintings,' I commented to my friends as we browsed through the first gallery. 'He seems to be a one-trick pony.' De Chirico's work featured oversized classical heads and weird classical buildings with an oddly distorted perspective that made me tilt my head and say, 'Huh?' The foregrounds were often decorated, Dali-esque, with rubber gloves or bananas.

There were the stark, monochromatic still lifes of Morandi, who was fixated on bottles and vases; the abstracts of Balla; the cartoons of Sironi.

'Now, this is more like it,' I said as we came to some vibrant, realistic portraits by Federico Andreotti, who posed his models in aristocratic scenes, often wearing eighteenth-century dress.

'Airs and graces,' muttered Izzy. 'My father couldn't stand Andreotti. Wouldn't have him in the gallery.' She dismissed the artist with a wave of her hand, and moved on to a series of paintings by Cagnaccio di San Pietro – a woman applying makeup at a mirror; another of a woman wearing a red dress; an old fisherman; and the little boy with the bubble, the painting that had been featured on the flyer.

'I'd buy this in a minute,' I said, indicating *La Bolla di Sapone*. I couldn't take my eyes off it.

'Got twelve thousand dollars?' Naddie wanted to know. 'That's what the di San Pietros are going for these days. I looked it up.'

'Maybe if I'm good, Santa will tuck the painting into my stocking for Christmas,' I joked.

Izzy and Naddie moved on. The paintings were growing progressively more abstract and, to my way of thinking, less interesting, so Safa and I took a detour to explore the section on decorative arts.

We were leaning over a display case of exquisite porcelain drinking cups by Gio Ponte, one decorated with circus acts and the other with airplanes, when I heard somebody wail. Safa and I exchanged worried glances.

'That sounds like Izzy,' I said.

We raced back to the gallery where we'd left Izzy with Naddie. As I turned the corner, barging into a gallery that Safa and I had skipped, I saw Izzy holding onto the doorframe with one hand, pressing the other to her breast. 'I can't breathe!'

I guided her to a nearby bench and forced her to sit down on it. 'Is it your heart?'

'No, no. My heart's fine.'

'You're hyperventilating, Izzy. Put your head between your knees . . . that's right. Now breathe in. Breathe out. That's it.'

'I'll go find some water,' Safa said, and she disappeared around the corner of the gallery.

I sat down next to my friend, reached out and began stroking her back. 'Where's Naddie?' I asked.

'Restroom,' she gasped.

'In and out,' I repeated. 'In and out. Better?'

She nodded, and several silver strands that escaped from her bun trembled around her face.

'What is it? What happened?'

'I, I . . .' Izzy began.

Safa returned just then, carrying a Styrofoam coffee cup of water. She knelt on the tiles in front of Izzy, her skirt puddling around her. 'Here, drink this.'

Izzy took the cup in both hands and took a sip, then another, then handed the cup back.

'Better?'

'Yes, I think so. It's just . . . that painting,' she said, pointing to a wall of portraits, one of them featuring a young boy kneeling with his arms wrapped around a dog. The animal had thick, curly brown and white fur. His large brown eyes stared out at the viewer, just like those of its pint-sized master.

'The one of the boy and the Portuguese water dog?' I asked, just to be certain.

Izzy nodded vigorously, dislodging even more hair from the confines of her bun. 'It's not a water dog, Hannah. It's a Lagotto Romagnolo named Pecorino, and that little boy is my brother.'

Needless to say, lunch at Sofi Crepes was forgotten as we sat in the gallery's cafeteria over pre-made sandwiches and bottles of designer water in pastel colors, discussing what to do.

While Izzy was a study in anxious indecision, Safa had donned full battle gear, prepared to march up to the gallery's office and put them on notice that they were in possession of stolen property.

'That's no good,' Izzy complained. 'They're not going to say, 'Oh, we're *soooo* sorry, we didn't know,' take the portrait off the wall, tape it up in bubblewrap and hand it back to me, are they?'

Safa looked crestfallen but reluctantly agreed. 'I guess you're right. We don't want to give them a head's up or the painting might disappear.'

Naddie and I concurred, urging caution. 'You need an attorney,' I said.

Izzy stared back at me blankly.

'Do you *have* a lawyer?' Naddie asked.

Izzy thought for a moment then shook her head. 'Only in Pennsylvania, and his specialty was real estate and probate.'

I patted Izzy's hand. 'I have a brother-in-law who's an attorney in Annapolis. He rejoices in the name Malcolm Gaylord Hutchinson, but everyone simply calls him Hutch. Would you like me to call him? If he can't take the case he will certainly know someone who can.'

Izzy looked up at me with red-rimmed eyes. Until then she'd been able to hold her tears in check but suddenly the floodgates opened. 'Yes, please,' she sobbed.

Safa grabbed a wad of napkins from a dispenser and tucked them into Izzy's clenched fist.

Ragazzo con Cane, I thought. Boy with dog. An unassuming title, a modest painting, yet tangible proof of Izzy's life before the Nazis. It had hit her like a blow to the stomach. Simple oil pigments dabbed onto a rectangle of canvas, yet representative of everything Izzy had lost: her father and mother, her brother, even her country.

Izzy cried until the tears would no longer come, and like good friends we sat there handing her napkins, making comforting noises, and let her.

TWELVE

'Jews, Free Masons and those opponents of National Socialism who are affiliated with them . . . are the authors of the present war against the Reich. The systematic spiritual battle against these forces is a task made necessary by the war effort.

I have therefore directed Reichsleiter Alfred Rosenberg to carry out this task . . . His staff for the occupied territories is authorized to search libraries, archives, lodges and other . . . cultural establishments for relevant material and to have this material requisitioned for the 'Weltanschauung' tasks of the NSDAP, and for future scientific research by higher educational institutions. The same regulation applies to cultural treasures which are the property or in the possession of Jews, which are ownerless, or the origin of which cannot be clearly established.'

Adolf Hitler, Decree of the Führer, 1 March, 1942.

Well before nine the following morning Izzy and I waited in my brother-in-law's Annapolis conference room while he arranged for his receptionist to bring us coffee. I'd rushed out of the house wearing slim jeans, a tank top and open-toed sandals, without applying makeup or blow-drying my hair, but compared to Izzy I looked like a cover model. She'd dressed in tennis shoes and a lime-green jogging outfit. She'd drawn her hair into an untidy ponytail at the nape of her neck and her eyes were nearly swollen shut from crying.

I knew Izzy's painting wouldn't be going anywhere soon; the exhibit would be running through January, according to the brochure, so there was no particular need to rush. Izzy had been so agitated, however, that I felt we had to get the ball rolling. When I called him at home the previous evening, Hutch's calendar, by some miracle, was free, so I'd made the appointment for Izzy and me to come in.

'The painting is by Clotilde Padovano,' Izzy explained when Hutch returned to the room and sat down at the conference table opposite us. 'It's one of a pair, and the other is hanging in my town home.'

I watched as Hutch scrawled 'Padovano' on the yellow legal pad in front of him. 'You said your father was an art dealer?'

'Yes. He owned the Galleria Rossi in Rome. When the Nazis came he was forced to sell. The paintings went for a fraction of their actual value but my father had absolutely no choice. If he hadn't sold they would have been stolen outright.'

'Who bought the paintings from your father, Mrs Milanesi?'

'I don't know. There were several buyers, maybe a half dozen or so. Because we lived over the gallery I saw these people come and go but I never knew their names. I was very young at the time,' she added.

'Is the picture owned by the Baltimore Art Gallery, or is it on loan from another museum?' Hutch asked.

'It's owned by the gallery; at least, there was no label on it to indicate otherwise.' She sat back in her chair and sighed. 'I wonder where it's been all these years and how it got from our home in Rome into a gallery in Baltimore.'

'The provenance will tell us that,' Hutch said. He scribbled something down on his pad then added: 'I'm sure the gallery believes it was purchased legally. As you probably know they're very careful about establishing provenance. Galleries have researchers to handle that sort of thing. The Baltimore Art Gallery is thoroughly reputable. They *will* have bills of sale.'

'A bill of sale is meaningless, Mr Hutchinson, if it's filled out while the seller has a gun pointed at his head.'

'True,' Hutch agreed. 'I've done a bit of research and there are a number of jurisdictions that have accepted that fact. The American Association of Museums recently issued guidelines that require extra scrutiny on all acquisitions that changed ownership between 1932 and 1945, especially if the work in question was previously owned by Jews.'

I felt a sudden chill that had nothing to do with the air conditioner kicking in. 'What's the next step, Hutch? Do you contact the gallery, let them know that a claim is being made and find out who sold them the painting?'

'Let me make a few calls, Hannah.' He turned to Izzy. 'It could be simple, Mrs Milanesi, or it could be complicated. Most likely it will take someone with more expertise than I.'

A tear rolled down Izzy's cheek. 'I don't want any money, Mr Hutchinson. Except for the single painting I have at home, I have nothing, *nothing* that once belonged to my family. That painting . . .' She paused, then took a deep, steadying breath. 'That painting may *legally* belong to the gallery, but not morally. It was as good as stolen.'

Izzy wrapped both hands around the mug of coffee on the table in front of her, raised it to her lips and took a sip. 'And I just thought of another thing, Mr Hutchinson. We didn't get to see all the pictures in the gallery. There could be more of my father's paintings there, maybe on display, or maybe even in storage.'

Hutch clicked the retractor on his ballpoint and said, 'Hmmm.'

Hmmm is not the response one wants to hear from one's doctor or lawyer.

We waited him out.

After a thoughtful silence, he said, 'I need to ask you a few questions.'

'Please, anything you need to know, Mr Hutchinson. Go ahead.'

'These confiscated paintings were hanging in your father's gallery, right?'

She nodded.

'Do you know if they were your father's property or were they simply hung there, on consignment from various artists, waiting to be sold?'

'I don't know the answer to that. But the portrait of my brother
– that particular painting hung on the wall in our dining room,
and it's the companion piece to mine.'

'You told me you secreted your painting in your suitcase?'

'My parents did, yes.'

'Why didn't your parents do the same thing for your brother?'

'They did but he was too young to appreciate it, Mr Hutchinson.
Before we left home *Abba* asked Umberto which painting he
wanted and my brother picked a charcoal drawing of a horse.'
She smiled sadly. 'Umberto loved horses. When we were on the
farm, he had a favorite. Albina.'

'Do you still have that drawing?' I asked my friend.

'Umberto slept with Albina at his side, Hannah. You
understand?'

I did. My niece, Julie, still had her 'lovie,' a bedraggled,
threadbare rabbit named Abby. Julie was fourteen, but her mother
still tucked Abby's pitiful remains into the toe of her sleeping
bag whenever my niece went on an overnight. There was no
chance the fragile drawing had survived Umberto's loving.

Hutch swiped at his cheek, visibly moved. 'Mrs Milanesi, I'm
no expert in art law. It's an amalgam of personal property law,
contract law, estate law, tax law and intellectual property law relat-
ing to the acquisition, retention and disposition of fine art.' After
getting that sentence out he had to take a deep breath. 'The first
thing that occurs to me, and this is basic, is to ask do you have
proof that your family once owned these particular works of art?
Is there anything – a sale catalog, perhaps?'

I bounced in my chair. 'I seem to remember that the Smithsonian
keeps a collection of art auction catalogs, maybe even on micro-
film. We could check there.'

Izzy raised a hand to cut me off. 'I don't think we'll need to
do that, Hannah. When our children were in their teens Bruno
and I took them to Italy so they could see where, where . . .
well, back to their roots.' She paused for a moment, swallowed
hard, then continued. 'One of the places we visited was the
farmhouse where my brother and I were sheltered by the DeLucas.
The DeLucas had long since passed away, but amazingly the
farm was still there, being managed by their son. He invited us
in and after a short visit he gave me a scrapbook that my mother,

Letizia Rossi, had made. He told us that he found it under the
floorboards in the bedroom, in the same space where my brother
and I had hidden from the Nazis. Mother had taken photographs
of all the paintings, you see, room by room by room, and pasted
them on the pages of the scrapbook, writing by hand under each
photograph what it was in white ink. I have the scrapbook packed
away somewhere at home.'

'Ah, that's excellent.' Hutch relaxed into the cushions of the
chair and tapped the point of his pen absent-mindedly against
the table. 'I think you should bring the scrapbook in as soon as
possible. We'll make several copies then store the original in the
safe. How does that sound?'

Izzy nodded. 'Very good.'

Hutch stood. 'Until later, then. I have several hearings to attend
in the next couple of days, but if I'm not here simply leave your
mother's scrapbook with my paralegal. I'll tell her to expect it
and she'll know just what to do. In the meantime,' he said as he
walked us to the door of the conference room, 'I'll check with
a colleague in D.C. to see what the best plan of action may be.'

Izzy shook Hutch's hand. 'Thank you, Mr Hutchinson.'

'You're very welcome. And Mrs Milanesi, don't even *think*
about contacting the gallery yourself.'

'No, of course not.'

'We don't want the painting to suddenly, say, disappear.'

As we headed down the hall, Hutch called out after me,
'Hannah! Will you stop by Mother Earth and tell Ruth I'll be
bringing pizza home for dinner?'

I tipped an imaginary hat.

Izzy and I ambled down Main Street and tried the door of
Mother Earth, the New Age store owned by my sister, but she
wasn't in. A sign taped to the glass read, 'Back in Five Minutes,'
so we waited for ten, admiring some wind chimes in the window,
but when Ruth didn't show we left.

We returned to the parking garage where I'd left my car, saying
very little. After we'd climbed into the vehicle and closed the
doors, Izzy turned to me and asked, 'Do you think there'll be a
big fight over this?'

'I honestly don't know, Izzy. My opinion? No matter what
the museum might have paid for that painting of your brother,

it belongs with you. They'll need to do the right thing. And if they don't . . .' I patted her knee. 'Then maybe Hutch will make them.'

THIRTEEN

'Depression is not a normal part of aging. Studies show that most seniors feel satisfied with their lives, despite having more illnesses or physical problems. However, when older adults do have depression, it may be overlooked because seniors may show different, less obvious symptoms. They may be less likely to experience or admit to feelings of sadness or grief.'
National Institute of Mental Health: www.nimh.nih.gov

A couple of days went by before I was able to return to the memory unit.

I found Nancy Harper in bed with the covers drawn up to her chin, her fingers braided neatly across her breast which was rising and falling with every slow, even breath. At first I thought she was napping, but when I tiptoed closer I noticed that her eyes were open and she was staring at the ceiling. Gone were the carefully enhanced eyebrows and the blusher on her cheeks. Her hair was a tangle of unruly curls, white at the roots, and the lovely, decorative combs she favored were nowhere to be seen.

'Nancy? It's Hannah. How are you doing today?'

'Who?'

'Hannah Ives. I've come to read to you if you feel up to it.'

'Go away.'

'Are you hungry? Can I bring you a snack?'

'I said go away.'

As I was considering whether to take her summary dismissal seriously or not, she turned on her side and inched up the sheets until she was in a sitting position. After grabbing her pillow and savagely punching it into submission, she settled back against the flowered pillowcase and said, 'I don't want you. I want Frank.'

Was she having a lucid moment? Did she mean 'Frank' as in 'Frank the man I married,' or did she mean, 'Frank, the guy across the hall whose real name is Jerry'?

'Do you want me to see if I can find him?' I asked.

Her eyes locked on mine. 'Frank will know what to do.'

'I'll go look for him then,' I said.

Outside in the hallway I paused, trying to remember which of the fourteen rooms that extended along both sides of the corridor belonged to Jerry Wolcott. On the unforgettable occasion when I'd seen him last he'd been in Nancy's room. Fortunately, each room had a framed name plate screwed to the wall outside the door, so I had to walk only a few yards before I found his: *Jerry Wolcott from Pikesville, Maryland. I am a retired banker. I enjoy golf and watching the Baltimore Ravens play football.* It was illustrated with crayon drawings and magazine cutouts by someone who clearly loved him; a grandchild, perhaps.

The door was shut so I knocked gently. 'Mr Wolcott? Jerry?' I knocked again, more loudly this time, figuring the old guy might be hard of hearing. 'Jerry?'

When he didn't answer I pushed the door open and peeked inside.

Except for a chair, an end table and a bed stripped down to the mattress, the room was empty. I stiffened, stepped back and took a deep breath as the significance of the empty, sterile room sank in. Jerry Wolcott, Nancy's beloved companion, had passed away.

I hadn't known the man all that well but the realization still stung. I pulled the door shut behind me and leaned against the chair rail in the hall, digging my fingernails into my palms, unsuccessfully fighting off the tears.

That was where Elaine Broering, the memory unit supervisor, found me a few minutes later as she was chugging down the hallway on her way back to her office from visiting one of the residents.

'It gets to you, doesn't it?' she said. Elaine pulled a clean tissue from the pocket of her Donald Duck scrubs and handed it to me. 'Like a Girl Scout, I come prepared,' she said with a comforting smile.

I pressed the tissue gratefully against my eyelids. 'Thanks.'

'Can I help in any way?'

I shook my head. 'Nancy was asking for him, so I went to look. When I saw his empty room . . .' I took a breath then let it out. 'When did he die?'

Elaine touched my arm. 'Mr Wolcott isn't dead, Hannah. He's been transferred to the memory care unit at Ginger Cove.'

A wave of relief washed over me, followed almost immediately by a flood of questions. 'But why?'

'The family thought it was best.'

Best? I couldn't imagine why. Calvert Colony was a state-of-the art facility and Jerry had, by all accounts, been happy here. It couldn't have been a financial issue, I thought to myself. I knew from talking to Naddie that although the buy-in plans for Ginger Cove and Calvert Colony varied in some of the finer details, the bottom-line, long-term costs were relatively the same.

'But doesn't his son's family live nearby, on East Lake Drive? You'd think they'd want their father to stay as close as possible.'

'It was his son's decision, Hannah. I can't have an opinion about that.'

'Nancy must be devastated,' I said.

Elaine opened her mouth as if starting to say something, then her lips slammed shut around it. Her eyes locked on mine, as if weighing the pros and cons of telling tales out of school.

'It was the sex, wasn't it?' I said, answering my own question.

Elaine sighed, confirming my suspicions. 'You'll read about it in the newspapers soon enough.'

Newspapers. Plural. I didn't like the sound of that. 'Don't tell me . . .' I began.

She nodded. 'Nancy's family is suing Calvert Colony, claiming she was raped and that we failed to protect her from a dangerous predator.'

'But that's nonsense! Those two are truly in love. You know that and so do I.'

Elaine nodded. 'It's a damn shame. You should have seen Nancy before Jerry came into her life. Baggy double-knit pants with elasticized waistbands, soup-stained sweatshirts, shoes if she felt like it – and she usually didn't. We'd have to force them on her. After Jerry she dug into her closet again. Pulled out some classics – St Johns, Ahni, the Barbara Bush pearls. Insisted on having her hair done every week. Now?' She shrugged. 'Well, you were in her room. You saw her.'

'She's in bed.'

'Can't say I blame her. We check on her every thirty minutes, of course. Make sure she's up, taking her meals, at least here in the unit. But it fries my grits that the Wolcott family didn't warn us. They just showed up one day last week and hustled Jerry out, right in front of Nancy. He's yelling, "What's going on? Where are you taking me?" and she's looking lost and confused.' She pressed a hand to her chest. 'Honestly, it broke my heart. She's spent the last four days staring out the window, waiting for Jerry to come back.'

I pictured Nancy as she was a week ago wearing a classic, bright yellow shirtwaist dress, tripping the light fantastic with Jerry, who looked pretty spiffy himself in an oxford shirt and jaunty bow tie. 'Oh, stop!' I said, flapping a hand in front of my face. 'You're going to make me cry again. It's a goddam tragedy. Romeo and Juliet. Abelard and Heloise. Star-crossed lovers thwarted at every turn by well-meaning but callous . . .' I paused. 'Not sure I want to call them "grownups."'

'Well, if it were *my* mom or dad I'd be grateful they found somebody to spend the rest of their lives with.'

'Sometimes grieving spouses do make poor decisions,' I said, thinking of the horrible woman my father had taken up with not too many months after my mother died. But someone had hated Darlene enough to take her out of this world before Daddy could make an even bigger mistake by marrying her. 'But in this case,' I continued, 'I can't think of two people more perfectly matched.'

A uniformed staffer pushed through the double doors butt first, dragging a vacuum cleaner. Elaine asked the woman to start work at the other end of the hallway, then said, 'Once Tina gets going we won't be able to hear ourselves think. Do you have to be anywhere?' When I shook my head, she said, 'Come with me.'

A few minutes later I was seated across from Elaine at a small, round table in the corner of her office, and she'd called out for tea. Sun poured through a picture window that looked out over a small, staff-only parking lot constructed of porous pavers through which grass was already beginning to grow. 'Why exactly did Jerry's son take him away?' I asked.

'You'll hear it from some of the other residents anyway so I guess it's OK to tell you. Jerry actually proposed to Nancy and when his son found out about it, well, all hell broke loose. He called Nancy a golddigger. Ridiculous.'

'Hasn't he heard about pre-nups?' I asked.

'Well, exactly. And since Nancy's still married to the real Frank, even though she doesn't remember him, it's kind of a moot point.'

'More to the point, how does *Frank* feel about the relationship?' I asked.

'Exactly. Have you met our director, Tyson Bennett?'

I nodded. She hadn't answered my question, so I wondered where she was going. 'We spoke. Briefly. He was making the rounds in the dining room last time I ate there.'

She smiled. 'That's Tyson. Very hands-on. Progressive. When it was clear that a relationship was blossoming between Nancy and Jerry, Tyson called a staff meeting. He believed that Nancy and Jerry's relationship was beneficial to their well-being and so did our resident psychologist. I agreed, certainly, and thought we should support it. The nursing supervisor, however, recommended keeping them apart, and even suggested prescribing drugs to help curb Jerry's sexual urges. But Tyson is opposed to chemical restraints so that got vetoed PDQ.

'Anyway,' she continued, 'Tyson decided to call both families in and talk to them about it. At the time, Nancy's husband, Frank, was totally supportive, whatever makes her happy and all that.'

'Like Sandra Day O'Connor,' I commented. 'I remember reading an article in the *New York Times* about it. Her husband, John, had Alzheimer's disease and totally forgot her. He took up with another woman in the long-term care facility he was living in. Justice O'Connor said it was a relief to find him relaxed and happy, holding hands with his sweetheart whenever she visited.'

'Exactly.'

The tea arrived. Elaine selected a Tazo Cucumber White from a wooden caddy, poured hot water into her cup then dunked the teabag up and down in it. I wasn't really thirsty but selected a spicy ginger one that I hoped would lift my spirits.

'As for Jerry's son,' Elaine continued, 'I think he was OK with the relationship as long as it remained on *his* terms,' she said thoughtfully, ticking them off on her fingers. 'Like, you can eat meals together. And dance. Holding hands and cuddling is OK, but kissing is off-limits, and, for heaven's sake, don't wander off to the privacy of your room and do what the rest of us do.' She took a sip of her hot tea then set the cup down on the saucer. 'He insisted that his father's heart wasn't healthy enough for sex. Ha! I'm sorry, but if you've made it to age eighty-eight, having sex won't kill you. It may even help prolong your life.'

'What did he expect his poor father to do?' I wondered aloud. 'Lie around all day watching reruns of *Gilligan's Island*, waiting for the arrival of Oscar the Death-Sniffing Cat?'

Elaine chortled. 'We have pets and visiting comfort dogs here at Blackwalnut Hall too, but so far none have demonstrated the kind of supersensory ability that Oscar seems to have. It would certainly make my job easier.'

'If it's true that touch is often the last sense to deteriorate,' I said, getting back to the subject of physical contact, 'I can understand why massages, facials and mani-pedis can be so therapeutic, especially for your dementia patients. Massages with Garnelle at Spa Paradiso are my main vice,' I added. 'They feel so good they ought to be illegal.'

'I hear her hands are insured by Lloyds of London.' Elaine grinned. 'Seriously, though, human touch is super critical. No matter how old you are you never outgrow the need for that kind of loving, physical comfort. Tyson believes that the elderly have a right to intimacy,' she continued after a moment. 'We don't treat it like a behavioral problem. The staff here are trained to monitor developing relationships, particularly among our residents with impaired memory, to make sure they're mutually enjoyable. I don't know about you, but I hope to have another shot at it when *I* get to be ninety.'

'Even in the short time I've been volunteering here,' I said, 'it became obvious to me that Nancy and Jerry's relationship was exactly that – mutually enjoyable. As for the sex? It looked entirely consensual to me.'

'Well, the Maryland Office of Health Care Quality might want to argue with you about that. Seems they have initiated an investigation.'

'I've heard about it. They've asked me for an interview. But what I don't understand is if it wasn't Tyson, who reported it and why? Was Nancy injured?'

'Of course not! When you brought the incident to our attention, I grabbed Heather and we went down to Nancy's room right away. Nancy and Jerry were still, uh, involved. It took two of us to separate them, and neither of them was happy about it! Jerry thought we were attacking Nancy and tried to protect her, while Nancy was screaming bloody murder. I haven't heard such language since my husband was working on our tax returns.' Elaine leaned forward and whispered, 'If anyone needed a doctor, it was *me*. Nancy bites.' She extended an arm where a ragged, red semi-circle confirmed her claim. 'Thank goodness my tetanus shots were up to date.'

'Ouch,' I said.

'After we got Jerry calmed down and settled back in his own room we called the doctor to take a look at Nancy,' Elaine continued. 'Aside from a bit of redness on her thighs and . . .' she cleared her throat, 'you know where, which would be entirely normal under the circumstances, there was nothing at all wrong with her.'

'So, I don't understand. What is there for the State of Maryland to investigate?'

'They claim that Nancy's advanced dementia made it impossible for her to give informed consent.'

I recalled, with some embarrassment, the cries of pleasure that I had – albeit unintentionally – overheard; sounds that everyone in America was familiar with thanks to Meg Ryan's famous Katz's Deli performance in the movie *When Harry Met Sally*.

'What nonsense,' I said. 'Nancy was a willing participant, otherwise she would have been screaming – and she knows how to scream, that's for sure – or trying to fight Jerry off.' I pointed to Elaine's wound. 'Exhibit A. But, she was doing none of those things. She may not remember who the president is, or that she already has a husband, or even what day of the week it is, but she definitely wanted to have sex with Jerry.'

Elaine sighed. 'Honestly, I'm worried. If this lawsuit goes

against us we'll be in danger of losing our Medicare/Medicaid certification and that would be a serious blow, financial and otherwise.'

'You'd think there'd be a clearer policy on this sort of thing,' I said. 'Isn't anyone paying attention? Think of all the baby-boomers who are rapidly joining the ranks of the elderly and terminally confused.'

'That's just it, Hannah. The people who brought us the sexual revolution are now living together in nursing homes instead of communes. And, call me a revolutionary, but if they want to smoke pot and shag, I say, let 'em.'

Back in the day, my older sister, Ruth, had been a make-love-not-war, flower-in-the-riot-gun kind of gal. If ever the time came for her to check into a nursing home, I pity anyone who tried to prevent *her* from having sex.

As I drove home to my empty house, I couldn't help thinking that this was going to end up badly for everyone involved.

FOURTEEN

'Wherefore seeing we also are compassed about with so great a cloud of witnesses, let us lay aside every weight, and the sin which doth so easily beset us, and let us run with patience the race that is set before us.'
                                    King James Bible, Hebrews, 12:1.

I hadn't even rolled out of bed the next morning when the telephone on my bedside table burbled. It was Hutch, getting straight to the point. 'I thought Mrs Milanesi was going to bring in her mother's scrapbook.'

'She didn't?' I threw the duvet aside and padded barefoot to the bathroom.

'No, she didn't. I can proceed without it, of course, but having a copy of that scrapbook could grease a few wheels.'

I promised Hutch I'd follow up with Izzy right away.

Izzy picked up on the first ring, sounding breathless. 'Hello.'

'Izzy, this is Hannah Ives. My brother-in-law just called asking about your mother's scrapbook. He's wondering when you're going to bring it in. I'll be happy to drive you into his office, if that's helpful.'

'Oh, Hannah, I can't find it!'

'What do you mean, you can't find it?'

'I always keep it in my bottom dresser drawer. After I showed it to Naddie, though, I put it on the table in the hallway, ready to take to Mr Hutchinson. But it's not there now.'

'Maybe you put it somewhere else?' I suggested.

'Maybe, but I don't think so.'

'When was the last time you saw it, before you put it on the table in the hallway, I mean.'

'A couple of nights ago. I took it to dinner so I could show it to Naddie.'

I suppressed a sigh of relief. At least Naddie would confirm that the scrapbook existed, that it wasn't simply a figment of Izzy's imagination.

'Maybe I belong in the memory unit.' Izzy began sobbing.

'Don't be silly,' I soothed. 'Most of the time you're sharp as a tack.'

'No, I'm not. I've lost my best hairbrush. I mislay my reading glasses all the time. I can never find my tweezers. But they can all be replaced. Nothing can replace my mother's scrapbook. Nothing! I'm just sick about it.'

'What does the scrapbook look like, Izzy?'

'It's green leather with "Fotografie" embossed on the front. The pages are black, with punched holes, and it's all bound together on the narrower side with a black shoelace.'

Ah. I'd had a smiliar scrapbook in junior high, full of photos I'd clipped out of teen magazines of heartthrobs like Paul McCartney and Davy Jones.

'I distinctly remember bringing it home from dinner at the colony and putting it on the table, ready to take to Mr Hutchinson. Naddie even brought over a huge Ziploc bag for me to put it in. I didn't know Ziplocs even came that big. We sealed it up and I stuck one of my mailing labels on the outside, just in case.'

'Don't worry, Izzy. We'll find it. I'm going to call Naddie and we'll come over and help you look.'

Izzy protested, saying she was too embarrassed but, like good friends everywhere, we didn't listen. Twenty minutes later I'd picked up Naddie and we were standing on Izzy's stoop.

'Come in!' she called from inside when I knocked.

I turned the knob and went in. 'Don't you lock your doors, Ysabelle?'

Izzy emerged from the kitchen looking surprised. 'No, why would I? Calvert Colony is safer than Fort Knox.'

Obviously. I stole a glance at Naddie, who was already poking around among the magazines on the coffee tabletop.

'I've looked everywhere!' Izzy wailed.

Well, not *everywhere*, I thought, channeling my mother, or you would have found it.

While Izzy sat in an armchair like a lump, quietly sniffling into a ragged tissue, Naddie and I turned her town home upside down, searching closets, under beds and sofas, between cushions and even the trash can and recycling bin Izzy kept under the sink.

'I'm just sick about this,' Izzy sobbed when we rejoined her in the living room, empty handed.

'All is not completely lost,' Naddie said, surprising us both. If you remember, Izzy, when you showed me your mother's scrapbook at dinner the other night I took photographs of several pages with my iPhone, including the page with the painting featuring Umberto.'

Naddie slipped the iPhone out of the pocket of her slacks and powered it on. Perched on the arm of Izzy's chair, she leaned over and thumbed through the photographs. I stood behind the chair and looked over her shoulder.

Naddie had photographed six pages in all, each page featuring at least two paintings.

'Naddie,' I said, 'you are a treasure.'

'I just can't understand what happened to it!' Izzy whined.

I finally voiced what I had started thinking ever since I found myself rooting through the newspapers and empty pizza boxes in Izzy's recycling bin. 'Somebody stole it, Izzy.'

'But who would do that?'

'I don't know, but I think it's a much more reasonable explanation than you losing your mind.'

'Have you had any visitors?' Naddie asked.

Izzy shook her head miserably.

'A cleaning lady?'

'I wish.'

Naddie got up from the arm of Izzy's chair and sat down next to me on the sofa. 'What's your brother-in-law's email address, Hannah?'

I gave it to her and watched while Naddie tapped each photo, selecting it, then emailed the lot to Hutch. With a whooshing sound, they were on their way.

'Thank you, thank you, thank you,' Izzy said. 'How fortunate that you took those photos!'

'Better that than nothing,' Naddie said. Turning to me, she said, 'So you think the scrapbook was stolen?'

'It's the obvious conclusion.'

'But who would do that?' Naddie wondered.

As far as I knew, the list of suspects was short. 'The only people who are aware of the existence of Letizia Rossi's scrapbook are Hutch, Izzy, Naddie and me.' When I finished ticking the names off on my fingers, Izzy flushed.

'What is it?' I asked.

'I brought the scrapbook to dinner to show Naddie, as I said. We were there early, so before they served the appetizers I opened the scrapbook up on the table – that's when Naddie took the photographs. When Safa came in, she had to see it, too. That meant Masud saw it as well, of course. Pretty soon we had attracted a bit of a crowd.'

'That's true,' Naddie said. 'Then Izzy started telling everyone about how she was going to get her painting back.'

I suppressed an anguished moan.

'Even that horrible Richard person was there,' Naddie added. 'He was Christie's guest at dinner, sitting all lovey-dovey at a corner table for two.' Naddie stabbed a finger at her open mouth and made a gagging sound.

'"So great a cloud of witnesses,"' I muttered.

'Indeed,' Naddie said.

'But I still don't understand,' Izzy said. 'What would anyone at Calvert Colony want with my mother's scrapbook?'

Hutch, I knew, had kept the identity of his client confidential, so even the staff at the Baltimore Art Gallery – the only people I could imagine having any interest in it – wouldn't know where to come looking for it.

'It's a puzzlement,' I said.

FIFTEEN

'*The OHCQ licenses and certifies Maryland state health care facilities. Through licensing, a facility gains the authority to operate or do business in the state; through certification, a facility obtains the right to participate in the Medicare and Medicaid programs. The OHCQ uses state and federal regulations . . . to determine compliance. When problems or deficiencies are noted, the OHCQ initiates administrative action against facilities that violate rules and regulations. If a facility fails to correct problems and is unable or unwilling to do so, the OHCQ may impose sanctions such as license revocation, fines, bans on admission, or other restrictions on the operating license.*'
Maryland Department of Health and Mental Hygiene, Office of Health Care Quality, *http://dhmh.maryland.gov/ohcq*

The team the Maryland Office of Health Care Quality sent to interview me consisted of two overworked civil servants, a middle-aged man wearing a rumpled gray-and-white seersucker jacket and a woman, clearly his supervisor, whose sour expression told me she'd rather be anywhere but in a super-chilled conference room on a blistering hot August day.

The meeting was straightforward. I walked into the room and sat down. A tape recorder, with my permission, was turned on. Yes, I saw Nancy Harper and Jerry Wolcott engaged in sexual intercourse. Yes, I recognized them. Of course, I was sure it was Jerry. No, I could not be mistaken. Tattoo, you know. Yes, the sex appeared to be consensual. Yes, I reported the incident to the memory unit authorities.

End of story.

Following that ordeal, I decided that, come hell or high water, I would find poor Nancy Harper and do something, anything, to coax her out of the debilitating funk she had slipped into. She was clearly grieving the loss of Jerry; everyone was talking about it. She no longer appeared in the lounge during Charlie Robinson's popular sing-alongs, staff said. She refused to cooperate with any of the volunteers, including me. Getting her to meals was like pulling teeth and, once there, she'd simply sulk over her plate, poking experimentally at the food with her fork but eating nothing. As a result, unit staff told me, she was losing weight. Not good for a woman who weighed only a hundred and twenty-one pounds to begin with. Her advance directive, I learned, prohibited force feeding, so persuasion was the only tool left to us.

Steeling myself for another rejection, I knocked on the door of Nancy's room. When she didn't answer, I peeked in. Nancy sat in a chair by the window, barefoot but otherwise fully dressed, staring out into the Tranquility Garden. 'Hello, Nancy.'

She sat as inscrutable and still as one of the stone Buddhas poking his belly out of the shrubbery in the peaceful garden below.

'How are you doing today?'

I knew it was a dumb question the minute it fell out of my mouth. She felt like shit, that's what. And unless I could bring Jerry magically back into her lonely life, there was very little I could do about fixing it.

'The garden's very serene, isn't it? Anything special going on out there today?'

She turned her head in my direction but her eyes remained unfocused, disturbingly empty.

'He went away,' she said.

'I know, sweetie,' I said, swallowing hard and stepping closer. 'No wonder you're sad.'

'What's done is done, and that's all there is to say.'

'Would you like me to read to you today?'

She turned her attention to the window again, gazing out over the trees and into the distance. The entire Baltimore Ravens football team could have come charging through the Tranquility

Garden, hooting and hollering, and I doubted Nancy would have noticed.

'How 'bout we go for a walk?'

'I don't like these shoes.'

She wasn't wearing any shoes, but I didn't argue. At least she was talking to me. 'Do you want me to find you another pair then?'

Nancy shrugged but she'd clearly understood. 'When they don't want me to go out, they hide my shoes in the closet.'

'Well, let's look in the closet, then, shall we?'

With Nancy in suitable footwear and her arm tucked through mine, we strolled out of the memory unit and down the long hallway that led to the lounge. That Nancy was as popular as the high-school homecoming queen was evident. Other residents greeted her all along our way.

Hi, Nancy.

Good to see you out and about, Nancy.

Missed you in art class, Nancy.

(I'll bet, I thought, thinking about her last, uh, monumental sculpture.)

After a while I noticed hints of a smile tugging at the corners of Nancy's mouth.

At Sweet Tooth we were waylaid and summoned inside by the Easy Rider himself who sat at a table for four, putting the moves on Christie McSpadden and another woman I didn't recognize who used our entrance as an excuse to make a quick escape.

The colonel sprang up like a Pop-Tart and offered Nancy his seat.

I had to laugh. 'No, thanks, Colonel. Please, go back to whatever you were doing. We're just getting some ice cream to take out into the garden.'

'Nancy likes Oreo milkshakes,' the colonel volunteered, stooping a little so he could look Nancy straight in the eyes. 'Don't you, sweetheart?'

I consulted with my friend. 'Does an Oreo milkshake sound good to you, Nancy?' The staff had told me she'd refused to eat lunch (again!), even though it was her favorite, macaroni and cheese, so I figured the poor thing would be hungry.

A tiny smile and an almost imperceptible nod.

That was all the confirmation the colonel needed. He bowed gallantly from the waist, executed a perfect about-face and marched off to the counter to place our order.

I sat Nancy down at the table next to Christie and pulled up a chair for myself. When Colonel Greene returned he set our treats on the table and said, 'You're friends with the Abazas, right?'

'With his wife, Safa, yes. I don't know Mr Abaza at all, really.'

'He's making trouble,' the colonel said, retaking his seat.

'What kind of trouble?' I asked, playing dumb.

'I like it here,' he said. 'I don't want to move.'

Something wasn't tracking. 'Why on earth would you have to move, Colonel Greene?'

He laid an ice-cold hand on mine. 'Nate, please.'

'OK, Nate.' I smiled and retrieved my hand. 'Do you *want* to move?'

'God, no, but if Calvert Colony loses its license, assisted living and the memory unit will have to close down, and without the insurance money coming in . . .' He made a slashing motion across his throat.

'Surely . . .'

'Insurance money. That's what keeps this place afloat, trust me. I cashed in everything to buy into Calvert Colony and it would be pennies on the dollar – pennies! – if the place goes belly up.' He slapped the table so hard it nearly knocked over Christie's Diet Coke. 'And all because of a little slam-bang-thank-you-ma'am. Jerry and Nancy are good folk and look what's happened to them.' For a moment I thought the colonel was going to slap the table again, even harder. 'I just don't get it.'

Ah ha, I thought. It didn't take long for word about the investigation to get around. Not surprising, though, since people like me were being called in for interviews.

'I'm taking steps to protect my investment,' he said.

'Steps? What kind of steps?' Christie wanted to know.

'A little friendly persuasion,' he said, looking grim.

I didn't like the way the conversation was going. 'Nate . . .' I paused to consider my words carefully. 'I don't think there's

much anyone can do now that the incident's been reported and
the health department's already involved.'

'Him and his big, blabby holier-than-thou mouth.'

I frowned and opened my big, blabby mouth in protest. 'We
don't know . . .'

The colonel cut me off. 'See this?' he said, making a fist and
thrusting it in my direction. It was hard to miss an opal set in
a gold signet ring so large it should be registered as a lethal
weapon. He rapped it three times on the Formica tabletop.

Ring knockers. Service academy graduates. We had them at
the Naval Academy, too.

'West Point. Class of 1956.' *Tap-tap-tap*. 'I have buddies who
fought guys like Abaza in Operation Desert Storm. They're not
our friends. *None* of them.'

'That's right,' Christie chimed in. 'Dickie's writing a book.
His experiences in Afghanistan would make your hair stand on
end.'

The colonel winced.

'Seems to me that Al-Qaeda is the enemy,' I said, 'or the
Taliban. Not Muslims in general.'

'Don't be naive, Hannah. Look around you. They're out there
trying to kill Americans every single day.'

'They're cowards,' Christie said. 'You've seen the videos,
Hannah. They wear masks.'

I wondered how much of this diatribe, if anything, Nancy
was picking up on, but she seemed oblivious, sipping content-
edly on her milkshake, quietly humming along to a fifties tune
playing softly in the background.

Still, the colonel had wound Christie up. 'What kind of person
hijacks a schoolbus and shoots a thirteen-year-old girl in the
head?' she sputtered. 'And what was Malala Yousufzai's crime?
Huh?' Christie paused but didn't wait for an answer before
practically shouting, 'She wanted to go to school!'

'The shooter and the cleric who ordered that attack are hiding
out in Afghanistan,' the colonel informed us. 'It's one of the
most corrupt governments in the world. The U.S. has squandered
billions of dollars there. About as effective as giving a teenager
a bottle of booze and the car keys.'

'Savages,' Christie grunted. 'You can't make peace with savages.'

The colonel reached across the table, covered Christie's hand with his own and squeezed. 'Kindred spirit,' he said, winking.

Paul and I had friends, former midshipmen, who'd lost their lives in Afghanistan. At some visceral level I agreed with the colonel, but I refused to tar the Abazas and our other Muslim friends with the same brush used to tar the Taliban. Nothing was going to budge this old vet from his anti-Muslim platform, however, so I decided to retreat from the battlefield before I said something I ended up regretting.

I pasted a smile on my face and said, 'Be a sweetie and fetch me a couple of plastic lids and one of those cardboard caddies, would you, Nate? I promised Nancy a walk in the garden, and so far I'm failing miserably.'

The blast of hot air that hit us as we stepped out of the building with me carrying the caddy nearly took my breath away. I urged Nancy along the path as quickly as I could, seeking a spot in the shade where we could finish enjoying our shakes. I remembered the stone bench in the cherry grove and headed that way – through the flowerbeds, up the path and over the bridge spanning the lily pond where the rowboat and the remarkable glass sculptures lay.

The Tranquility Garden was beautifully designed, so perfect in every detail, I thought as we settled onto the bench, that not a single leaf or blade of grass would *dare* to be out of place. Elves undoubtedly swept through the garden while the rest of us slept, putting everything to rights.

I slipped fresh straws out of their paper sleeves, tucked the trash into my pocket, jammed the straws through the plastic lids, then handed the Oreo shake to Nancy. She put the straw to her lips and began sipping happily.

'Ahhhh, perfect,' I said to nobody in particular as I took a sip of mine. Plain chocolate, thank you very much, as rich and delicious as a Dove bar.

But not everything was perfect. Something was off in the garden today. A wrong note, a discrepancy, a flaw in the carefully staged landscape around me.

It was the rowboat, I decided. When we sat there before, hadn't it leaned at a slightly different angle? And the glass balls had completely filled it, surely, but now some of the smaller ones had tumbled out, littering the ground.

I squinted. Was that a shoe? Had one of the residents lost . . .?

'I'll be right back,' I said to Nancy. Her head bobbed as she took another sip of her Oreos and cream. She closed her eyes, smiled with pleasure and took another sip. You do good work, Hannah, I thought as I rose from the bench.

Slowly, still casually sipping on my milkshake, I approached the rowboat. When I was about ten feet away I could see that the shoe was a sandal. It had a sock-clad foot in it and, as I moved closer still, I saw that the foot was attached to a leg wearing khaki trousers.

Paul's parting words echoed in my head: 'You, too, Hannah. And no dead bodies, OK?' *Shit.* Was I cursed, doomed to stumble over bodies for life, rerun after rerun like Jessica Fletcher on *Murder She Wrote*?

I should back off now, I knew. Take Nancy by the hand, return to Blackwalnut Hall. Call 9-1-1. But . . . perhaps he – she? – was alive and needed help.

I glanced back at Nancy and was relieved to see she was still concentrating on her milkshake, oblivious.

I approached the rowboat cautiously and leaned far to the right to get a better view.

The leg belonged to Masud Abaza, who was beyond any help on this side of paradise.

Safa's husband lay face up, his sightless eyes staring at the sky, the tremor in his hands stilled forever. Blood had congealed on a vicious wound to his temple and stained the manicured grass under his head. It seemed obvious that some savage blow had killed him, and yet, protruding a good two feet out of the center of Masud's chest was a giant purple icicle. An art installation gone bad, I thought, suppressing an insane urge to giggle. As if a blow to the head wasn't sufficient, Masud's killer had uprooted one of the artist's decorative glass reeds and driven it straight into the poor man's heart.

SIXTEEN

'Gardens of perpetual bliss: they shall enter there, as well as the righteous among their fathers, their spouses, and their offspring: and angels shall enter unto them from every gate (with the salutation): "Peace unto you for that ye persevered in patience! Now how excellent is the final home!"'

Quran 13: 23-24

My own heart thumped, leapt and turned within my chest. I hugged myself hard, trying to calm its frantic pounding. I closed my eyes and counted slowly to ten, breathing steadily. When I opened my eyes again it was as if nothing had changed. The sun still shone, the birds still sang, the honeybees still flitted from flower to flower and Nancy Harper was still occupied with her milkshake, staring at a pagoda-shaped bird-feeder – Grand Central Station for chattering finches and a pair of cardinals – and humming quietly to herself.

I reached into my pocket for my cell phone and hastily dialed 9-1-1. 'Stay where you are,' the emergency operator told me after I had explained the situation. 'An officer is on his way.'

The next call I made was to the memory unit. Heather, the attendant on duty, told me that Elaine Broering was in a meeting.

'We have a serious situation,' I told Heather. 'Please ask Elaine to meet me in the Tranquility Garden right away.'

Elaine didn't waste any time. She joined me in the garden where I had settled myself down next to Nancy, keeping her occupied with one-way small talk.

'What's wrong?'

I gestured with my head. 'Over by the rowboat.'

Elaine took a few steps in that direction and pulled up short. 'Jesus! Is he . . .?'

'Very.'

'This is dreadful, simply dreadful,' she said after taking a closer look at the body. 'I've never, not in all my years . . .' She took several deep breaths then blew them out slowly through slightly pursed lips. 'We'll need to find Tyson Bennett and inform him right away. He'll want to begin damage control. And locate Safa, of course. Oh, Lord, poor Safa!'

Elaine thrust her hands into the pockets of her scrubs and rocked back and forth on the soles of her sensible shoes. 'First the Health Care Quality people, then the lawsuit and now this. It's bad, Hannah, very bad.'

'What's bad?' Nancy wanted to know. 'What are we talking about? Have I forgotten something?'

'Come on, Nancy,' Elaine said, seguing smoothly from unit manager into caregiver mode. 'It's almost time for dinner. They're serving lasagna today, and I know how much you like lasagna.'

Nancy offered me her empty paper cup then stood up. 'I make lasagna with meatballs. Frank likes it that way. Meatballs and lots of mozzarella cheese. Do you like meatballs . . . I forget your name.'

'Hannah. My name is Hannah.'

'Hannah,' she repeated thoughtfully as Elaine linked her arm in Nancy's and started to draw her away.

Suddenly, Nancy jerked her arm free. 'Is someone in trouble?'

Elaine bowed slightly, then cocked her head so she could look straight into Nancy's eyes. 'No, no one's in trouble. Why?'

Nancy waved in the direction of the open field then chugged off. 'There's a police car,' she trilled. 'Maybe it's Frank!'

Elaine shot an oh-help-me look over her shoulder and trudged after her.

I scuttled further on down the walk until I was even with the pavilion. I could see the police car now, just pulling into the parking lot. Elaine waved both arms over her head to attract the driver's attention then chopped them in my direction, like a flight attendant pointing out the emergency exits.

The head gardener of Calvert Colony was going to have a conniption, I thought, as I watched first the dark blue Crown Vic, then an ambulance, and finally a white Chevy crime scene van bounce across the field, ripping up the lawn and sending divots flying. One by one they braked to a halt about twenty feet from where I stood.

I introduced myself to the patrolman, who emerged from the

Crown Vic, and showed him where Masud's body lay. I withdrew to the shade of a cherry tree while he, too, ascertained that the gentleman was dead, a fact that was confirmed for the fourth time by one of the paramedics who knelt by the body, pressed his fingers against the victim's neck then shook his head. The paramedic waved off his partner, who had been busily hauling a gurney out of the back of the ambulance, then went to talk to the driver of the crime scene van while the patrolman dealt with me.

'Let's sit down for a minute, shall we?' he suggested.

After we got settled on the bench that Nancy and I had so recently vacated, the patrolman eased a notebook out of the breast pocket of his navy blue uniform, jotted down my name and contact information then asked me what happened.

So I told him.

While we talked, two guys from the crime scene team began cordoning off a wide area around the body with yellow tape. I was busily explaining Nancy Harper's condition – yes, somebody'd been with me, but no, she hadn't seen anything and wouldn't have been a reliable witness in any case – when a familiar voice drawled, 'So, we meet again, Mrs Ives.'

The last time I'd seen Detective Ron Powers he'd been coordinating the investigation into the abduction of my grandson, Timmy. He was a little bit grayer around the temples now, perhaps, but had the same serious gray eyes and the same half-inch scar that only emphasized the resolute squareness of his jaw. A veneer of designer stubble gave the detective a rugged, outdoorsy look, but I didn't know whether he was being fashion forward or whether it was due simply to the lateness of the day.

I managed a smile. 'It's a curse, Detective Powers.'

'Did you know the victim?' His eyes flicked to a notebook in his hand. 'Masud Abaza?'

'Vaguely. I know his wife, Safa, much better. They own one of the town homes here at the colony. The folks at reception can tell you which one. I've never been to their home. Masud seemed to prefer his own company.'

One of the crime scene techs called Powers over, so the detective excused himself. They stood over the body, consulting calmly, as if seeing a body pinned to the ground with a stalk of glass like a butterfly on a specimen board was an everyday occurrence.

When he finished talking to the tech, Powers rejoined me. 'Can you think of anyone who hated Mr Abaza enough to do this?'

While waiting for the cops to arrive, I'd made a mental list. 'There was a whacko in a balaclava who Masud caught spraying graffiti on the *musalla*.'

'*Musalla?*'

'It's kind of a prayer hut.' I waved. 'Over there. I'm surprised you don't know about the graffiti. It was reported.'

'Vandalism's not my department,' Powers said, scribbling.

'Masud and Mister Balaclava got into a tussle, but by the time I arrived on the scene Masud was dusting himself off and the guy in the balaclava had disappeared into the woods.'

'Anyone else?'

From a life-long, in-depth study of television crime drama I've learned that the spouse of a murder victim is always the first suspect, so I thought I'd set the record straight on that point from the get-go. 'Not his wife. Safa seemed to be devoted to the guy. They'd been married for thirty-some years.'

Powers raised a dark eyebrow. 'Where have I heard that before?'

'He was having some sort of running disagreement with the chef, Raniero Buccho, though,' I hastened to add. 'On two occasions, I overheard them arguing.'

'What were they arguing about?'

'The first time, I'm not sure. I wasn't close enough to make out their words. But the second time Masud seemed to be reaming Raniero out for being a little too friendly with his wife. Because of their religious beliefs – they're Muslim – he found Raniero's behavior disrespectful. Although Masud's definition of "disrespectful" was pretty broad.'

'As in . . .?'

'Well, simply talking to Safa, really. Smiling, joking, touching her arm. That kind of thing.'

'Did Mrs Abaza have a relationship with this Raniero guy?'

I flashed back to the day I'd surprised Safa alone in the kitchen with Raniero. Although I'd been slightly suspicious at the time, Safa was a friend, and I didn't want to jump to conclusions. She *could* have been consulting with the chef about the menu, as she had claimed.

I kept my eyes steady. 'As I said, she seemed devoted to her husband. She converted to Islam for him, you know. She's going to be devastated.'

Powers nodded. 'I've sent an officer to find her.'

'You're not going to make her . . .' I started to panic, thinking how I would feel if I had to see Paul lying dead on the grass with a glass spike driven through his chest.

'No. We have your identification – that's good enough for now. She can do the formal identification later, or another family member can, after we get him, uh, cleaned up.'

'They have a son, and a daughter, maybe one of them would . . .' I paused to get the little wheels within my brain spinning. 'I'm not sure where the son lives, but the daughter is local. Chevy Chase. Potomac. Someplace like that. Sorry, I'm blanking. Maybe the son can identify his dad?'

'I wouldn't worry about that, Mrs Ives. I'm sure that Calvert Colony has all the contact information we need.'

'You're right, of course they will,' I said, breathing deeply.

Outside the boundaries of the crime scene tape colony residents had begun to gather. Two Calvert Colony security officers, dressed in khaki uniforms, paced back and forth between the entrance to the garden and the parking lot, keeping the curious at bay. I spotted Naddie, keeping pace alongside one of them, pumping him for information, no doubt. I had to smile. *You go, girl.*

All that energy! I felt suddenly drained. 'Is there anything else you need me for, Detective? This whole situation has been pretty upsetting and I'd like to go home now, if possible.'

'Of course.' He closed his notebook, slapped it against his open palm. 'No worries. If something comes up I'll know where to find you.'

If something comes up. I trudged wearily back over the bridge and along the walk, thinking that the only witness to the fact that *I* hadn't murdered Masud Abaza was Nancy Harper and her poor, befuddled brain. Not that *I* had any motive to murder the poor man.

As I neared the crime scene tape that was stretched between the garden gateposts, a security officer spotted me and lifted the tape so I could duck under. I ran straight into the comforting arms of Nadine Smith Gray, friend, co-conspirator and surrogate mother. Sometimes a gal needs a soft shoulder to cry on.

SEVENTEEN

'Warsaw, Ky., Nov. 26 – In the Gallatin circuit court W. J. Castleman was acquitted by a jury for killing Dr G. W. Ferrell about a year ago in this county. The two men were playing croquet and got into a trifling dispute in which the lie was passed, and Castleman struck Farrell on the head while Farrell was advancing on him, producing concussion of the brain and almost instant death.'
Mayville Public Ledger, November 26, 1900.

The killing of Masud Abaza precipitated a media feeding frenzy. 'Is Anti-Muslim Violence Spiraling Out of Control?' asked Wolf Blitzer from the CNN Situation Room, while Fox News bulletins were screaming, 'Retired Professor Murdered in Anti-Muslim Hate Crime!'

It was all over the regional papers, too, of course, capturing the front pages of both the *Baltimore Sun* and *The Washington Post*, and the story was feuled anew several days later by whoever leaked the details about Balaclava Man and the graffiti, until political shenanigans in our nation's capital pushed all other news aside. Our local rag, the *Annapolis Capital*, stuck with the story a few days more – 'Police Probe for Motive in Deadly Attack on Local Man' and 'Bizarre Murder Weapon Baffles Police' – but eventually a lack of any progress in the case caused even the interest of the *Capital* to wane.

According to a story in the paper, the Office of the Baltimore Medical Examiner had demonstrated commendable respect for Islamic burial customs, setting other work aside in order to concentrate on Masud's autopsy in a heroic attempt to meet the twenty-four-hour turnaround between death and burial that was generally proscribed by Islamic law. They didn't quite make it. Masud's body was released to his family within seventy-two hours, and the beloved husband, father and grandfather had been buried privately, with only men in attendance, in the George Washington Islamic Gardens off Riggs Road in Adelphi. As I had suspected, it had been a blow to the head that had killed him. The glass spike had been – well, no other word for it – overkill. Somebody had been seriously unhappy with Masud Abaza.

As I'd told Detective Powers, number one on my list was the guy in the balaclava who'd gotten into a tussle with Masud over the graffiti. I had no way of knowing for sure, but that act of mischief had all the earmarks of Christie's boyfriend, Richard Kent. I'd left Richard in the lobby with Christie when I went to the memory unit that day, but Naddie told me later that their date had been a short one. He'd left after an hour, so Richard could have easily attacked Masud while I was reading to Lillian Blake.

Had Masud and Raniero finally come to blows over Masud's imagined – perhaps confirmed? – suspicions about the relationship between his wife and the master chef?

Masud had been making trouble for Tyson Bennett, too, over the incident with Nancy and Jerry. If Bennett were holding Masud responsible for the possibility that Calvert Colony might lose its accreditation, and his spotless reputation along with it, things might have gotten ugly between them. It seemed unlikely that he would have been able to persuade Masud to stay quiet on the issue. And what if Masud had threatened to leave Calvert Colony and take all the other Muslims with him?

If you added the Islamophobes like Christie McSpadden and Colonel Nate Greene, who'd also been upset for his friends and didn't want to have to move from the colony in the event of it being shut down, and even the old guy I'd met on the porch that first day, the list grew even longer.

Could I eliminate Jerry, who'd been separated from the love of his life for no good reason? No. Stranger things had happened.

I shook myself back to reality. My iPhone was beeping.

A text message from Paul, my seafaring husband: *WTF?*

He must have come ashore and picked up a newspaper. I had some explaining to do.

A week after the murder I decided to pay a condolence call on Safa Abaza, but when I knocked on the door of her town home she didn't come to the door. From the helpful woman at reception I learned that Safa had left Calvert Colony and was staying, at least temporarily, at her daughter's home in Potomac, Maryland. With a nudge-nudge-wink-wink, I-won't-say-anything-if-you-don't, the receptionist gave me Laila Kazi's phone number.

After three attempts at talking to Laila's voicemail I managed to reach the actual daughter on the phone.

'Mother can't come to the phone right now,' Laila explained. 'She's in her *Iddah.*'

In her Iddah? Was Safa in her room, her car, her boat, her cottage in the back yard or what? 'Uh . . .' I started to say, when Laila rescued me from ignorance.

'*Iddah* is Mother's official period of mourning,' she informed me cooly. 'It generally lasts for four lunar months plus ten days.'

During *Iddah*, I learned, her mother would wear plain clothing and no makeup, perfume or jewelry. She'd stay at home, seeing no one, except for emergencies, of course. Apparently talking to me wasn't one of those emergencies. After asking Laila to convey my sincerest condolences to her mother, I hung up. I sent a handwritten sympathy note to Safa at the Potomac address, but decided that, for the moment anyway, there wasn't much more that I could do.

The next time I returned to Blackwalnut Hall I found Angie McSpadden and her mother in the lobby trying to organize a game of croquet. Angie was dressed casually in Bermuda shorts and a yellow tank top, but Christie, her mother-in-law, had stepped out of a TravelSmith catalog wearing gray slacks and a pebble-print tunic in shades of gray, purple and magenta with matching purple tennis shoes.

'Your mother-in-law looks nice today,' I told Angie, *sotto voce.*

'Go figure,' she replied. 'I'd been after her for weeks to get her hair done, then all of a sudden, like, it's an emergency. Had to drive her out to Karen James on Maryland Avenue because the salon here was totally slammed.'

'Is she going on a date?' I asked, thinking about Richard Kent.

Angie groaned. 'She lives in hope. But I haven't seen Dickey-boy in a couple of weeks. He's off on some secret mission. Like I'm buying that shit.'

'I'd like to play, if you've still got room,' I said.

'Sure. You'll make a foursome, but we still can add two more.' She scanned the lobby hopefully. 'Croquet, anybody?'

It was then I noticed that someone had parked Nancy Harper in the lobby. Looking thin, washed out and withdrawn, she slouched in an overstuffed chair pulled up as close to the fish tank as the built-in benches would allow. She stared with no sign of interest into its aquamarine depths.

'Let's ask Nancy,' I suggested. 'I know she can play. She was out on the court a couple of weeks ago.' *With Jerry*, I thought, with a pang. 'You just have to keep reminding her what direction she's going in. I'll play and keep an eye on her, if you like.'

Despite encouragement from me, Nancy stubbornly refused to budge, and nobody else in the lobby was dying to volunteer, so I hauled out my cell phone and called Naddie. 'Want to join us for croquet?' I asked.

She had been watching the Food Channel on TV, but readily agreed. 'Sure, why not. They're making sushi out of live sea urchins. I can live a long and happy life and never taste that.'

When it came to croquet, Naddie was a catch. She'd been a member of the crack Ginger Cove team that had trounced the Naval Academy midshipmen the previous year in a match that had been covered by *Sports Illustrated* magazine. At Ginger Cove croquet wasn't a game, it was blood sport. Team members played year-round on two AstroTurf courts. During inclement weather, aficionados moved inside to a ballroom court, laid out with specially weighted wickets. Naddie had even dated – briefly – their Imperial Wicket, who was a spry ninety-one. The average age of his team, from newbies to veterans, was eighty-one, but it would have been a mistake to underestimate them. Their win-loss record against the navy was 12-7 and, until next year, at least, the geezers remained in possession of the coveted Generation Gap Cup.

Calvert Colony, by comparison, was a bit low tech. The courts were laid out, end to end, on two meticulously manicured, fifty-by-one-hundred-foot swatches of lawn adjacent to the tennis courts. Oversized white wickets were staked out on each court in the traditional double diamond design. Although the white stood out clearly against the close-cropped green of the grass, red flags had been tied to the tops of the starting and finishing stakes to capture the attention of the more visually challenged.

The croquet set – one of two snazzy models imported directly from Jacques in London – was stored in a garden shed adjacent to the courts in wheeled, wooden caddies. By the time Naddie joined us I had already located one of the caddies, dragged it from inside the shed, and we players were busily selecting mallets, arguing about colors and hurling good-natured insults at one another.

I snagged blue, won the coin toss, cued up my ball and gave it a good whack, sending it sailing through the first two hoops. Angie followed, and then her mother, who managed to tap my ball. Instead of taking the extra stroke to which she was entitled, Christie chortled like the witch from Hansel and Gretel, placed her ball against mine, held it there with the toe of her purple shoe and *thwack*, 'sent' my ball into the underbrush. *Damn*. I hated that rule.

When my turn came again I trudged into the taller grass, dropped down to my hands and knees and narrowed my eyes, lining up the shot. If I angled it just right, I calculated, the ball would hop over a tuft of grass, bounce up onto the court and, if the croquet gods were in my favor, come to rest somewhere in the vicinity of the third wicket.

I swung the mallet experimentally, not quite connecting with the ball, then swung it again, testing, preparing for the shot. As I concentrated on the mallet at the spot where it would make contact with the ball I noticed something clinging to the surface of the wood. Not wanting a pesky clump of dirt to spoil my aim, I swept the mallet up and squinted, turning it into the sunlight for a better view. Something dark stained the wood, and imbedded in the stain were several strands of coarse, dark hair.

'Your turn, Hannah! What *are* you waiting for?' Naddie taunted.

Christie flapped her elbows, clucking like a chicken.

A Southwest plane on a landing approach to BWI droned overhead.

These sounds and others merged, surged and faded as the significance of what I was seeing sunk in.

'Naddie! Come here a minute,' I called when I finally caught my breath.

Naddie wandered over, swinging her mallet casually like a cane. 'Seeking advice from the croquet pro already?'

Carefully balancing the handle of the mallet on the palm of my hand, I offered it up for her inspection. 'What does this look like to you?'

Naddie stared, moved in for a closer look then drew back as suddenly as if she'd been slapped. 'Blood, would be my guess, and hair.'

'Damn. That's what I thought, too.'

Our eyes locked. Without another word, we each sensed what had to be done.

'Sorry, gang,' I sang out. 'Just got a text from my daughter. Gotta go. I'm sure you can carry on here with out me.'

Naddie laid a hand on my arm, patted it reassuringly then turned away. 'Look out, here I come!' she called. 'Christie, you are going to be toast!'

Carrying the mallet gingerly so as not to smudge any latent fingerprints other than my own, I made my way back to the staff parking lot at Blackwalnut Hall, lay the mallet down on the clean concrete next to my LeBaron, and, for the second time in a week, called 9-1-1 and asked to be put through to Detective Ron Powers.

'We can't go on meeting this way, Mrs Ives.' Detective Powers's smile didn't quite reach his eyes.

'Sorry.' Although what I had to be sorry about, I couldn't imagine. *I* was the one who found his missing murder weapon, after all. At least I believed it was the murder weapon.

As we talked, the croquet mallet lay like an exclamation point on the ground between us.

Powers squatted, resting his butt squarely on his heels. 'A croquet mallet! Well, I'll be damned. The medical examiner thought it might have been a baseball bat, or one of those old-fashioned wooden hammers.' He looked up at me. 'I probably shouldn't be telling you this, Mrs Ives, but I know you'll eventually weasel it out of me anyway, or out of your brother-in-law down in Chesapeake County.'

I raised my eyebrows. '*Moi?*'

He straightened and loomed over me. 'There were wood fibers in the wound, but the lab is having trouble identifying them.'

'*Lignum vitae,*' I said.

His eyes widened. 'I beg your pardon?'

'*Lignum vitae.* Tree of life. It's a hard, resinous wood, one of the hardest woods there is, actually. It doesn't even float.'

'And you know this because . . .?'

'It's the national tree of the Bahamas, for one thing. My husband and I lived on an island in the Abacos for six months while he was on sabbatical.' I felt my face flush and fessed up. 'Actually, I read about it on the information booklet that was attached to the croquet set. Jacques uses aged *lignum vitae* in the construction of their mallets, and . . . well, we had a *lignum vitae* in our yard on Bonefish Cay, so it kind of caught my attention.'

Power leaned in for a closer look at the mallet, but didn't touch it.

'Did you find any fingerprints at the crime scene,' I asked, 'like on the glass reed?'

'Sadly, no. Whoever grabbed it wiped it clean afterwards.'

He rose, straightened and adjusted the waistband of his khakis. 'Can't tell much just by looking. Could be animal blood, could be human. The hair . . .' He shrugged. 'We'll have to get it to the lab. Where's the rest of the set?'

'My friends are over at the croquet courts playing with it now. The colony has two sets, actually, and they keep them in a kind of garden shed between the croquet and the tennis courts.' Before he could ask, I added: 'The door wasn't locked, Detective, so anyone could have had access to them. The only reason I picked up this particular mallet is because I wanted to play with blue.'

'We'll need to take the sets away, too.'

'Of course,' I said, thinking, well, there goes any prayer of a Calvert Colony championship season. 'Want me to show you where they are?'

'Thanks. But first, can you keep an eye on it for a minute while I get something from my car?'

I nodded but paced uneasily like a mother lion protecting her cub until Powers returned carrying a large white paper bag.

He slipped the mallet carefully into the bag, secured the flap and initialed it, then said almost conversationally, 'We'll need your fingerprints, of course, for purposes of elimination.'

'I was arrested once,' I confessed. 'They're in AFIS.' When his eyebrows shot up into the stratosphere, I said, 'It was a mistake.'

'Of course it was,' he said evenly, but I had the feeling that the minute he got back to his office he'd be tracking my tarnished record down like a bloodhound.

'One should never get into arguments with people who later turn up dead,' I said, flashing back to what had happened between me and the late, unlamented Naval Academy company officer, Lt Jennifer Goodall.

'A good rule,' he agreed. 'Especially in this case.'

'Ah . . .' I thought about the arguments I'd recently overheard. Raniero Buccho. Balaclava Man. Was somebody's goose about to be cooked?

EIGHTEEN

'It should be noted that many people at the death of a dear person will bring flowers and wreaths and after proceeding with the funeral will take the flowers and wreaths to the home of the deceased. They buy the best flowers and wreaths to show their deep sympathy and concern. To do this is forbidden – whether presenting it at the funeral, accompanying the funeral with it, or bringing it to the deceased's house. This is an imitation of non-Muslims, and is an evil innovation which should be strictly avoided. Those who do

*such a thing will have no reward from Allah. To the contrary,
they will be questioned for such meaningless waste.'*
Shaykh Abdul-Fattaah Abu Ghuddah (RA), *Haq Islam,*
Sending Flowers and Reading Quran During Funerals, 9.4

The following day I went to read to Nancy and stopped to
check in with Elaine. To my surprise, Heather was sitting
in the unit manager's office. As my shadow darkened her
door she glanced up from the chart she was annotating, grinned
and said, 'Hi, Hannah.'

'Hi, Heather. Is Elaine around?'

Her face flushed. 'Sorry, but she's on administrative leave.'

'Why? I don't mean to be nosy,' I said, thinking *yes I do,*
'but what happened? A family illness or something?'

'It's just until this whole thing with Nancy is settled.'

'What do you mean, "settled"?'

'There's going to be an official hearing. Honestly, I'm really
worried, Hannah. Elaine could lose her license.'

I plopped myself down in the guest chair. 'Oh, no!'

'They're saying she didn't follow proper procedures after
Nancy was . . . well, you know.'

I didn't understand, and I said so. 'But Elaine reported it to
Tyson, didn't she?'

Heather shook her head. 'No, that's the problem. She *didn't.*'

So Tyson hadn't even known what was going on. 'Then who
told the board?'

Heather and I stared silently at one another. The way I
looked at it, there were only six people who knew what Nancy
and Jerry and been up to in her bedroom that day. Nancy and
Jerry themselves, of course, if they could even remember the
incident. Elaine and Heather, me and . . . Safa. Safa had
assured me earlier that she hadn't blown the whistle on Jerry
and Nancy. But she *had* mentioned the incident to Masud. It
was looking more and more likely that Masud Abaza was the
WikiLeaks of Calvert Colony. The colonel certainly suspected
as much.

The only way to find out was to ask Safa.

If I called I might be put off again. I decided to simply pop
in instead, hoping that whatever the rules for *Iddah* were, if I

transgressed, perhaps my ignorance of Islamic law would give me a pass.

Safa had mentioned that her daughter, Laila, worked outside the home, so I planned to arrive around mid-morning when I figured Laila would be at work.

First stop was Whole Foods, where I selected a fruit basket to take to the grieving widow, not knowing whether my first choice, Godiva chocolates, were halal. Before I pulled out of the parking garage I tapped Laila Kazi's address into the GPS and, forty minutes later, pulled up to the curb in front of her home. I sat for a minute, studying the house – a modern, two-story colonial – before picking up my cell phone and giving Laila's number a call, imagining, as it rang, that I could hear the phone ringing inside the house.

To my surprise, a child answered. 'Kazi wesidence.'

I smiled. 'Hello. My name is Hannah. Is your mother home?'

'No.'

'May I speak to your grandmother, then?' I asked, taking a stab at the relationship.

Without taking the phone away from her mouth, the child yelled, 'Grandmother, for you!' then banged the instrument down on some hard surface. After a minute or two, while I stayed on the line rubbing my ear and hoping I hadn't been forgotten, Safa picked up.

'This is Safa Abaza.'

'Safa, it's me, Hannah.'

'Hannah!' She sounded genuinely pleased to hear my voice. 'Thank you for your kind note.'

'I felt . . .' As much as I'd rehearsed coming over in the car, when the moment came I seemed to be at a loss for words. 'I really wanted to see you, Safa, but then I talked to Laila and she explained about your *Iddah* and, well, I wasn't sure what was permitted.'

'I would like to see you, Hannah. We didn't really get to talk . . . afterwards.'

'I know.'

'When are you free?'

'Right now, as a matter of fact. I'm calling you from my car. If you look out your window, you'll see me.'

Safa laughed out loud. A few seconds later I saw the living-room curtains twitch. 'Please, come in, then.'

'I wouldn't be breaking the rules?'

'Don't be silly. I can have visitors, as long as they're women, or men in my immediate family.'

As I climbed out of the car balancing the fruit basket in my arms, I wondered how long after Masud's death that sort of foolishness would continue. The girl had been born in Texas, for crying out loud. Stepping from flagstone to flagstone as I made my way up the walk, I imagined Safa returning to Calvert Colony, meeting the retired CEO of a Fortune 500 company – suitably widowed, of course – casting aside her hijab and running through the Tranquility Garden with her apricot hair streaming like a banner behind her.

The object of my fantasy met me at the open door wearing a white hijab, a shapeless magenta maxi-dress and flip-flops. She engulfed me in a hug – *so good to see you* – then invited me to follow her into the kitchen. A child of around four sat on a tall stool at the butcher block island, drawing circles on a piece of paper with a green crayon. 'This is my granddaughter, Yasmine.'

That the little girl's name was Yasmine I might have guessed. She wore a bright purple T-shirt with her namesake's Disney princess printed on it.

'I brought you some fruit,' I said, proffering the basket.

'That was sweet of you, thanks,' Safa said, taking the basket from my hands and setting it in the exact center of the island. She fingered some of the fruit through the cellophane. 'Oh, I love blood oranges. Can I make you some tea?'

'That would be lovely.'

Safa picked up the electric kettle and filled it with water from the tap. 'Yasmine, why don't you go color in your mother's office so Hannah and I can talk?' She switched on the kettle, removed two cups from the dishwasher and set them down on the counter.

Yasmine crammed the crayon she was using back in the box, hopped off the stool and said, 'Can I play on your iPad, Grandmother?'

Safa smiled indulgently. 'Of course.'

Yasmine snatched the device off the counter where it had been charging and skipped off into the adjoining room.

When the kettle began to scream for attention, I said, 'Have the police made any progress in finding Masud's killer?'

Safa filled the teapot and set it in front of us to steep. 'Sadly, no.'

'I keep asking myself who could have done such a terrible thing.'

'I ask myself the same question, every minute of every day.'

I was tempted to tell Safa about the evidence I had found on the croquet mallet, but I had promised Detective Powers that I'd keep that information to myself. 'Everybody at Calvert Colony is jumpy,' I said instead. 'If it can happen to Masud it can happen to anyone.'

'Not just anyone,' Safa said. 'I think the newspapers were right. It was a hate crime.'

As I sipped my tea I reviewed my list of potential suspects: the colonel, Christie, Richard Kent, Tyler Bennett and Balaclava Man – who may, of course, have been one of the men. After a few moments, I asked, 'Safa, are you sure you didn't report what we saw to the Office of Health Care Quality, between Nancy and Jerry, I mean?'

She studied me over the rim of her teacup, pale eyebrows gracefully arched. 'No, of course not. That's not my job.'

'Then who did, I wonder? It wasn't Elaine or Tyson.'

Safa's gaze was steady, unwavering. In that moment I knew it was Masud – it had to be. And she knew that I knew.

'Masud can, uh, could be compulsive. When I told him about the rape, he marched off to see Tyson Bennett. Demanded that he *do* something, although between you and me, Hannah, I'm not sure what Mr Bennett could have done. You can't chain old people to the beds, after all.'

As I sipped Safa's fine Earl Gray tea, I mused that Masud was *exactly* the kind of person who might chain an infidel to a bed, but the man was dead, so I chided myself for being so judgmental and moved on. 'So what happened between the two of them? Did Masud say?'

Safa set down her mug, stirred in another half teaspoon of sugar, then laid the spoon to one side. 'Masud told the director that perhaps we'd made a wrong decision in moving into the colony, that maybe it wasn't a safe place for a woman to be.'

'Ah.'

'Mr Bennett insisted that Jerry's sex with Nancy had been consensual, and that, he said, was that.' She shrugged. 'Perhaps Masud called the Health Care Quality people after hearing that Mr Bennett didn't plan to report it, or perhaps not. I really don't know. But maybe Masud was right. Maybe Calvert Colony isn't a safe place for a woman like me to be.'

'Does that mean you're not planning to come back?'

'I'm needed here.' She bobbed her head in the direction of the next room where the familiar sounds of Angry Birds – *deedle-deedle-ha-ha-ha-squawk-squawk-squawk* – followed by the computerized sound of broken glass testified to a touchingly familiar, normal twenty-first-century home environment.

'They've been a great comfort to me, my family,' she said.

'I'm crazy about my grandkids, too, Safa, but you have many friends at Calvert Colony. We miss you.'

'After the incident with the graffiti, Masud wanted to move right away.'

'I can understand that, but where did he plan to go?'

'That's just it. The waiting list at Ginger Cove is a mile long and, well, they don't cater to our special needs.' She smiled. 'I put my foot down, Hannah. I told Masud that the only way I was leaving Calvert Colony was feet first. I *love* my town home.'

'Good for you,' I said, admiring her gumption.

'Underneath all this,' she said, indicating her baggy dress and hijab, 'there's an opinionated Southern Baptist from Texas named Linda.'

I laughed out loud.

Safa's face clouded. 'I made every effort to be a good Muslim wife, Hannah, but no matter how hard I tried, Masud wasn't entirely convinced that my conversion was sincere.'

'I saw how he treated you outside the kitchen that day, Safa. Frankly, I was concerned.'

'Masud was a jealous man, but his behavior that day was an aberration, I assure you. Masud never hit me, Hannah.'

I searched her face, seeking the truth. 'I would never make

a good Muslim,' I told her. 'I have too many male friends, and I enjoy their company, even when Paul isn't around.'

'That was the hardest part of conversion for me.'

'Sometimes I don't play by the rules either,' I said, thinking about finding Safa alone in the kitchen with Raniero.

'We have a lot more in common than you might think, Hannah Ives.'

I reached across the butcher block surface and squeezed her hand. 'I know.'

NINETEEN

'There is a curious respect for legal formalities. The signature of the person despoiled is always obtained even if the person in question has to be sent to Dachau in order to break down his resistance.'
John C. Wiley, U.S. General Counsel in Vienna,
March, 1938.

I f I had to write a caption to illustrate the next few days, it would be this: *Woman waits vainly for the telephone to ring.*

Not that I expected Detective Powers to keep me in the loop on the progress of his investigation into the murder of Masud Abaza, but I still hadn't heard back from Hutch about what, if anything, he'd learned about Izzy's valuable painting currently on exhibit at the Baltimore Art Gallery. I was within hours of dropping into my brother-in-law's downtown office in full-blown pester mode when he phoned.

'I have news.'

'Good or bad?'

Hutch snorted. 'A little of both, I should think. When can you and Mrs Milanesi come by?'

Right now, was the correct answer, but I needed to consult with Izzy, so we tentatively settled on eight o'clock the following morning, and I'd call him if that turned out not to be convenient.

Izzy and I arrived right on time the following day; the receptionist escorted us into the conference room where Hutch was waiting. A stack of photocopies sat in front of each of our places, along with a bottle of spring water. A tray of donuts, each neatly sliced in half, sat in the center of the table. Hutch didn't usually provide refreshments. Perhaps he was laying in supplies for a marathon.

'Please sit down, ladies.' He paused, then added, 'Coffee?'

'If it's no trouble,' I said, reaching for a cruller.

Hutch nodded in the direction of the credenza where a Keurig coffee machine sat in splendid isolation, surrounded by a selection of individual K-cups. 'My new toy. Help yourself. The French roast is particularly good, but there's decaf as well.'

'None for me, thanks.' Izzy selected a half moon of cinnamon, and had taken a nibble when Hutch tapped a set of printouts of photos that I knew had come from Naddie's cell phone.

'First of all, Letizia Rossi's scrapbook. Has it been found?'

Izzy shook her head sadly.

'Pity. Well, then, let me say how valuable these photographs have been. I had an expert enlarge and crop them, so we have records of at least fourteen of your family's paintings. Over the past several days I've spent a good deal of time with the director of the Baltimore Art Gallery and her staff, who have, in my opinion, been fully cooperative.

'Naturally,' he continued, 'they claimed to be totally surprised that *Ragazzo con Cane* might have been stolen during the war. They tell me that it, along with a couple of other smaller works, were donated to the gallery in 2011 and 2012 by Benjamin Pfaff, a prominent Baltimore philanthropist.'

Izzy sat up straight in her chair. 'There's more than one?'

'Let's take it a step at a time, Mrs Milanesi. Why don't we refer to the packet in front of you?'

I sat down with my coffee. The documentation had been put together as carefully as a PowerPoint presentation. Hutch walked us through the printout, page by page. Each page was like a thread, drawing us inexorably into the next, gradually stepping back in time. I picked up the document and fanned the pages, eager to skip ahead to see where they led, but Hutch gave me the evil eye, so I decided to go with the flow.

'As I said, Pfaff donated the painting to the Baltimore Art Gallery in 2011, presumably taking a tax write-off in the amount of $250,000, which was the appraised value of the painting at the time.'

Next to me, Izzy gasped.

'On the next page, we have a bill of sale from the Crown Gallery on North Howard Street in Baltimore, detailing the sale of the painting to Mr Pfaff two years prior for $130,000. So far, so good.' He flipped to the next page. 'Here, we find that the work was taken on consignment from the estate of a certain Muzio Buccho, and he . . .'

I felt like the wind had been knocked out of me. 'What?'

Hutch raised a hand, palm out. 'You're getting ahead of me, Hannah. Now, the executor of the estate, if you'll look at the next document, please, is Muzio's daughter, Filomena.'

I turned to the next page as instructed. It was a photocopy of the relevant page of Muzio Buccho's will, and there, printed in clear, unambiguous capital letters was the name Filomena Buccho.

I couldn't believe it. '"Of all the gin joints in all the towns in all the world . . ."' I quoted.

Izzy simply stared, nodding vigorously. She knew that line from *Casablanca*, too.

Hutch tapped the tabletop with the tip of his pen, a nervous habit. 'You know her, Mrs Milanesi?'

'I do. She manages the dining room at Calvert Colony.'

'Unbelievable,' I said.

Hutch shrugged. 'It happens.'

'So Filomena's father, Muzio, brought the paintings with him when he immigrated to Argentina . . .' I asked.

'Not Muzio,' Hutch interrupted. 'A guy named Vittorio Piccio. Does that name sound familiar?'

Izzy frowned. 'Not really.'

'Well, I did a little digging, and this guy Piccio was a notorious art thief, working hand in glove with the Nazis. If you'll look ahead to the next page, you'll see that it was Piccio who was hired to do the official inventory of the contents of an art collection owned by an art dealer in Rome named Giacomo Rossi just a couple of months before the poor fellow was forced to sell out.'

Izzy cried out, 'That was my father!'

'I expected that.' Hutch waited for Izzy to regain her composure, then moved swiftly on. 'Not only that, but Piccio had the unmitigated gall to charge your father a *fee* for doing the inventory. You'll see his itemized receipt. Time, travel, lodging . . . God, just when I think I've seen everything . . . It makes me ill. But the important thing,' he continued, 'is that this inventory actually exists, and we have a copy of it here. There are one hundred and twenty-three paintings and drawings listed, Mrs Milanesi, some of them, like *Ragazzo con Cane*, specifically by name.'

'That *proves* my father owned them.'

'It does. And the scrapbook that your mother made is further confirmation of that ownership – photographic evidence, if you will. I do hope it can be found.'

'But how did that particular painting get into the hands of Filomena Buccho?' I wanted to know.

'I'm coming to that. If you'll flip forward to page ten, you'll notice that we have copies of a customs declaration form dated 1948 when Piccio entered Argentina, and *Ragazzo con Cane* is listed on it then. Piccio paid a small duty of around four percent on the painting based on the clean bill of sale from your father, Giacomo Rossi, dated September 18, 1943.'

Izzy's head was bent over the bill of sale, studying it closely, slowly tracing the loops with an index finger. 'That *looks* like my father's signature but it could be a forgery.'

Hutch nodded. 'Point taken. Moving on, though, after 1948, the works drop out of sight until ten years later, in 1958, when *Ragazzo Con Cane* and a dozen other works previously owned by your father showed up as part of a larger sale that took place in Buenos Aires. That's when Adriano Buccho, Muzio's father and Filomena's grandfather, acquired the works. The rest of the catalog . . .' He shrugged. 'The sale attracted a lot of attention because of the Fattoris and the Signorinis being offered. They were popular Italian Impressionists. Perhaps you know them.'

Izzy frowned. 'So, this accounts for only thirteen of my father's paintings. Where is the rest of his collection?'

'It's possible that the Piccio family still owns them.'

Izzy raised an eyebrow. 'I hear an "or" in your voice, Mr Hutchinson.'

'Or they could have been sold and are now scattered in galleries and private collections all over the world.'

Izzy took a deep breath and let it out slowly. She straightened her back. 'OK, so what's the next step?'

'Well, that's complicated. As you can see from these documents, which the museum freely provided, by the way, your father *legally* sold his paintings to Piccio.'

'Yes, but that doesn't mean anything if the works were extorted from my father in the first place. Father might as well have had a gun aimed at his head!'

'If we can prove that he was coerced we might be able to persuade the gallery to compensate you for the painting.'

'Compensate? I don't want compensation! I want that painting back. It's my brother!' Izzy began to sob.

I grabbed the box of tissues off the credenza and set it gently in her lap. While she dabbed at her eyes, I asked, 'What other paintings does the gallery have that once belonged to Izzy's family?'

'Two smaller ones, much less valuable. But they were also bought by Benjamin Pfaff and donated to the gallery in the following year.'

Benjamin Pfaff. It'd been so long since his name was mentioned in this tortuous chain of custody that I'd practically forgotten about him.

'They're listed on the next to the last page.'

Izzy blew her nose, tucked the used tissue into her pocket then bent over the photocopies. 'I remember this one,' she said, pointing to a reproduction of a girl holding a bowl of cherries. 'It hung in my parent's room. And this little one, this still life . . .' she tapped the page with her finger. 'This was in our drawing room, on the wall over my mother's silver tea service.' She looked up. 'They will be pictured in my mother's scrapbook.'

'Do you think the museum will give them back?' I asked.

'Truthfully? Because of the bill of sale it will be a tough

case to make. But it's not unheard of. There's case law in New York that supports our position. Basically it says that a thief cannot pass good title. If we can prove that Piccio was a thief . . .' His voice trailed off. 'I should warn you, though, Mrs Milanesi, that if we have to take this to court it could be expensive.'

'I don't care about that. I just want my family's paintings back.' She leaned forward toward him, arms stretched in supplication across the table. 'Will you help me?'

'Of course I will.'

I signaled a time out with my hands. 'Wait a minute. Help me get this straight. Adriano Bucco bought thirteen paintings at that sale, right?'

Hutch nodded.

'And they were handed down from Adriano to Muzio and finally to Filomena and her brother.'

'Presumably.'

'The Baltimore Art Gallery has three of the Buccho paintings, so where are the other ten?'

'We'll hope to find that out, too.'

I wanted to hug my brother-in-law but I settled for a profuse thank you, then added: 'As much as I want to go back to Calvert Colony and shake Filomena until the truth drops out, I don't suppose that would be a good idea.'

'No, you'll have to let me handle that,' Hutch drawled. 'Remember that Filomena Buccho may have absolutely no idea that her grandfather had been purchasing art that was stolen from the Jews. As far as she's concerned her family legitimately owned the art. It'd been in her family for three generations. It will have been a part of her life since childhood.'

'Still . . .' I began.

Hutch raised a cautionary hand. 'I tried to contact Filomena this morning, by the way, but she's a little busy just now. The kitchen at Calvert Colony is in turmoil. It seems that her brother has been taken in for questioning over the murder of Masud Abaza.'

TWENTY

'*Rester éveillé. Le plus longtemps possible. Lutter contre le sommeil. Le calcul est simple. En une heure, je fabrique trente faux papiers. Si je dors une heure, trente personnes mourront.*'

Adolfo Kaminsky, 1925.

[Keep awake. As long as possible. Struggle against sleep. The calculation is easy. In one hour, I make thirty false papers. If I sleep one hour, thirty people will die.]

I had promised I would keep the information about the provenance of Izzy's art collection to myself. Ditto my discovery of the bloodied croquet mallet. But, sharing that information with Naddie didn't really count, did it?

'Don't tell anyone,' I cautioned after my long tale was done.

'Don't tell anyone what?' she said.

I loved that in a woman.

We were tucked away at a corner card table in the lobby of Blackwalnut Hall. The cards were spread out for a game of gin rummy but neither of us had played a card. I kept my eye on Nancy, who was looking paler and thinner than ever, as we listened to Charlie Robinson play the piano. It was Gershwin Day, and happily even Nancy was humming along – '*the Rockies may crumble, Gibraltar may tumble*' – and drumming her fingers silently along the arms of her chair as if it were a keyboard.

'What I don't understand,' I commented to my friend as Robinson launched into the next tune, 'is if Filomena and Raniero inherited all these valuable paintings from their father's estate, what are they doing working *here*?'

'It costs a lot of money to start up a restaurant,' Naddie said. 'Two, three hundred thousand dollars would be a drop in a bucket. I can't imagine they got much more than that for the three paintings.'

'Still sounds like a fortune to me.' I smiled dreamily, thinking what I might do with such a windfall if an unknown Monet or Picasso happened to turn up in my attic.

'So, who do *you* think killed Masud?' I asked Naddie, changing the subject. 'If you were writing the novel, I mean.'

Naddie considered my question thoughtfully, tapping her tented fingers against her lips.

'I hate thinking this, but how about Safa?' I prompted. 'He treated her like chattal, so it's possible that she snapped.'

'I think we can eliminate Safa, Hannah. She was in the computer room at the time, teaching a class on how to use Facebook. Six septuagenarians and her electronic signature on the Internet make for a pretty solid alibi.'

I hadn't known that, and felt relieved.

'Tyson Bennett?' I asked, looking at her sideways through my lashes to judge her reaction.

'Tyson?' she sputtered, then laughed. 'Mr Straight-Arrow? No way.'

'Safa tells me that Masud threatened to turn Tyson in to the Office of Health Care Quality for the unit not following proper procedure when we discovered Jerry having sex with Nancy. Maybe Tyson wanted to shut him up.'

'Not likely, especially since it's clear that Masud followed through on his threat. I've spoken to Tyson, and according to him he *did* report the incident to the Health Care Quality officials. Another staff member in the unit told him. After that . . .' She shrugged. 'There's no reason for Tyson to go after Masud.'

'Except in anger,' I said. 'Like Elaine Broering. She's out of a job because of Masud.'

'We don't know that yet. Isn't Elaine simply on leave? Besides, I can't think of anyone less likely to commit a murder than Elaine. She's one of the most gentle, caring people I know. You have to be to work in the memory unit.'

I thought back to my first substantial conversation with Elaine and had to agree. 'Nancy bit her, did you know that? Elaine simply shrugged it off in an "it-goes-with-the-territory" sort of way. I like her a lot, so I find it hard to picture her as a killer.' I paused. 'But then, a lot of women fell for Ted Bundy.'

'How about Richard Kent?' Naddie suggested. 'Or Mr Easy Rider?'

I shrugged. 'Possible, I suppose, but I think they just hated Muslims in general, not Masud specifically. Richard is a sure bet for the graffiti, but murder?'

We sat quietly for a moment, enjoying the sing-a-long. 'I Got Plenty of Nothing' seemed especially appropriate after what Naddie and I had just been discussing.

After the song was over, I said, 'I'm fond of Raniero, too, of course, and I'd like to think it isn't simply my lust for his spaghetti *putanesca* that keeps me from pointing an accusatory finger.'

'I wonder what the police have on Raniero?' Naddie said. 'You mentioned the arguments he had with Masud. Do you think it might have been a fight over Safa gone bad?'

'I don't. I witnessed a lot of yelling, and a few punches were thrown, but nothing ever got too physical.' I gazed out the window for a moment, collecting my thoughts. 'If Safa and Raniero *were* having an affair, though, it's conceivable that Raniero lost it when he saw how badly Masud was treating her.' I picked up one of the playing cards, turning it over and over between my fingers. 'Besides, how likely is it that Raniero would come across Masud in the Tranquility Garden? The more I think about it, the more I'm starting to believe that Masud was *lured* there.' I ticked the items off on my fingers. 'One, it's secluded, especially at mealtimes when almost everyone is in the dining room. Two, by choosing to use the croquet mallet it was obviously premeditated since the croquet sets are stored in a shed some distance away and would have to be carried into the garden. And three . . .' I flapped my hand. 'I don't have a three.'

'I do,' Naddie said. 'If it happened at lunchtime, as the rumor mill has led us to believe, wouldn't Raniero's absence in the kitchen have been noticed?'

'Yes!' I said, doing an arm pump. 'Naddie, you are brilliant!'

'Hardly.' She inclined her head toward my ear. 'And here comes someone else whose absence during mealtime would certainly not have gone unremarked.'

I followed her gaze. Filomena was chugging our way like a

determined steam engine. 'Do you mind if I interrupt your card game for a moment, ladies?'

'Of course not.' Naddie waved at the empty chair. 'Please.'

'I need your help, Mrs Gray,' Filomena said, pulling out the chair and sitting down in it.

'Me? And how can *I* help you, my dear?'

Filomena folded her hands on the table in front of her and leaned toward Naddie. 'You write the detective stories, right? You know about the police and things.'

Naddie cocked her head. 'A little, dear, but remember, what I wrote is fiction not fact. Sometimes I simply made it up. It's one of the reasons I gave up writing police procedurals, to tell the truth. Too much forensics in crime novels these days. I'm much more interested in the characters, in their relationships. I let the cops do what they do somewhere off the page.'

Filomena waved Naddie's objections away. 'I am worried. I think they are going to put my brother in jail.'

'According to what I've heard, they've simply taken Raniero in for questioning, Filomena. That doesn't mean he's going to be arrested. If he has nothing to hide . . .'

The deer-in-the-headlights look on Filomena's face said it all.

Naddie and I exchanged worried glances. Naddie leaned forward and cocked her head. 'Are you telling us that Raniero *does* have something he doesn't want people to find out about?'

Filomena lowered her gaze, confirming my suspicions. 'Mr Abaza, somehow he found out what Raniero was doing.'

'What was Raniero doing?' I asked, bracing myself for an avalanche of sordid details about a love affair with Safa.

'I know nothing about it, of course. It is the chef's job to plan the menus and order the supplies. I just pay the bills.'

Filomena needed prodding. 'Tell us. What was Raniero doing?' I repeated.

She took a deep breath then puffed it out. 'Raniero, he is taking what you call backkicks.'

'Kickbacks,' I corrected.

'Yes, kickbacks. He is giving me invoices for meats that are kosher and that are halal when they are not. They are cheaper. And Raniero and the meat man, they are splitting the difference and putting the money in their pockets.'

That was a shocker. 'How much money are we talking about, Filomena?'

She studied the chandelier, as if the answer were written on one of the cut-glass crystal pendants. 'Since Calvert Colony opened? Many thousands, maybe. Special meat is very expensive.'

Although Masud was quite the busybody, it seemed unlikely to me that he'd be involved behind the scenes in the kitchen. While Safa . . . I flashed back again to the day I'd run into Safa scooting out the kitchen door. She'd *said* she'd been discussing the menu, and specifically mentioned a meat delivery. Could she have been aware of Raniero's scam with the meat and told her husband, rather than been indulging in an affair?

'But, wouldn't *you* be the most likely person to stumble over what Raniero was doing, Filomena? How on earth did Mr Abaza get involved?'

She straighted her spine and rotated her shoulders. 'Ah, Mr Abaza, he parks his golf cart over by the kitchen, where there is good shade so the seat is not so hot when you sit on it, you know? One day, Raniero tells me, he is late. Mr Abaza is climbing into his golf cart when the delivery truck comes, so he starts talking to the meat man.' She tucked a wayward strand of golden hair behind her ear. 'I don't know exactly how, but Raniero tells me afterwards that he's in trouble and we can't afford to lose this job.'

'We?'

'If Raniero goes, I go. How do you Americans say? That's how we roll.'

I wondered why Filomena was telling us this. You'd think she'd want to protect her brother, not point one of her well-manicured fingers at him. 'So, are you saying that your brother murdered Mr Abaza to shut him up about the kickbacks to the meat man?'

'I do not know, Mrs Gray. I only know about the meat.'

'Do the police know . . . about the meat, I mean?' I asked.

Filomena screwed her pretty face into a frown. 'Raniero, I think he is confessing. That is why I am telling you.'

'You don't know that, Filomena,' Naddie said gently.

Her face suddenly went pale.

'Why did he do it?' I asked. 'Cheat Calvert Colony on the meat, I mean?'

Filomena looked distinctly unwell, but shrugged. 'We need the money for the restaurant, maybe?'

I frowned. Skimming money off the top of the meat bill seemed like small potatoes to me, but over time perhaps it added up. Or perhaps the funny business with the meat was just the tip of the iceberg. Perhaps Raniero had found other unorthodox ways to 'economize.' As if selling works of art that had been in their family for three generations wasn't enough.

Filomena stopped chewing her lower lip. 'What do I say when the police ask me about Raniero, Mrs Gray?'

Naddie reached out and patted the worried woman's hand. 'You tell them the truth, my dear.'

TWENTY-ONE

'[They] never cared to report, nor to return: they longed to stay forever, browsing on that native bloom, forgetful of their homeland.'

Homer, *The Odyssey,* Book IX, Lines 99–104.

'What do you think about that?' Naddie asked me after Filomena had gone.

Charlie Robinson segued from 'I Got Rhythm' to 'Nice Work if You Can Get It' while I mulled over the conversation.

'Something's off. Masud must have been upset to learn that the meat he'd been eating was *haram* rather than *halal*. I can easily imagine him flying into a blind rage and killing Raniero over that, but not the other way around.'

'But Filomena thinks Raniero may have killed Masud to keep him from spilling the beans about the kickbacks,' Naddie reminded me.

I shook my head. 'We know the guy is a tattletale. After talking to the meat man Masud would have made a beeline for

Tyson Bennett's office and Raniero would have been out on his ear.'

'But he didn't see Tyson,' Naddie said. 'Raniero was still working up to the point of being taken in for questioning.'

'And why didn't he?' I asked, trying to follow Naddie's train of thought.

'Because he wanted to use the information as leverage. There was something he wanted from Raniero.'

'Stop messing with my wife, or else?'

'Maybe.'

'Yes!' I was practically leaping out of my chair. And then I sobered up. 'But was that the something?'

'Hannah, my dear, I don't have the slightest idea.'

I pondered what Naddie had said until I thought my brain would explode. I was only half listening to 'Someone to Watch Over Me' when Naddie shook my arm gently. 'Look.' She jerked her head sideways.

Standing at the reception desk, dressed casually in khaki slacks and a bold Hawaiian shirt, was Richard Kent.

I had Angie on speed dial.

'Hi, Hannah, what's up?' she said without preamble.

'Dickie's back.'

'Shit.'

'I thought he was on some secret mission for the CIA,' I said as I watched Richard sign in on the tablet.

Angie snorted. 'As if. He now works for a contractor at the amputee clinic in Bethesda.'

'I presume he's here to see your mother-in-law, but she hasn't shown up yet, Angie. When she does, what do you want me to do?'

'Remember what you said the last time about following them?'

'In a rash moment, yes.'

'Would you? Please? I don't trust him one tiny bit.'

'I don't know, Angie,' I said. 'Everybody knows he's taking her out. He signed in, for heaven's sake.'

Suddenly Christie popped through a door into the lobby, all Talbot petites, Ann Klein, a Coach bag and smiles. She took

Richard's arm. As they walked out the front door, Richard eased a ball cap out of his back pocket and put it on.

I caught my breath: a gray baseball cap with a blue star. Damn. Richard was a Dallas Cowboys fan. Hadn't Masud told me . . .?

'No problem, Angie. I'm on it.'

I pocketed my phone and shot Naddie a look of desperation. She waved me off. 'Write when you get work!'

The sacrifices I make for my friends.

Richard was driving a generic white Dodge Avenger – probably a rental – so at least Christie wasn't behind the wheel. From the partial cover of a hedge, I observed him opening the passenger-side door then waiting until she slipped in and fastened her seatbelt before closing the door with a solid *thud* behind her.

I hustled over to my car and followed the Dodge out of the parking lot and down Bay Ridge Avenue. I nearly lost it at the light at Hillsmere Drive, but caught up with the rental car again a few lights later.

When they got to the intersection of West Street and Forest Drive I knew they were headed for the Annapolis Mall.

Restaurant or food court? I wondered as I dogged their tail around the perimeter road of the enormous shopping center. Christie's hands were actively waving, giving directions. Eventually Richard pulled into the parking lot at the Nordstrom end of the mall. Dickey-boy was going to splash out, it seemed. Stony River? California Pizza Kitchen? I parked a few spaces over and waited until the couple was safely inside the Cheesecake Factory. A thought struck me . . . I strolled casually over to Richard's rental car and tried the trunk.

To my astonishment, Richard had neglected to lock the car. The trunk popped open revealing a carry-on suitcase, two paperback books, a black jacket and, underneath the jacket, a balaclava.

Gotcha, Balaclava Man!

It was a gorgeous day so I sat down outside the Cheesecake Factory at a table for two, snagged a passing server and ordered iced tea and a sandwich. While I waited for my drink I called Detective Powers and left a message about Richard and the balaclava, then swapped texts with Angie.

At mall. CCFactory.

OMFG.

Srsly.

Pix?

I figured there wasn't any way I could take a picture of the happy pair without calling unwanted attention to myself, but I thought I could give it a try, so I texted back *IAM* and headed into the restaurant. If I were going to drink that tall glass of iced tea I desperately needed to find a restroom, anyway.

As I came out of the ladies' room I spotted them, sitting in a booth across from one another, sharing a platter of Thai chicken lettuce wraps and toasting each other with cosmopolitans served in oversized martini glasses. Christie was gazing at Richard with the same look of adoration that the three kings had bestowed upon the Christ child. World War Three could have broken out around her and she wouldn't have noticed. I hauled out my iPhone, aimed and took the shot.

Back at my table I sent the picture to Angie with no comment, dawdled over my chicken parmesan sandwich, ordered a refill on the tea then finally paid the bill and moved back to my car. Fifteen minutes later the couple emerged, arm in arm, laughing. Once again I followed the car around the perimeter road and into the parking lot of the Wells Fargo bank on Jennifer Road, next to Fuddruckers.

While Richard kept the engine running, Christie climbed out of the car, toodled over to the ATM and slotted in her card.

The next stop was the liquor store in the Festival mall at Riva. From a parking spot in front of Petco, I watched Richard enter the store alone, then emerge carrying something wrapped in a brown paper bag. After a discussion inside the car, Christie strolled over to the ATM next to the grocery store and made another withdrawal.

As they proceeded eastward on Forest Drive, stopping at two more ATMs along the way, Richard drove with the exaggerated caution of the professional drinker, sticking to the far right lane, never exceeding twenty-five miles an hour. I loafed along on their tail, wondering who was going to give out first – Christie's money or me.

TWENTY-TWO

'One time I dated this guy named John. He lived in a classy condo in Washington, DC. Early on, he showed me his family tree. I thought this was odd, but so what, he was a fun guy. A few months into the relationship, he said, "I cannot date you anymore. Your name does not fit into the family tree." WTF? Since when is "Sue" considered strange? The accepted names included Agnes, Agatha, Bertha, Beulah, and Hortense. Oh, and my family had to have come to Virginia prior to 1750. I don't recall being upset when John dumped me, just relieved. I wonder if he's still single considering all of his family rules?'

'Sue,' Anonymous Facebook posting.

It must have been the shortest love affair in history, with the possible exception of Britney Spears and Jason Alexander whose 'til-death-us-do-part lasted all of fifty-five hours.

I'd followed the couple back to Calvert Colony. Richard let Christie out at the front entrance, then went to park his car.

By the time I'd parked and returned to Blackwalnut Hall Christie was standing on the balcony of the old hotel, Juliet to a Romeo who was staggering one painful step at a time up the staircase behind her. 'But, Christie, I *love* you!'

'No, you don't! You're only interested in money.'

What a surprise.

Richard grasped the railing, his head bowed as if it were too heavy for him. 'That's not true,' he whined into his chest. 'I love, love, love you.'

He dragged himself painfully up another step. 'We're going to get married! What's mine is yours, baby.'

'A lousy disability check from the VA?' Christie screamed from her vantage point at the top of the stairs. She disappeared, but I could still hear her. 'I don't think so!'

Halfway up the staircase Richard stumbled and fell to his

knees. His head lolled. Suddenly, he threw his head back and yelled, 'Christie!'

'Don't you Christie me, buster. Go away and leave me alone.'

With a burst of energy only a professional drunk could muster, Richard lurched up the stairs. When he reached the top, he leaned against the railing, swaying dangerously, gathering strength for whatever was next on his alcohol-fueled agenda.

The man was a danger to himself and others, I thought. I waved, caught the attention of the receptionist and pantomimed dialing the phone. She gave me a thumbs up. It had already been done.

I had started up the stairs to see if I could help when Christie breezed past coming down, nearly knocking me over. 'Sorry.' She flushed. 'I think we need to call security.'

'The receptionist just did.'

Upstairs, Richard leaned over the balcony rail, calling down. 'Christie, come back. I love you!'

'This is so embarrassing,' Christie said. 'I can't *believe* I've been so stupid. Everyone must be talking about me behind my back.'

'No, they aren't,' I reassured her, although everyone was, of course.

As we stood together, watching and waiting for security to show up, Richard eased one leg over the railing. 'If you don't come back to me, I'm going to jump! I swear I will.'

I stepped forward, but Christie grabbed my arm and pulled me back. 'He's so full of shit! You can't believe a word he says.'

'But what if he does?' I hissed.

Richard was straddling the rail now. 'I mean it!'

Christie pulled herself up to her full five-foot-seven and screamed, 'Go ahead and jump, then. See if I care!'

'No, don't!' I shouted back.

A khaki uniform swam into my peripheral view. The cavalry had arrived. 'Sir, what seems to be the problem here?' the security guard boomed, and started to climb the stairs.

Richard's voice was calm, conversational. 'I'm going to jump.'

'I can see that, sir, but how will that solve anything?'

Richard didn't answer, but remained where he was, teetering drunkenly on the railing.

'He's bluffing,' Christie said.

'Shut up, Christie!' I struck the stupid woman sharply on the back.

'I'm going to jump and it'll be your fault.' Richard slumped, suddenly drained of bravado. 'You think I'm worthless? That's how much you know, you heartless bitch. Four hundred and fifty thousand dollars, that's what. That's what you're giving up by not marrying me.'

'What's he talking about, Hannah?' Christie demanded.

'I'm not sure, but if he's still active duty, it could be the military death benefit, or a life insurance policy.'

'Going, going . . .' Richard began.

Possibly sensing that this boozehound was deadly serious, the guard sprinted up the staircase but before he could get anywhere near him Richard yelled, 'Gone!' and launched himself into space, his arms spread like a bird. He hit the rim of the aquarium with a hideous *clonk* and tumbled, head first – *sploosh* – into the fish tank.

The only creature that didn't seem surprised was Scooter, the cownose ray. Richard sank slowly to the bottom where his body draped itself lifelessly over the coral head. Scooter dived, nudged him curiously, shimmied over this strange new creature, then moved on.

There were several seconds of silence, and then the shouting began.

'Somebody get him out of there!'

'He could still be alive!'

'Get a ladder!'

'Back, back everyone!'

The security guard streaked past me, shouting, 'I'm on it!'

And somebody pulled the fire alarm.

As the alarm *whoop-whoop-whooped* deafenly around us, Christie buried her head in my shoulder and sobbed, 'I didn't . . . he wouldn't . . . how could?'

I held her close, rubbing her back while the receptionist and one of the security guards ushered the residents who had been sitting in the lobby into the dining room.

I stayed put, conforting Christie.

Ten minutes later the paramedics arrived to discover the

security guard standing on a ladder usually used for changing light bulbs, straining to reach Richard's body with a life hook hastily borrowed from the swimming pool. His skin glistened with sweat; his uniform shirt was soaked with saltwater.

'Come down off the ladder, man. Nothing you can do for the guy now.'

That I even heard the paramedic's remark was a miracle of selective hearing as Christie had crumpled to the floor and was keening like a professional mourner at a Chinese funeral.

Angie burst in about then. After a hasty consultation she dragged her mother-in-law away to the health center where (I learned later) she'd been given an injection to help her sleep and put to bed.

The job of retrieving Richard's body was beyond the expertise of the paramedics, who called for the Underwater Recovery Team that the state of Maryland kept handy. When the URT barged into the lobby about ten minutes later, the guy in the lead screeched to a halt and sputtered, 'How did he . . .' turning what was almost certainly a snigger into a cough. 'Jesus, Mary and Joseph,' exclaimed his partner, and made the sign of the cross.

'Gives new meaning to swimming with the fishes.' It was the colonel, coming up behind me. 'She-it. Go out to the movies for the first time in ages and miss all the excitement.' He elbowed my arm to get my attention, then winked. 'First date.'

Thinking this was hardly the time to discuss the colonel's love life, I ignored him.

The divers got to work. They set up a portable air compressor and donned their masks while the colonel observed, offering a running commentary worthy of an announcer on the Discovery Channel. I tuned him out.

One diver slipped into the tank, sleek as a shark. He eased Richard's body into a sling that fit under his arms and guided the operation by holding on to Richard's legs while his partner hauled on the rope attached to the sling.

'Not from around here, then?' said the colonel when the body was laid out on the marble floor. He stood on tiptoes in his black leather boots, craning his neck for a closer look.

'No, he's not. He came to visit Christie McSpadden. Sort of

a pen pal,' I added, not wanting to embarrass Christie any further. 'He was in the army serving in Afghanistan.'

'A jumper?'

I knew he didn't mean parachuter. 'Apparently.'

'She-it.'

'PTSD would be my guess,' I said.

The colonel's back stiffened. 'Bullshit. Bunch of slackers. In my day . . .'

I thought I would have to wait to find out how it was back in his day, but after a brief pause, presumably to collect his thoughts, the colonel launched into a rant. 'I know people who can get you one hundred percent disability benefits, easy as that.' He snapped his fingers. 'Tell 'em where to go and what to say when they get there. It's a scam. You got a half million vets out there right now claiming PTSD. Makes me sick. There are vets with *real* issues, you know. Paraplegics, amputees, traumatic brain injury. Jeesh. And here you go,' he indicated the body bag that contained what was left of Richard, now lying on a gurney. 'This guy never looked like boots on the ground to me. Probably one of those sissies stationed at a home base somewhere, shot themselves in the foot at the motor pool. Or they're all hands over their heads in the mess hall shouting, 'Incoming, incoming!' Bull*shit*! I held my best buddy in my arms, saw his eyes roll back, the life leak out of him.' He paused to take a deep breath, then shook himself almost like a dog and said, 'Sorry, I don't usually go on like that. Must be off my meds.'

I turned, reached out and hugged the man. I couldn't help it. My father had served with distinction in Vietnam and he knew, first hand, what real war was all about. Maybe if I hugged this guy it would help him stow his demons back in the box. Beneath my arms, I felt him tremble.

'Colonel,' I said after a bit.

'Yeah?'

'You can let go of me now.'

He sprang away like a teenager who'd been caught in a clinch. 'Sorry.'

I managed a smile. 'No need. It's quite all right. I'm a military brat, so I know where you're coming from.'

He poked my shoulder with his index finger and channeled

his best John Wayne. 'I knew there was something about you that I liked, Little Lady.'

The Easy Rider had returned.

'But you're wrong about Richard Kent,' I told him gently. 'He was a medic in Afghanistan. Watched *his* friend die.'

'Sorry,' he said, his face clouding over as his head bent low. 'I didn't know.'

'Not many people did,' I said.

I caught up with Angie in her mother-in-law's apartment, where Christie was sleeping soundly. Angie closed the door between the living room and the bedroom and invited me to sit down.

'So, what happened to the lovebirds?' I asked. 'Did she tell you?'

'By the third ATM, she figured it out. The money was supposedly so they could elope to Las Vegas.'

'At the Graceland Wedding Chapel, I presume, married by an Elvis impersonator to her hunka-hunka burning love.'

Angie laughed. 'Something like that.'

I melted back into the upholstery, suddenly exhausted. 'That's certainly what I'll want for *my* second wedding.'

'When she turned him down, Richard explained that he was the beneficiary of a trust fund from his grandfather but the money only came to him when he married.'

'So he picked your mother-in-law.' I sat up straight in the chair. 'Not to cast aspersions on Christie, my dear, but he had flowers, candy and charm going for him. And I'll give him at least a seven in the looks department. Couldn't he find somebody a *teeny* bit younger?'

Angie's look said *get real.* 'I think the younger girls were smart enough to figure out that Richard didn't exactly play for their team, if you know what I mean. He probably flunked the tryouts.'

'Ah, I missed that, Angie. My gay-dar must be on the fritz.'

'I missed it, too, but Christie didn't. Richard must have figured he wouldn't have to sleep with someone as old as my mother-in-law, so when she came on to him he turned her down.' Even in the dim light, I could see her roll her eyes. 'Poor Christie.

She wanted a *real* relationship, with sex in it and everything. Go figure.'

'Don't we all?'

'And I don't think she believed him about the trust fund, although I certainly do. Why else would he want to marry my mother-in-law?'

'Do you think he was really a medic, fighting with the army in Afghanistan, Angie?'

'That part, at least, is true. Christie said it screwed him up, big time.'

I thought about the ball cap. 'How long had Richard been hanging around, before he showed up here, I mean?'

Angie shut her eyes, considering my question. 'He arrived about two weeks ago, I think. Christie said she met him for the first time at Grump's for a hamburger.' She grunted. 'At least she was smart enough to pick a public place.'

'So, that was *before* Masud was killed.'

Angie's face paled. 'Ohmygawd! Richard just hates, uh, hated Muslims. He called Mohammad a seventh-century Charlie Manson.'

'What a smooth talker,' I said.

A guy with PTSD and a hatred of Muslims. A guy who had almost certainly spray painted anti-Muslim slogans on the wall of the *musalla*, if the balaclava in the trunk of his car was anything to go by. A guy who had tussled with Masud. I asked the obvious question: 'Do you think Richard might have murdered Masud Abaza, Angie?'

Her gaze didn't waver. 'Words of wisdom from Richard Kent: "Give a Muslim a rock and they'll throw it at an embassy."'

TWENTY-THREE

'Research. . . is expensive. For objects with no prior indication of Nazi looting, the costs range anywhere from $40 to $60 per hour, and the time needed to document just one object can vary enormously, from a week to a year, and if initial

*research suggests an object has a history that may include
unlawful appropriation by the Nazis, time and expense can
double or triple. One museum spent $20,000 plus travel
and expenses over the course of 2 years to have a researcher
resolve the history of just three paintings.'*
Edward H. Able, Jr, Review of the Repatriation of Holocaust
Art Assets in the United States, Hearing Before the
Subcommittee on Domestic and International Monetary
Policy, Trade, and Technology of the Committee on Financial
Services, U.S. House of Representatives, July 27, 2006.

'I've thought of something, Hannah.'

I shifted the cell phone to my left ear and stared at the numerals on the bedside clock: 23:45. I'd been asleep for only an hour.

'What is it, Izzy?' Little men with hammers were pounding nails into my head.

'I was going over the packet of materials your brother-in-law prepared for me, and I saw something that I hadn't noticed before.'

'Ummm.' I staggered out of bed, flipped on the bathroom light and rummaged through the medicine cabinet, looking for aspirin.

'It's the original bill of sale, the one the Nazis made my father sign.'

'Uh huh,' I mumbled, attempting to twist the cap off the aspirin jar without dropping the phone in the toilet.

'It's a forgery.'

I dropped the bottle, spilling the aspirin into the sink. *Damn.* I was wide awake now.

I sat down on the toilet seat, cradling my aching head in my hands. 'A forgery? Are you sure? At the meeting with Hutch you said it looked like your father's signature.'

'That's not important. What's important is that my father didn't sign it, he *couldn't* have signed it. The bill of sale is dated September 18, 1943. I don't know what made me do it, but I checked the universal calendar, Hannah. September 18 is a Saturday. *Shabbat.* Not even for the Nazis would my father work on *Shabbat.*'

'That's great, Izzy,' I said, trying to infuse my voice with an enthusiasm that was being sapped by the little men in my head, who were now hurling miniature thunderbolts at one another. I scooped two aspirin out of the sink and chewed them up whole. 'It's really great. I'll let Hutch know. It might make a difference.'

'You'll call him? You'll call him now?'

'Just as soon as I hang up the phone.'

After Izzy thanked me profusely and wished me a goodnight I staggered down to the kitchen, filled the teakettle with water and switched it on. While I waited for the water to boil, I texted my brother-in-law.

9/18/43 = Sabbath. BS forged?

By morning my headache had thankfully vanished. When I checked my phone there was an I heart U text from Paul and Hutch had texted me back – K. Thx – but I didn't hear another peep from my brother-in-law for three more days.

When the call finally came, it was early morning and I was in the shower. I put the phone on speaker. 'Hutch, glad you called. Do you have any news?'

'I do,' he said, sounding as pleased as if he'd just been invited to the White House for dinner. 'Can you find Izzy and bring her to my office at, say, ten this morning?'

I grabbed a towel and started rubbing briskly at my hair. 'I don't see why not. Can you give me a head's up?'

'It's very good news, Hannah. The Baltimore Art Gallery might well have come to this decision on their own, but the information you gave me about the date on the bill of sale was probably the clincher. Izzy is getting her paintings back.'

I leaned against the cool tile wall, slid down it until I was sitting on the bathmat. 'All three?'

'All three.'

'I don't believe it.'

'Believe it. The fax came through this morning. I'm holding the letter right here in my hot little hand.'

'Izzy and her family are going to be over the moon.'

'It won't be immediate, you understand. There'll be papers to sign, and . . .' He paused. 'Look, you'd better prepare Izzy for a press conference. This is big news and there's going to be a lot of hoopla. The gallery's publicity machine is going to swing into action. Izzy's face is going to be all over the media.'

'Shall I tell her to buy a new dress then?'

'Absolutely.'

'How about the other paintings? There were thirteen in the Piccio sale, as I recall.'

'They could be anywhere by now, Hannah, and tough to track down. The best thing to do is register them as stolen. There's the Art Loss Register in London, plus databases at Interpol, Scotland Yard and the FBI. The next time someone tries to sell one it should crop up in the database. But don't worry, I'm going to take care of that for her.' He paused, and I could almost hear him smile. 'No charge.'

'How about the paintings pictured in her mother's scrapbook, Hutch, the one hundred and ten paintings that weren't part of the Piccio sale?'

'Let's hope the scrapbook turns up. Right now, the only evidence we have of the Rossi family's ownership of all hundred and twenty-three works is on that inventory Piccio made back in 1943, and some of it's rather vague. "Still Life with Oranges" or "Study #3" doesn't tell us very much, even if we know who the artist was. And another thing,' he said. 'A few of the works in the Rossi collection had never been cataloged. They were painted when the artist was a relative unknown, so nobody knew the works even existed, let alone what they looked like.'

'Hutch, do Raniero and Filomena Buccho know about this?'

'Unavoidable. The researchers contacted them both, first individually and then together. Just so you know, there's going to be no blame attached to the Buccho family. It's impossible to say what Adriano Buccho knew when he bought those paintings back in fifty-eight, of course, but we're convinced that Raniero and his sister had no idea that the paintings were stolen. It's just their rotten luck that both Ysabelle and the paintings ended up in the same museum at the same time.'

'I'm relieved to hear it. The last thing Raniero needs right now is another charge hanging over his head.'

'Has he been arrested for Masud Abaza's murder, then?'

'Not yet. He's back at work, but his sister expects him to be carted away in handcuffs at any minute.'

'Too bad.' After a beat, my brother-in-law added more jauntily than the turn in our conversation warranted, 'And if he needs an attorney, you have my number. I'll have a referral for him.'

Because we were celebrating Izzy and I ordered wine with our crab cakes in the dining room that day. Filomena hadn't been on duty when we came in, but she showed up at our table, chilled Sauvignon blanc and corkscrew in hand. 'Susanna said you asked for wine. How nice! It is a special occasion?'

Uh oh, I thought, this might be awkward, but Izzy dove right in.

'It is,' Izzy said. 'As you may have heard from the Baltimore Art Gallery, I'm getting my paintings back.'

'Oh! I am so very glad.' Filomena set the wine bottle down on the table and started to remove the seal. 'You must believe me when I tell you, my brother and I, we had *no* idea. No idea at all.'

'Did your grandfather buy any of my father's other paintings, Filomena, maybe at another sale?' Izzy's voice cracked. '*Abba* had so many.'

Filomena jammed the point of the corkscrew into the cork and began twisting. 'I know what the lawyer said, Mrs Milanesi. But when my father died there were only those three. The boy with the dog, the still life with the water jug and lemons, and that nice one of the girl holding a bowl of cherries.' She extracted the cork. 'That was my favorite.'

'Only three?' Izzy asked.

Filomena scowled. 'You don't believe me?'

Izzy cheeks flushed and she apologized. 'Sorry, I didn't mean for it to come out that way.'

'There were only the three. I swear to you that. If my father had owned more than three, I would have sold them all, and Raniero and I would have no trouble paying for the restaurant. You see?'

I did see. Hutch had told us there had been a lot of interest in the Piccio sale. Clearly, another buyer or buyers had purchased the rest of Giacomo Rossi's paintings from Vittorio Piccio. If

Izzy had the scrapbook, Hutch could supplement the data he was entering about the paintings in the international databases by including indentifying photographs. But even with the inventory, the scrapbook and the databases she'd have to wait for the paintings to surface again, which might be years, or even never.

Filomena screwed the bottle into a pewter bucket filled with ice. 'You call me if you need anything else, OK?' She turned to leave, thought better of it, and turned back. 'I am so happy for you, Mrs Milanesi. It is not right what the Nazis did to your father.'

Izzy went home to take a nap while I trotted over to Spa Paradiso for a good long soak before it was time for me to show up in the memory unit. I'd promised Nancy I'd look at her drawings, not that she'd remember, but a promise was a promise. I eased into the hot tub until the water was up to my chin; the bubbles danced, exploding all around me, tickling my nose.

Now that the question of Izzy's paintings had been settled, my mind wandered back to whoever had murdered Masud Abaza. Had the murderer died in the Blackwalnut Hall fish tank? Or was his killer still at large? What was Safa's role in all this? Did she say something to Masud that inadvertently set into motion a chain of events leading to his murder?

Nor was Masud's slate squeaky clean. Why hadn't he reported Raniero's jiggery-pokery with the meat supplier?

I closed my eyes, relaxed my limbs and focused on my mantra – *kerim, kerim, kerim.*

The jets had shut off automatically and the water had grown as tepid as my brain so I climbed out of the hot tub, dried off and headed to the locker room to get dressed.

When I arrived at the memory unit Nancy was busy, sitting happily with Eric in the lounge watching television. On the screen Richie Cunningham was making out with Fonzie's girlfriend. This wasn't going to end well, I thought with a grin. I hadn't seen *Happy Days* since I was in college, so I sat down for a minute to reminisce and – guilty – liberate some Hershey's Kisses from the candy bowl.

At the break, WBAL reported about the lack of progress in

the Abaza murder. While I watched, sucking on a chocolate, a picture of Masud filled the screen.

'Look, at that,' Nancy said, waving a finger badly in need of a manicure. 'That's the man from the garden.' She smiled and patted Eric's knee. 'He looks like Frank.'

Except for their abundant salt-and-pepper hair, I didn't think Masud looked the least bit like Jerry. But . . . hadn't Nancy mentioned seeing a man in the garden before? And Lillian had heard noises over by the trees . . . What if it wasn't her 'babies' she heard 'squabbling?' I had to draw Nancy away from the television while she appeared to be alert and relatively lucid.

I would tell Paul later that the Devil made me do it.

The television, I knew, was controlled by a remote kept out of residents' reach in the nurse's office. With Nurse Heather as a willing co-conspirator we switched off the TV.

'Oh, no!' Heather cried. 'The cable seems to have gone out.'

Eric rose stiffly to his feet. 'Fuck that,' he said.

'Nancy,' I said, materializing at her elbow. 'Weren't you going to show me your drawings?'

Back in Nancy's room I easily found the portfolio Mindy had mentioned resting on the bookshelf next to a basket of postcards that Nancy – or one of her family members – had been saving.

Mindy had been right. The pencil drawings were perfection. I recognized Nancy's dog, Rosco, the Buddah in the garden and a magnificent tulip poplar. For the poplar, she'd used the sides of the paper to draw closeups of its four-lobed, heart-shaped leaves and its distinctive tulip-shaped blossoms. There were seven drawings of the tree in all, but one in particular captured my attention. Standing under the umbrella of its branches, pressed up against its slightly furrowed bark, a couple stood, locked in an embrace. The woman's back was to the artist, while the man's head was bowed. His hair had been meticulously rendered – Nancy'd drawn every strand – and it certainly could be Masud, but in spite of the detail, the couple was too far away to identify.

Holding the drawing I wandered over to the window and pulled the drapes aside. In a corner formed by the hedge of the Tranquility Garden where it met the wall of the secret garden the dementia patients used stood a lush tulip poplar, a twin to the one in the drawing in my hand. A perfect spot for a rendezvous, I thought, tucked out of sight of anyone except the patients here in the memory unit. If they noticed any hanky-panky, who were they going to tell? And who would believe them?

I leaned forward, propped my elbows up on the sill, laced my fingers and rested my chin on top of them. 'The garden's really beautiful at this time of year, don't you think so?'

'I love gardens,' Nancy said. 'But Frank does the weeding because my knees are so bad.'

'I don't see Frank in the garden today. I wonder where he is?'

Nancy tapped the glass. 'He likes it there.'

'Where?' I asked her. 'By the cherry tree?'

'No, the *liriodendron tulipifera*.'

'Ah, the tulip poplar. Does he stand there often, Frank, I mean?'

'It is what it is,' she said cryptically. Suddenly she turned to me, her eyes wide and wild. 'Where's Frank?'

I reached out and patted her hand. Poor Nancy. If Jerry wasn't where she could actually see him it was as if 'Frank' had vanished. Although sometimes yesterday made an appearance, tomorrow, tonight, this afternoon, soon . . . those concepts seemed foreign to her. 'You ate breakfast with Frank,' I fibbed, and hated myself for doing it. 'He's probably in the bathroom.'

'It's not fair,' she said after a moment.

'What's not fair?'

'If she can have a boyfriend, I can have a boyfriend!'

'She?'

'That cheerleader. Think's she's so smart!' Nancy drew out the 'O' in so, turning it into four syllables – O-O-O-O – wagging her head from side to side as she spoke.

I decided to wait her out. After a bit, she said, 'It's not allowed, you know. Teachers aren't supposed to mess around with students.'

'So, you saw a teacher messing around with a cheerleader?'

'Oh, yes, I certainly did.'

'What does the cheerleader look like?' I asked, not really hoping for an answer that would make any sense.

'I see her all the time, that blonde,' Nancy said. '"Only her hairdresser knows for sure!"' she sing-songed. 'Bitch.'

Somewhere in Nancy's past a cheerleader had done her wrong, and she wasn't about to forget it.

'Where do you see the cheerleader?' I asked, hoping to get her back on track.

'She has a board job. In the dining hall. At least *I* don't have to wait tables.' She gave me a slow wink. 'My father is very rich.'

So, Nancy was back in college. I'd waited tables at Oberlin College – Dascomb Hall, if you'd like to know – and I'd often felt looked down upon by the more privileged few. Oh, the tricks I played when they got my goat! Maybe Nancy's cheerleader had done the same to her.

'She was supposed to be working, but no, she was having sex. And I know sex when I see it,' Nancy said dreamily.

It wasn't Jerry having sex with a pretty blonde in the garden, I knew, but someone Nancy thought looked like Jerry. Masud Abaza? 'The man from the garden,' she had said when Masud's picture had popped up on the television screen. And unless I was mistaken, the only person working the dining room who would qualify as a cheerleader waiting tables was our own young blonde, Filomena.

Were Masud and Filomena having an affair, improbable though it may seem? Or was it some other transaction altogether? Whatever, Detective Powers needed to know.

When Detective Powers finally returned my call, I shared my suspicions with him and got the detective's equivalent of 'thank you for sharing.'

'You're not listening to me, Detective Powers.'

'I am. The question is, where's your proof?'

'Nancy Harper saw Masud and Filomena together in the garden.'

'Correct me if I'm wrong, but are you referring to the Nancy Harper who is a patient in the dementia unit?'

'Well, yes, but just because you have dementia doesn't mean you're blind. She's forgetful, not blind.'

Powers snorted. 'Even a public defender fresh out of law

school would make mincemeat out of her testimony, even assuming she was judged competent to take the stand in the first place, which I doubt.'

'She drew a picture of what she saw, Detective. She's an accomplished artist.'

'Mrs Ives.' He paused. 'I could draw a picture of Hilary Clinton having sex with the Jolly Green Giant, but that doesn't mean it actually happened.'

'Right.' I hung up, thinking I'd have to go to Plan B. Whatever Plan B was.

TWENTY-FOUR

'In compliance with the order of the Fuehrer for protection of Jewish cultural possesions, a great number of Jewish dwellings remained unguarded. Consequently, many furnishings have disappeared . . . In the whole East, the administration has found terrible conditions of living quarters, and the chances of procurement are so limited that it is not practical to procure any more. Therefore, I beg the Fuehrer to permit the seizure of all Jewish home furnishings of Jews in Paris, who have fled, or will leave shortly, and that of Jews living in all parts of the occupied West, to relieve the shortage of furnishings in the administration in the East.'
Albert Rosenberg, Secret Documentary Memorandum for
the Führrer, Berlin, 18 December, 1941.

It took a couple of days to arrange everything to my satisfaction.

In the meantime, I continued to eat lunch in the dining room with Naddie, fury bubbling up in me, white and hot, as Filomena flitted from table to table, smiling and greeting residents as if she didn't have a care in the world.

'Here she comes,' Naddie whispered. 'It's showtime.'

When the hostess was within earshot, I leaned over the

portfolio I'd spread out on the table between us and said, 'Look, Naddie, aren't they amazing?'

Naddie leafed through the drawings with deliberate care, pausing to examine each in turn, sometimes holding one up to the light that cascaded from the chandelier.

'Nancy doesn't recognize her family,' I nattered on, 'but when it comes to drawing her mind's as sharp as ever.'

'Stunning!' Naddie agreed. 'I wonder where she trained?' She tapped the drawing on the table in front of her. 'I like this one very much.'

'It's the tulip poplar in the Tranquility Garden,' I told her. 'And here's a nice one of the garden gate.' I chuckled. 'What else to do when you look out your window all day?'

'Makes me want to hang up my paint brush,' Naddie complained.

'Fat chance,' I said. I scrabbled among the drawings until I found the one of Nancy's dog. 'She draws from memory with incredible accuracy. Look at this! It's her dog, Rosco. According to the nurse in the memory unit, Nancy had Rosco as a child over sixty years ago.'

Naddie studied me over the top of her reading glasses. 'Are there more? We should definitely include some of Nancy's work in the art show this coming fall.'

'She's got a whole portfolio in her room.'

As we talked I kept one eye on Filomena, who was fussing with the napkins on an adjoining table, folding and refolding. 'Filomena!' I called, waving her over. 'Take a look at Nancy's drawings. Aren't they wonderful?' I pawed through the pile, selected one of the tulip poplar and handed it to her.

'Lovely,' Filomena said, handing the drawing back. 'It's too bad she's . . .' Filomena tapped her temple. 'You know.'

'A shame,' I agreed. 'But music and art can unlock the most amazing memories, even in patients with advanced Alzheimer's disease.' I grinned up at her. 'You've heard Nancy play the piano. It's as if she's young again.'

Filomena smiled then bowed slightly. 'You must excuse me now, ladies, but I have work to do. Susanna will come by in a moment to take your order.'

Naddie and I inhaled our Caesar salads while tag-teaming

Filomena to make sure she didn't slip away. I skipped dessert and hurried back to the memory unit while Naddie went off in the opposite direction to play her part.

In Nancy's darkened room, lying in her bed with a blanket pulled up to my chin, I sensed, rather than saw someone open the door and slip in. While I held my breath and counted to twelve the figure stood quietly at the foot of the bed, then turned toward the coffee table where I'd carefully arranged Nancy's portfolio so that it was clearly illuminated by the single bulb of her Tiffany-style floor lamp.

Filomena.

Through half-slitted eyes I watched her paw through the drawings, pausing to examine one or the other more closely. She gasped quietly then drew back. She'd come to the drawing of the couple having sex under the tree. After a moment she closed the portfolio and patted the cover as if to say *you're mine now*.

I expected that she'd take the drawings with her, but Filomena had other plans. She picked up a pillow from the sofa and crept slowly, but deliberately toward the bed.

As she drew nearer I tensed, muscles screaming to bolt. I wrapped my fingers even more tightly around the weapon clutched in my right hand, hidden under the covers.

Filomena held the pillow in both hands. I could hear her ragged breathing, feel her breath hot on my cheek as the pillow began to descend.

When it was six inches from my face, survival mode kicked in. I thrust my weapon into her abdomen, found the trigger and pressed.

Filomena shot back and crumpled to the floor. The pillow flew into the dark. As she lay on the carpet, spasming, her eyes wide and staring, I slipped out of Nancy's bed, holding the stun gun in front of me in case I needed to zap her again, but the first two-and-half million volts the manufacturer had promised in the guarantee printed on the box seemed to have done the trick.

I turned on the bedside lamp and leaned down. Filomena was still breathing, thank goodness, but she'd lost control of her bladder. I circumnavigated the spreading puddle that was soaking into the carpet, borrowed the sash from Nancy's terrycloth bathrobe and tied Filomena's legs together at the ankles. I used a clove hitch with an extra wrap. Paul would have been proud of my knotsmanship.

Then I punched speed dial on my cell phone. 'Detective Powers,' I said when he picked up. 'I need to report an attempted murder.'

I reached Naddie at Spa Paradiso, where she'd taken Nancy for a massage. 'Mission accomplished,' I told my friend, who'd been standing by, waiting for my call. While I debriefed Naddie I stared daggers at Filomena, waiting for her to stop twitching and come around.

'You murdered Masud, didn't you?' I said finally, when Filomena's tongue had begun working again. 'Why?'

She stared at me for a moment, and I thought she'd decided to stay silent. But then she slurred: 'I was tired of having sex. The first time wasn't so bad, in his home when his wife was teaching her computer class, but then he wanted it anytime and just about anywhere.' She snorted. 'He didn't get much variety at home. I think it excited him to be a bad, bad boy.' She flexed her fingers and winced. 'Masud suspected his wife was sleeping with my brother . . . that is, how do you say, a big laugh. But Masud, he believed it, and wanted to teach Safa a lesson.'

'Was she? Sleeping with Raniero, I mean?'

Filomena laughed out loud. 'Not unless my brother had decided to, how do you say, bat for both teams.' She shifted uncomfortably. 'Raniero has a boyfriend in New York City. Can I sit up?'

'OK,' I said, 'but don't expect me to help you.'

I watched as she pulled her knees up and scooted backwards along the carpet, away from the wet spot in which she had been lying.

Filomena leaned her head back against the dust ruffle of the sofa. 'So, I told Masud "no."'

'And?'

'He didn't like it. But he knew about the meat – that's how it started in the first place.' She smiled. 'He could have gotten me fired.'

'So you blamed the kickbacks on your brother?'

Filomena shrugged. 'Raniero or me, it does not matter. For either one it is *final de la carrera*.'

'Your confession will clear Raniero's name, Filomena. He will be fine.'

Filomena laughed. 'Who is confessing?'

I pointed to Nancy's bookshelf. In the space I'd made between *Madame Bovary* and *Jane Eyre* sat a plush bear. 'See that teddy bear?' I said. 'It's a wireless nanny cam. Nadine Gray has been at the spa, recording everything that happened tonight.'

Filomena used her arms to push herself up into a sitting position. 'Bitch!'

I waved my Lady Lifeguard. 'Stay where you are, Filomena, or I'll zap you again, I swear.'

'Pink?' said a gravelly voice behind me. 'Your stun gun is *pink?*'

'A portion of the proceeds go to breast cancer research, Detective Powers. Just doing my part.'

After reading Filomena her rights, Detective Powers and a female police officer led her away. Filomena's face was streaked with tears and her hands were shackled behind her with a pair of plastic tie handcuffs. When she saw me she ducked her head, refusing to meet my eyes.

I opened my mouth but Powers silenced me with a death ray. I stepped aside to let them pass and followed a respectful distance behind as they trundled their prisoner through the lobby, down the front steps and tucked her into the back of the police car.

Power's partner climbed into the front passenger seat. Powers opened the driver's side door, paused, looked up at me looking down at him from the porch, and came to a decision.

Seconds later he stood next to me on the porch. Officer Powers seemed to be weighing how much to tell me. Suddenly he squared his shoulders and said, 'It took us a long time to process those goddam glass balls, but we found a handprint out there, on a ball from the rowboat. It belongs to Filomena.'

I frowned. 'But Filomena could have touched those balls at any time. I'm sure *I* touched one when I first went out there with Nancy.'

'Yes, but two of the partials we found were made with Masud Abaza's blood.'

I stared at Powers for a long moment. 'I see. So you didn't really need me to . . .'

He cocked a forefinger. 'Exactly.'

'And another thing,' he said. Powers rapped on the window until his partner rolled it down. He leaned in, reached across her lap and lifted a large Ziploc bag off the dashboard. 'Do you know a Ysabelle Milanesi?'

'It's Izzy's scrapbook! Wherever did you find it?'

Powers nodded toward the back seat of the patrol car where Filomena sat, head bowed, still refusing to meet my eyes. 'We executed a search warrant on her apartment. Found it there.'

'Izzy will be over the moon,' I said. 'Do you know how important it is?'

'Old photos. I figured it had sentimental value.'

'Much more than that, Detective. When can she have it back?'

'I'll let you know. If it's needed as evidence in the Abaza murder, it'll be a while. If not . . .' He shrugged. 'Sooner rather than later, I should think.'

'Take good care of that, Detective Powers. It's all Izzy has left of her family.'

'I promise.'

TWENTY-FIVE

'The Inner Harbor is a historic seaport, tourist attraction, and landmark of the city of Baltimore, Maryland, USA. It was described by the Urban Land Institute in 2009 as "the model for post-industrial waterfront redevelopment around the world."'
Announcement of 2009 ULI Awards for Excellence,
Urban Land Institute, Atlanta, April 24, 2009.

Angie and I sat on the porch like two old friends, quietly rocking. I'd brought my knitting with me: a sweater for my granddaughter, Chloe, that I'd started back during the summer Olympic Games, the ones in Beijing. The sun had slipped behind a cloud and there was a slight chill to the air, a harbinger of fall, which was just around the corner.

'How's your mother-in-law, Ange?'

'Surprisingly fine. I think she knew all along, deep down, that her relationship with Richard was a fantasy. Know what she said to me?'

'What?'

'"The tragedy of growing old is that I'm a young person in an old body."'

'Oscar Wilde?' I wondered.

'No. Christie McSpadden.'

I thought about Nancy Harper, living in her eighteen-year-old mind with no more worries than whether Frank was going to ask her to the prom. 'Well, on that cheerful note . . .' I began.

'Yeah, I know. It's almost time for lunch. I wonder when they'll have Raniero back? That mac and cheese yesterday. Bleah. Mother wanted me to join her today, but nuh-uh.'

'He might never be back, Angie. Last I heard he was working with a deal lawyer from Skadden Arps, trying to keep his restaurant plans from falling through.'

'What happened?' Angie asked.

'When Lawrence Levine found out it was being partially financed by the sale of artwork stolen by the Nazis, he decided to pull the plug.'

'Levine? Larry Levine the Quik Loan King? *That* Levine?'

'That's the guy.'

'No kidding. Figured it'd be bad for business?'

'That, too,' I said. 'He's Jewish. Lost his father and two sisters at Bergen-Belsen, so it's not surprising he wants to revisit the arrangement he made with the Bucchos.

'Hutch tells me that the project is pretty far along. The Bucchos bought an old warehouse on the waterfront in Canton near the Boston Street Pier. The architectural plans had made it through the Land Use and Urban Design division of the Baltimore Planning Commission, no mean feat that, so they were good to go. Filomena knew that if Levin found out about the investigation into the provenence of the art stolen from Izzy's father the deal might unravel. And once the press got ahold of the story . . .' I paused. 'She had to do something to shut Masud Abaza up. He knew about the paintings, of course, because of Safa. And she actually saw one of them in Izzy's scrapbook when Izzy foolishly brought it into the dining room. But Masud had something else on Filomena, apparently.'

'The whole thing with the meat inspections?'

'Yes. It was simple, really. He wanted to have sex with Filomena. She wasn't going to have it with him indefinitely.'

'There's one thing Raniero's gonna have to do for sure,' Angie said.

'What's that?'

'Change the name of the restaurant.'

'Why? What was he going to call it?'

'Filomena's.'

TWENTY-SIX

This be the verse you grave for me:
Here he lies where he long'd to be;
Home is the sailor, home from the sea,
And the hunter home from the hill.
'Requiem,' Robert Louis Stevenson, 1850–1894

Izzy and I were enjoying our ice-cream cones in our favorite spot on the front porch of Blackwalnut Hall when a Crown Vic pulled up along the drive. I thought we'd seen the last of Detective Powers, but to my surprise, an officer I didn't recognize climbed out of the driver's seat.

And he was not alone.

When I saw who he had with him I handed my cone to a startled Izzy, skipped down the steps and raced along the drive to meet them.

'Jerry!' I said, laughing. 'Where the hell have you been?'

Dressed in a blue-and-gold navy tracksuit, Jerry was grinning like he'd just won the lottery. 'Out and about, out and about.'

'So, he *does* belong here,' the officer added, chuckling.

'Oh, yes,' I fibbed. 'There are people here who've really been missing this guy.' I took Jerry by the hand and tucked it into the crook of my elbow. 'How . . .?

'Somebody spotted him wandering through Quiet Waters Park, looking confused. So they called us. He couldn't tell us his name or address, and he had no wallet or anything on him, but . . . you know those little laundry labels?'

I nodded. Oh, yes. Mother had sewed the embarrassing tapes that practically screamed 'Hannah Alexander is a bay-bee' into my camping clothes every summer.

'Well, we ran the name through DMV, checked him against the picture on the driver's license we found, got the address and brought him back here.'

'Thank you. Everyone will be so relieved.'

'He's not still driving, is he?' the officer asked, his face a mask of concern.

'Oh, no. He hasn't driven for ages, not since . . .' I tapped my temple. 'You know.'

'I heard the security around here was pretty tight,' the officer said as he accompanied Jerry and me up the sidewalk. 'I'm kinda surprised the old guy got away, you know?'

'I have a Hyundai,' Jerry said. 'Don't know where I parked it.' He patted his pajama pockets. 'Key's here somewhere.'

'He must have slipped out of his tracking device,' I said, tap dancing as fast as I could. When we reached the steps, I turned. 'Is there anything we need to do?'

'No, no. Just glad we have a happy ending here.' He gave me a two-finger salute, climbed back into his squad car and drove away.

I walked Jerry inside, heading straight for the memory unit where I knew Heather would be on duty. Holding firmly to Jerry's arm, I stuck my head around the corner of her door. 'Look who I have here!'

Heather shot out of her chair as if she'd been spring loaded. 'Oh my God! Jerry!' Even as she was hugging the prodigal son, she shot me a conspiratorial glance over his shoulder.

I nodded. We were in this thing together.

Heather held Jerry at arm's length, grinning. 'You are a sight for sore eyes. And I know someone who is dying to see you.'

Dying. I felt a pang. That was quite literally what Nancy Harper was doing. Dying. Wasting away of a broken heart.

'Where is she?' I whispered.

'Watching TV.' Heather bobbed her head in the direction of the unit's lounge.

As we walked Jerry into the lounge, I held my breath. What if he didn't recognize her? Or she him?

I needn't have worried.

'Frank!' Nancy shouted when her boyfriend's solid shape loomed between her and the image of Jack Lord on the oversized television screen. She rose from her chair, clapping her hands. 'Frank, Frank, bo brank, banana fanna ro rank, fee fie mo mrank, *Frank*!' she sing-songed, seamlessly regressing to a schoolyard chant.

'Hey, Toots,' he said. 'What's cooking?' He folded her into his arms, rested his chin on the top of her head and patted her playfully on the bottom.

When Jerry finally released her she looked into his eyes and touched his face gingerly with her fingertips again and again as if to convince herself that he was real.

'Is his room still available?' I asked Heather.

'As far as I know.' She winked. 'I'll get someone to make up the bed. And in the meantime . . .' She paused, letting me fill in the blank.

My stomach knotted. 'I'll need to tell Tyson.'

'Right. Let him work something out. That's why they pay him the big bucks.'

'Frank,' Nancy was saying as I turned to go. 'That show you like is on.'

When I left, Nancy and Jerry were cuddling on the sofa and watching *Hawaii 5-O*, as if he had never left.

'If the United States ever needs someone to negotiate with the North Koreans or solve a debt ceiling impasse with Congress, I've got the man for the job,' I was saying to Paul several days later. He'd returned from the sea and was dumping the contents of his laundry bag into the dirty clothes basket when I cornered him.

'Who?'

'Tyson Bennett, that's who.'

'Have I met him?' Paul wanted to know, holding up a pair of socks and studying them critically. 'Dirty or clean?'

I snatched the socks out of his hands and tossed them in with the rest of his stinky laundry. 'You sold beer at the Rotary crab feast together. There's a Labor Day party at Calvert Colony and we're invited, so you'll see him there.'

'OK, got that. So, why are we awarding this dude the Nobel Peace Prize?'

'He got them to settle the whole mess with Nancy and Jerry out of court, but most importantly, Jerry can stay with Nancy at Calvert Colony.' I brought Paul up to date on all that had happened since last we talked. 'After the police brought Jerry back to the colony, Tyson called in both families and held a meeting with Nancy and Jerry actually in the room. I have no idea exactly what transpired – Heather wasn't able to say because of patient confidentiality concerns and all that – but when they came out of the meeting the rape charges had been dropped.'

'What turned the tide?'

I shrugged. 'Maybe making the families and those bureaucrats at the Maryland Department of Heath all sit down together so they could see how sweet Nancy and Jerry are together, how *good* they are for each other. Or maybe everyone simply put on their big boy pants and worked out a deal.'

Paul lugged the laundry basket down to the basement with me following behind carrying a load of sheets. 'How about the nurse friend you were so concerned about. What was her name? Elaine? The one on administrative leave?'

'That has a happy ending, too,' I explained while stuffing the laundry into the washer. 'The Department of Health gave her a formal reprimand, but didn't yank her license, thank goodness. It might be an issue if she ever decided to look for another job, but as long as she stays at Calvert Colony where everyone worships the ground she walks on, it shouldn't be a problem.'

I poured liquid detergent into the dispenser and set the dial for a heavy duty load. We left the washer chugging away and adjourned upstairs to the kitchen where I poured us each a cup of coffee.

'You said Jerry was found wandering around Quiet Waters Park. Isn't that a long way from Ginger Cove?'

'Jerry's son didn't think that one through very well. He snatched his dad out of Calvert Colony in a fit of pique, really, but Ginger Cove had no vacancies, so he was keeping the old guy at home temporarily. One of the round-the-clock caregivers he hired fell asleep in the Lay-Z-Boy. Zing! Jerry opened the sliding glass door and got out of there. She didn't call the cops until nearly six hours later. She'd been driving around all that time looking for him.'

TWENTY-SEVEN

'Art is about family, it is about memory, and it is about history. It is about the history of paintings and drawings and sculptures, but more importantly, it is about the history of people. For many, it is the last tangible connection with a past that was destroyed and with a family that was lost.'
Gideon Taylor, Review of the Repatriation of Holocaust Art Assets in the United States, Hearing Before the Subcommittee on Domestic and International Monetary Policy, Trade, and Technology of the Committee on Financial Services, U.S. House of Representatives, July 27, 2006.

I t was supposed to be a picnic, but by noon the thermometer had climbed into the mid-nineties and barely a breath of air stirred the leaves. Seniors began to flag in the blistering heat, so when the skies darkened with the promise of rain the Labor Day festivities at Calvert Colony were moved inside.

I'd spent twenty minutes at home searching for the sandals that matched the sundress I'd bought in the Bahamas, so by the time Paul and I got to Blackwalnut Hall the party was in full swing. Uniformed servers carrying trays of wine and platters of canapés roamed the lobby, while classical jazz wafted out of the overhead speakers.

Paul snagged two glasses of Chablis from a passing server and handed one of them to me. 'Looks like they finally installed a grill on top of the fish tank,' he observed.

'Looks nice,' I said, sipping my wine and watching the kelp

undulate. 'Not that having it in place would have changed the outcome. Richard Kent would be just as dead.'

'But less wet.'

I scowled at my husband. 'Behave or I'll have to take you home.'

We wandered into the dining room, looking for my friends. 'If this is a preview of the restaurant Raniero plans to open,' Paul said as he took in the tables, groaning with food, 'I predict a long and successful career.'

Gourmet salads had been laid out on long, cloth-covered tables, but the platters were still covered with plastic wrap. I browsed along them anyway, rehearsing my plan of attack. Fresh-cut veggies, mushrooms vinaigrette, grilled asparagus, hearts of palm, tabbouleh – twenty hors d'oeuvres in all. 'This is going to be good,' I said as I checked out the figs stuffed with pistacios and ricotta.

The French doors stood open. 'Come on,' my husband said, and led me out into a carnivore's paradise. Three barbeque chefs bustled about the outdoor grills tending rumps of beef, legs of lamb, loins of pork and racks of ribs as well as sausages and chicken – burgers and hot dogs, too, if you must. The aromas were intoxicating. It was all I could do to get him back inside when Izzy *you-hooed* at us from the open door.

'Your brother-in-law is amazing,' she cooed. 'Hutch entered all my father's paintings into the lost art registry and, *voila*!' She waved a hand. 'One of them has already turned up. A Carlo Mattioli.'

I folded Izzy into my arms and gave her a crushing hug. 'That's wonderful! Where?'

When I released her she took a deep breath. 'Interpol located it at a gallery in Florida. It was part of a traveling exhibit from the Pinacoteca di Parini in Milan. The U.S. Attorneys have seized it, Hannah. It may take a while, but . . .'

'But what, Izzy?' Paul prodded.

'The Mattioli painting is a tree of some kind, dark and boring. So, I'm thinking that my children will be able to build that swimming pool in their backyard after all.'

While Paul chatted with Izzy about her grands, I escaped to get some more wine. On my return, Raniero breezed up and seized my hand, nearly causing me to dump the wine all over my dress. He pressed my hand to his lips, thanking me profusely in a charming mixture of English and Spanish for saving his career.

I had to laugh, the boy was so earnest. 'No, you did that all on your own, Raniero.'

A comma of blond hair had escaped from his toque and trembled charmingly over his left eyebrow. He was going to argue with me, I could tell. 'No, it was you who saw my sister for who she really was. I could forgive her many things, but how could she tell such lies about me? Filomena was taking the kickbacks from the meat man, not me. If I had known . . .' He moved so close to me that our foreheads nearly touched. 'But there was no way I could know. The meat man was using counterfeit stamps. He told the police it was my sister's idea.'

'That must have been hard, Raniero. I'm so sorry. How is she doing, do you know?'

'She has a lawyer.'

'And?'

'I do not talk to her, Mrs Ives.' I could see the sadness behind his eyes. 'Perhaps one day.' His eyes glistened with unshed tears. 'I must get back to work, or I will not have a job,' he said, releasing my hand at last. I flexed it behind my back, trying to restore the circulation.

'Tell me about the restaurant, Raniero.'

Surprisingly, his face brightened. 'It will take longer, but it will come. Our investors are solid.' He drove a fist into his palm to emphasize the point. 'Now, I must go check on the *asado*.'

After another twenty-five minutes of schmoozing, Tyson Bennett made the rounds, inviting his special guests to fix their plates and join him in the private dining room. Once we were all assembled, he stood at the head of the table and banged on the side of his water glass with his spoon to get our attention. 'Calvert Colony has had a rocky start,' he said when we'd settled down, 'but thanks to all your efforts, I believe we are over the hump. 'I'd like especially to thank Hannah Ives, who I'm hereby nominating for the volunteer of the year award.' He raised his glass and said, 'Here, here!'

'Here, here,' everyone echoed, and I felt my face flush.

'What nonsense! You haven't even been open for a year yet, Tyson.' I raised my glass. 'But I thank you, anyway.'

Tyson grinned. 'At Calvert Colony we plan ahead.'

After all the speeches we settled down to enjoy our dinners. As I sliced my grilled sausage into coins, I asked Tyson, 'Is Safa Abaza coming back?'

He stabbed a bit of sirloin and looked up. 'Probably not. Their place is on the market. Are you interested?'

'Not yet,' I laughed.

I was chasing the last of the tabbouleh around my plate with a roll and actively resisting the urge not to pick up my plate and lick it clean when Raniero came into the dining room carrying a package about the size of a laptop computer wrapped up in brown paper. He stood politely by the door, waiting to be recognized.

I waggled my fingers at Tyson and, when I'd got his attention, I bobbed my head in Raniero's direction.

'Raniero?' Tyson said.

'I have something for Mrs Milanesi.' He crossed the room to where Izzy was sitting and thrust the package into her hands, shifting nervously from foot to foot like a schoolboy, waiting for her to open it.

Izzy's puzzled face turned to delight as she stripped off the wrapping. 'Oh, *Dio mio!*'

'What?' I asked from across the table.

She aimed it my direction. It was an exquisite painting of a Madonna and child. I recognized it as one of the paintings in the scrapbook Izzy's mother had put together.

A single tear rolled down Izzy's cheek and splashed onto her pink blouse. 'I cannot believe this. Raniero. Where did this come from? Your sister told me that your grandfather bought only three of my father's paintings at that sale.'

Raniero considered her sideways through pale eyelashes. 'She was not telling you the truth.' He touched her shoulder. 'But this one, it is the last, I am sure of that. Filomena had a safety deposit box. I found the key. When I opened the box, there it was.'

Izzy covered his hand where it rested. 'How can I ever thank you for this?'

Raniero stood tall, straightened his jacket and said, 'Come eat at my restaurant, of course. Free. On the house.'

'What are you going to name your restaurant, Raniero?' Naddie wanted to know.

'I think I will name it after my mother: Graziella. It sounds good, no?'

Naddie favored her favorite chef with a grin. 'It sounds good, yes.'

'Why did Filomena steal Izzy's scrapbook?' Paul asked after Raniero had excused himself and returned to the chaos in the kitchen.

I shrugged. 'Filomena didn't know about Piccio's inventory, did she? Perhaps she thought that without the scrapbook Izzy's claim to the paintings could not be proven. Without photographic evidence the gallery might have dismissed her claims as simply the figment of an old woman's imagination and rejected them out of hand.' I took a sip of wine, trying to work it out. 'If the gallery didn't dig deeper into the provenance then the Buccho family's connection to the stolen paintings might never have been uncovered. Especially since we now know that she was holding back at least one painting.'

'How do we know there aren't any more?' Paul wondered.

'We don't.'

Paul polished off his chicken kabob. 'And I can think of another reason she wanted the scrapbook.'

'What's that?'

'To see if the painting she was holding back was pictured in it. Once the painting was connected with looted Holocaust art it would become completely worthless from a financial standpoint.'

'Bye bye, imported koa wood paneling.'

Paul saluted with the empty skewer. 'Exactly.'

After dinner was over, we were invited back to the main dining room for an evening of entertainment. Paul and I joined a cast of nearly one hundred at one of several small tables arranged, cabaret-style, around the room.

On a raised platform at the end of the room nearest the bar sat a pianist, a bass player and a drummer, all three looking snappy in navy sports jackets and chinos. At the far right stood a gentleman wearing striped suspenders and a remarkable Three Stooges tie that Charlie Robinson, the regular Calvert Colony piano player, would have been proud to own. He held a trombone to his lips and was warming up, working the slide.

Tyson stepped onto the stage and leaned into the mike. 'We've got a special treat for you tonight, ladies and gentlemen. Here, all the way from Jamestown, New York, is Barbara Jean and her band. Let's put our hands together for the coolest girl crooner this side of the Mississippi River, Bar-bra *Jean*!'

Smiling brightly, Barbara Jean dashed out of the bar area and took the stage. She wore a neon-blue, off-the-shoulder dress. Her hair, cut in a stylish, shoulder-length shag, shone like burnished copper in the spotlights.

The singer eased the microphone out of the stand and placed it close to her lips. 'Funny you should say that, Tyson, because the first song I'm going to sing for you tonight is, "I'm not cool yet, but I'm getting warm."' A wave of laughter arose from the audience, the piano played a riff and she began singing – low, slow and seductive.

After the first verse, Paul leaned into me. 'I think I'm in love.'

I took immediate corrective action with a sharp elbow to his ribs.

Our server kept the wine coming while Barbara Jean performed classic songs by George Gershwin, Cole Porter and Irving Berlin. Who doesn't swoon to 'Summertime,' could resist clapping your hands to 'Anything Goes,' or singing along with 'Puttin' on the Ritz?'

Heather, butt first, eased through the swinging door from the Tidewater Bar pulling Lillian in her wheelchair.

'"Super duper!"' Lillian sang along with the chanteuse.

Paul shot to his feet and pulled his chair aside, clearing a path for Lillian who was ensconced in her wheelchair like the queen of England, surrounded by her loyal entourage, a menagerie of pint-sized stuffed animals. More than a dozen were sprawled across her lap and tucked into the spaces between her hips and the arms of the chair.

'We've come to join the party,' Lillian beamed as Heather slotted the chair into the space next to me.

'We?'

Lillian held up a gray-striped cat and smoothed its acrylic fur. 'Me and my babies. They've been very good – no fighting and no biting – so I told them they could come to the party, too.'

Beanie Babies! Of course. The bull dog she held up next, and the psychedelic bear still had the original heart-shaped Ty swing tags clipped to their ears.

Lillian beamed. 'I told you I have *lots* of babies.'

'You certainly do, Lillian,' I said, giving myself a mental one-handed slap to the forehead and wishing that all mysteries were so easily solved.

The tables had been cleared of everything but our drink glasses and bowls of Chex Party Mix. Halo, Lillian's gold-winged white angel bear was reclining in my lap when Barbara Jean announced, 'And now for my final number . . .'

To quiet the groans of protest she paused, grinned and held up a hand. 'Sorry we have to leave, but we have a plane to catch in the morning. You've been a *great* audience, and to show my appreciation, here's a little ballad I've written especially for you. It's called "Tell Me Your Name."' She snapped her fingers, gave the downbeat, 'Hit it, boys!' and sang: *'Tell me your name if you love me, don't make me try to guess. I know I parked my car, somewhere not too far. I think I'll make it home if I walk west.'*

As the song continued, Barbara Jean strolled through the audience, carrying the mic. *'Our shelves are always jammed. We buy in bulk at Sam's, because we can't remember what we've got,'* she sang as she paused in front of me before moving on.

Paul nudged me with his elbow. 'She's got you pegged, Hannah.'

'Shhhh,' I hissed, elbowing him back.

As Barbara Jean continued, *'Though your name escapes me now, I love you anyhow,'* I sought out Paul's hand and held on tight, trying hard but failing to suppress my laughter.

'Do you think this song's a bit insensitive?' I whispered to my husband in one of the instrumental solos between verses.

'Are you kidding?' he whispered back. 'Look.'

I followed his gaze. Nursing staff clustered in the doorway, hugging themselves, rocking with laughter.

Nancy and Jerry sat side by side at a table for two, holding hands and giggling, whether at the song or each other it was impossible to tell.

Colonel Greene snaked his arm around Christie McSpadden's shoulders on Day Five of his campaign to help Christie 'get over her heartbreak.'

Chuck, wearing a checked, short-sleeved button-down shirt and long-sleeved cardigan, totally channeling Ritchie Cunningham from *Happy Days*, was chatting up one of the bartenders.

A couple of old dears parked near the stage in adjacent wheelchairs sang a song of their own composition, slightly off key.

Even Edith, the lady with the Bible, seemed to be laughing.

Clearly, Barbara Jean was among friends.

After the last notes of the song died away, two of the wait staff scurried about, helping to break down the set so Barbara Jean and her band could stow it away in their van. That done, they began tugging urgently on cables and wires, working them into new configurations. A custodian, hunched over and pushing with both arms, rolled the enormous flat-screen Wii into the room and positioned it near the stage. Additional cables and wires appeared, connecting the screen to an array of tall, black box speakers. One of the waiters, dressed in black jeans and a black turtleneck, sat down behind a control board and began fiddling with the dials.

Karaoke Night at Calvert Colony was about to begin.

Elaine Broering got the ball rolling. Her boots were made for walking, and we'd better watch out.

Tyson Bennett, like Frank Sinatra, stood tall, faced it all, and did it his way.

I smiled to myself. So true.

Tyson handed the mike off to the receptionist who stumbled her way through 'I'm a Believer,' which was popular at least two decades before the poor young woman had been born.

The party was in full swing when Paul brushed his lips against my cheek and whispered in my ear, 'I think it's time to go.'

But something had caught my eye. 'Wait, Paul! Look over there!'

Halfway across the room, Jerry had gotten to his feet, taken Nancy's hand and was tugging on it, urging her to join him up on the stage. She shook her head but he tugged harder, and she shrugged and finally got up, too. There was no telling what would happen next.

While Nancy stood with her back to the audience, nervously wringing her hands, Jerry had a brief consultation with the DJ, which seemed to satisfy him. Then he grasped Nancy by the upper arms and slowly turned her around until she was facing into the spotlight.

He leaned into the microphone. 'Ready?'

She giggled. 'Ready whenever you are.'

'I'm ready.'

'You go first.'

'No, you.'

I was beginning to worry that this exchange would go on forever when the DJ flipped a switch, the music started and the words to the song, in white letters so large they could be seen from outer space, began scrolling up the screen. The song was a long-ago classic by Sonny and Cher.

'Babe,' Jerry sang, 'I've got you babe.'

'I've got you babe,' Nancy sang in reply. The two sang the familiar refrain together, twice, three times. When they got to the part about kissing goodnight and holding tight and not letting go, well, I have to admit that I completely lost it.

Paul handed me his napkin and I buried my face in it, sobbing.

'I guess we'll stick around a little longer, then,' he said, signaling the server that his wine glass required attention.

'We need to make an appointment with Hutch,' I said as I drove Paul home.

Paul laid a hand on my knee. 'Why? Thinking of divorce?'

'After your performance tonight, I should.' One of the residents – an impeccably dressed woman who was well past her ninetieth birthday – had taken a shine to my husband, handed off the karaoke microphone to him and he'd spent several unsteady minutes wasting away in Margaritaville looking for a lost shaker of salt.

'What was I to do?' Paul drawled. 'As the song says, there's always a woman to blame.'

'That's why I relieved you of the car keys, stud muffin.'

'Why do we need to consult Hutch, then?' Paul wondered.

'Now that the museum is going to return the paintings to Izzy and her family, what else is there to talk about?'

'This has nothing to do with paintings, Paul. I've been thinking a lot lately about those advance directives we signed, gosh, over ten years ago now, back when we both thought I was going to croak.'

Paul squeezed my knee. 'Hush, Hannah. I *never* thought that breast cancer was going to get the better of you. I've never known such a fighter.'

'I have excellent doctors.' I turned right at the intersection of Bay Ridge and Forest Drive and headed into Eastport.

'I'm sure Emily can't even imagine that her aged parental units are still having sex,' I continued as we sailed through the green light at the Eastport Shopping Center. 'But, I'd like to add a clause to our advance directives that makes sure that if we end up in a nursing home, nobody will make us stay in separate rooms or get in our way when we decide to have sex. Because . . .' I paused. 'I'm quite sure that I'm going to want to have sex with you even if I have no idea who you are.' I reached over and patted his cheek. 'You're a handsome son of a gun, you know.'

'You're not so bad looking yourself,' he said, nuzzling my neck.

I swatted him away and adopted a more serious tone. 'And, should I shuffle off this mortal coil before you, I want you to know that it's OK if you want to have a girlfriend. I'll hate her, of course, but it's OK.'

'No thank you,' Paul drawled. 'You'd come back to haunt me.'

I beamed a smile at him. 'You can count on that, sweetheart.'